Flesh
and
Fantasy

Penny Stallings

with Howard Mandelbaum

ST. MARTIN'S PRESS
NEW YORK

Library of Congress Cataloging in Publication Data

Stallings, Penny.
  Flesh and fantasy.
    1.   Moving picture industry — California — Hollywood.
I.   Mandelbaum, Howard, joint author.   II.   Title.
PN1993.5.U65S7   791.43'0973   78-19391
ISBN 0-312-29586-3
ISBN 0-312-29587-1 pbk.
ISBN 0-312-29588-X prepack

Contents

Preface

Strip away all the phony tinsel of Hollywood, and you'll find the real tinsel underneath.
—Oscar Levant

It was always my intention while planning this book to play around with gossip—the Hollywood kind of gossip that's been around forever, yet never seems to lose its appeal. It struck me that there's a huge body of folklore surrounding the movies and movie stars which has gone, until now, largely unchronicled. I'm talking about the type of thing that we speculate about at home while we're watching the Late Show, like which star was a mob protégé or mogul's plaything or who's had a facelift and is sixty-five if he's a day. What fascinates me and, I suspect, others like me who come to the vintage movies of the thirties and forties for the first time on television or in revival theaters, is the way in which reality intersects with the fantasy that Hollywood conjured up about itself. With this thought in mind, I decided that, rather than our being preoccupied with the trivia of film technology and technique (which most movie books appear to assume), most of us are far more interested in the particulars of the lives and careers of the stars and the baroque machinations of the studio politic. That, if the truth be known, we'd much rather read about how Orson Welles spent his spare time, while filming the famous sleigh-riding scene in *The Magnificent Ambersons,* pawing his young star, Anne Baxter, than about how the Boy Wonder made the synthetic snow look so authentic. My original aim, consequently, was to compile a sort of catalog of movie related gossip—not necessarily the *Star* or *Hollywood Babylon* kind of gossip, but rather stories and anecdotes more directly related to the making and selling of movies themselves.

I originally expected to illustrate these accounts with the usual pictures that one finds in film books, shots of scenes extracted from various well-known movies. But in trying to track them down, I eventually ended up, with the help of several friendly collectors, stumbling upon a completely different kind of publicity shot, the sort of thing you used to see in movie magazines in the old days but that has since become extinct. For almost two years, I waded through thousands of never-before-published stills of remarkable quality and unrelenting naiveté. They were so odd, so far removed from anything we see nowadays, that I felt almost as if I'd unearthed the artifacts of some ancient civilization.

By comparing thousands of these photographs taken over a fifty year span and juxtaposing them with the information I'd accumulated through my research, an overview of the way in which Hollywood consistently restructured the real world emerged. I began to see that there were multiple and conflicting versions of reality in these photographs, all of which were at once true and untrue. I'd uncovered an aspect of my subject far more bizarre than that which had been manufactured for the public. It was these forgotten photographs, rare and touching souvenirs of a bygone era, that eventually shaped the material and attitudes which follow.

The first section of *Flesh and Fantasy* treats loosely the life span of a star (the studio version versus the truth) from childhood through grooming, fame, decline, and, finally, death. The second section continues to deal with the star-making machinery and Hollywood folklore to a certain extent, but here the focus shifts to the fantasy contained in the movies themselves and the mentality that fashioned it. In some respects, the final section, "Studio Tour," contains the most eccentric material to be found in the book, since it is presented without any intrusion by me exactly as the studios released it (publicity department copy intact) several decades ago.

As far as the gossip that accompanies these photographs throughout is concerned, we try not to disappoint you by telling only part of a story or disguising one of the characters ("a Certain Famous and Beautiful Star," etc.) as so many columnists and star bios have a tendency to do. We name names as often as possible, unencumbered by discretion or taste; but remember, when it comes to Hollywood folklore, word of mouth tends to edit out the truth from the final cut. But then, so what.

P.S.

Flesh

A STAR IS BORN

It was all beauty and it was all talent, and if you had it they protected you.
—Lana Turner

The Lanas, Lindas, Joans, and Mickeys were properties nurtured from childhood by the studios, packaged and sold with the utmost care for the maximum return. Identities were invented by publicity departments to be merged with a celluloid soul and fed to the public through fanzines and formula movies. Adolescence was postponed for some, accelerated for others. Social lives were cast, choreographed, and documented as carefully as screen images. The studio became home. The boss was daddy, flesh and blood parents became business partners, movie crews and stand-ins were playmates, and co-stars were lovers. Life was predestined, a role to be acted out according to the studio game plan, whether the cameras were rolling or not. But there was one liability that couldn't be found in the small print of a star's contract—these beautiful creations tended to crumble when they stepped out of the scripted fantasy of their Shangri-las into the real world.

The major studios were each headed by a Big Daddy who reigned supreme.

—Evelyn Keyes,
Scarlet O'Hara's Younger Sister

Louis B. Mayer, the head of MGM and the biggest Big Daddy of them all, told his young stars that they were all his children and must "come to me with all your problems, no matter how small." Because, no matter how small, a star's problems and emotional entanglements had a way of toppling the best-laid plans of the studio braintrust. Puppy love, for instance, could turn a million-dollar investment into a little drudge with one in diapers and another on the

way. The most efficient method of handling valuable star properties was to buy them while they were still very young, preferably in their teens, and keep them perpetually off balance throughout their indenture by training them to do one thing and one thing only: perform in front of the camera. Daddy's children were to stay just that—trusting children completely unaware of the most routine patterns of survival.

A young star's earnings were often funneled directly into expensive playthings by his parents and the studio. He was coddled one minute, bullied the next, and constantly reminded that the cold cruel world lay outside the studio gates. Work was life's *raison d'être*, and work meant competing with other members of the studio family for the public's love. The hunger for the spotlight, for being the center of the world's attention, would prove to be the most deadly of all the extravagant tastes cultivated by the studios in their talented charges.

An effective alliance could usually be formed between the studio head and the hungry parents of a younger star. For several years, Mayer allotted Judy Garland's mother a salary to match her daughter's; in return Mrs. Gumm performed various management chores, like seeing to it that Judy kept up the special diet of chicken soup and Dexedrine prescribed for her by the studio. And, of course, there was Judy's grueling schedule to be coordinated—one year in the life of the gifted teenager might include filming as many as three movies, recording dates, radio work, personal appearances, and high school classes. Mayer and mother understood the priorities of a young girl's career. Together they even went to the trouble of arranging Judy's first abortion, not long after her marriage to bandleader David Rose. Judy had desperately wanted to have this, her first child. But Mama and Mayer knew best.

Parents were so active in the professional lives of Hollywood child stars that in 1932 the California State Legislature felt called upon to pass the Child Actor or "Jackie Coogan" Law, making it illegal for Mom and Dad to appropriate the money, sometimes in the millions, that their talented progeny earned before reaching the age of consent. The bill, however, came as too little, too late, for its namesake. Jackie Coogan's mother had invested the $4,000,000 he'd earned as "The Kid" in futile get-rich-quick schemes.

Conniving parents tried to hold onto their meal tickets for as long as possible. A few, like Milton Berle's mother Ruthie, lived with their children all their lives. Their identities were completely wrapped up in their children's careers. When a movie mother lost a child to marriage, she was losing both prestige and a lifetime investment. Some, like the parents of Mary Astor and Judy Garland, sued their grown-up children for support in order to maintain the luxurious life styles to which they'd become accustomed while controlling their children's resources.

For seventeen years it was Mr. Mayer who guided me, and I never turned down a picture that he personally asked me to do. He was kind, fatherly, understanding and protective. He was always there when I had problems.
—Robert Taylor

Mayer was really a softie underneath it all. Didn't he shed real tears when June Allyson insisted on having her own way? And didn't he always point with pride to Judy Garland when escorting visitors around the lot and boast, "You see that girl...she used to be a hunchback. Do you see what I've made her into?"

Mayer was steadfast in his insistence that his children get the very best education. Besides, he was required to do so by law. Seventeen-year-old Elizabeth Taylor might have been playing passionate love scenes with Robert Taylor in *The Conspirator* every morning, but she put in her three hours with the three R's every afternoon.

Rarely has a less enthusiastic class of students been assembled than the little group that met daily in MGM's little red schoolhouse—Mickey Rooney, Elizabeth Taylor, Lana Turner, Judy Garland, etc. But the sweet picture that these wholesome kids in their classroom presented was pure Americana, perfect for staged publicity photographs of Mickey and Judy passing notes behind teacher's back (especially since Teach herself was straight out of Central Casting).Of much greater interest to the kids at P.S. MGM was the latest dirt from Hedda or Louella, or perhaps their daily wardrobe fittings and makeup sessions, not to mention studio-arranged birthday parties, dates, premieres, public appearances, and publicity stunts.

Like any father, Mayer must have found himself at a loss when dealing with the younger generation. Fresh from her triumph in *National Velvet*, Elizabeth Taylor informed him that he could go to hell for all she cared. Judy Garland eloped with David Rose after Mayer had sabotaged her first try with Tyrone Power. Teenaged Lana Turner refused to pay attention to his admonitions that she was headed for trouble with her racketeer boyfriends. And little Margaret O'Brien? When Mayer promised the talented tot that her fondest birthday wish would become his command—she asked for Lassie. What was a Big Daddy to do?

The system clucked, protected, nursed, and arranged for [everything]. Soothed us if we were upset, tended to our every comfort when we were working. That all this was likely to keep us in a childlike state well into middle age was not foreseen.
—Evelyn Keyes

Most of the stars who found themselves cast adrift after having options dropped by their studio homes discovered that they didn't really know who they were without the studios to tell them. MGM had been June Allyson's "mother and father, mentor and guide, my all-powerful and benevolent crutch." For Linda Darnell, who'd made her film debut at sixteen, leaving Fox after twelve years was like "leaving home"; suddenly, there was no one to run interference between her and the outside world, no familiar routine to follow each day. During Robert Taylor's twenty year reign as one of Metro's biggest draws, he'd been steered through life's little nuisances by unseen pampering hands; once it was over, he realized that it was the simple things, like answering the phone or making dinner reservations, that threw him. Judy Garland was only twenty-eight when Metro lowered the boom, but as far as she was concerned, her life was over. She reacted to the news by walking calmly into the bathroom and slashing her throat. Tragically, nobody had believed in the image the studio had invented for Judy more completely than Judy herself. In her mind she was the sincere but unattractive girl-next-door, of little value apart from a voice. When the studio abandoned her, she was sure that no one wanted her—or, more importantly, her talent—anymore.

But still, it was these special few who, for one brief, shining moment, were the repositories of the sum total of Hollywood's magic. And if they had it to do all over again, could they demur, even with the knowledge that tragedy is built into the formula?

ANNOUNCER'S VOICE: "We'll give you the rest of your life to make up your mind, little Judy Mildred Francis Turner of Wallace, Idaho. Will you trade in your own poverty-filled childhood as an itinerant miner's daughter for that of . . . the pampered and talented daughter of a mining engineer? Instead of an ugly murder by local gangsters, your father's death scene will be rewritten by the studio hacks as . . . a mining accident! You'll be discovered on a stool at Schwab's sipping a soda, instead of being hustled to the right people by a powerful mentor with underworld connections! And you'll be earning fifteen hundred dollars a week before you turn twenty-one, while the rest of Depression-struck America struggles to keep body and soul together.

It's up to you, little Judy Mildred Frances. You've got something special—something millions of people will pay to see—if you'll just take the chance. . . ."

GEORGE RAFT
in Paramount Pictures

Harry Cohn, former head of Columbia, once bet an actor $100 that the actor couldn't recite the Lord's Prayer. The actor accepted the bet. He then began reciting, "Now I lay me down to sleep . . ." Cohn tossed him a bill and conceded, "Awright you win; I didn't think you knew it."

(Judy Turner)

Lana Turner

(Dominic Felix Amici)

Don Ameche

(Phyllis Isley)

Jennifer Jones

Betty Grable

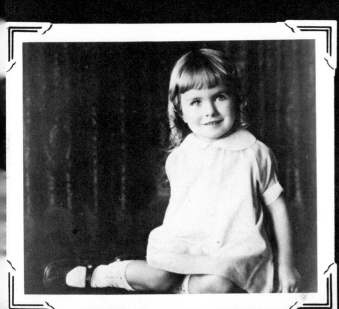

William Powell

Jane Russell

Fred MacMurray

PERIOD OF ADJUSTMENT

I was coming along in Rita Hayworth's wake. The various departments, believing her image to be the winning one, tried to make me over into a blonde replica. Hairdressing pasted tons of hairpieces, including one of Otto Kruger's old toupees, to my forehead. Wardrobe padded my breasts to match Rita's more generous proportions.

—Evelyn Keyes

The Stars of Tomorrow had to be pretty tough to survive the onslaught of the studio star-making machine. Young contract players were groomed and packaged, drilled mercilessly for their moment of glory on the screen. Meeting the camera's demands for perfection meant that bodies had to be toned and reshaped, faces redrawn, and regional dialects replaced by the Hollywood accent, which hovered between British, Yankee, and Brooklynese.

But for every overnight sensation, there were thousands who went back to their homes in the Midwest to marry the boy or girl they'd left behind. Other neverweres settled permanently in Hollywood to work full time at that job waiting tables (which they'd taken on temporarily, to make ends meet) and to spawn a population of surfers and golden girls with long, flowing hair.

Ann Evers, Wilma Francis, and Irene Bennett, recently signed by Paramount, get their first and most important lesson from studio dramatic coach Phyllis Loughton.

ATTENTION
NEW PLAYERS

DON'T look at the camera.
DON'T report late on the set.
DON'T overlook script studies.
DON'T talk during scene filming.
DON'T forget studio appointments.
DON'T lose your dressing room key.

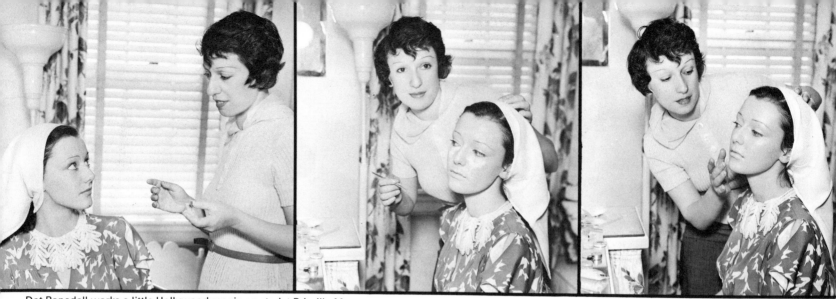

Dot Ponedell works a little Hollywood magic on starlet Priscilla Moran.

Ann Sheridan with Paramount gymnasium director Jim Davis

Under the trained eye of Sophie Rosenstein, Warner Brothers dramatic coach, Dolores Moran and Ross Ford learn the fine art of the screen kiss.

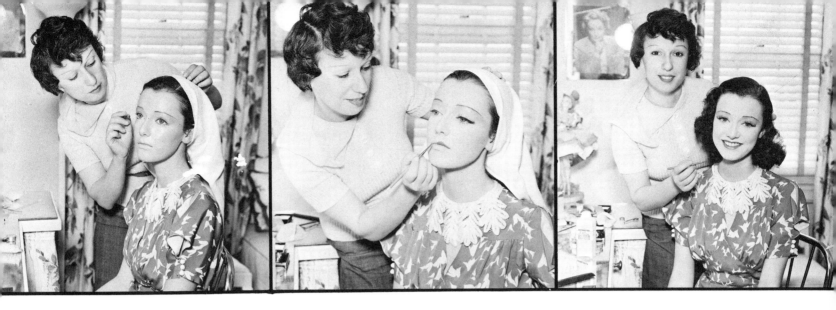

Ida Lupino with athletic instructor Richard Kline

Freddie Bartholemew with MGM athletic instructor

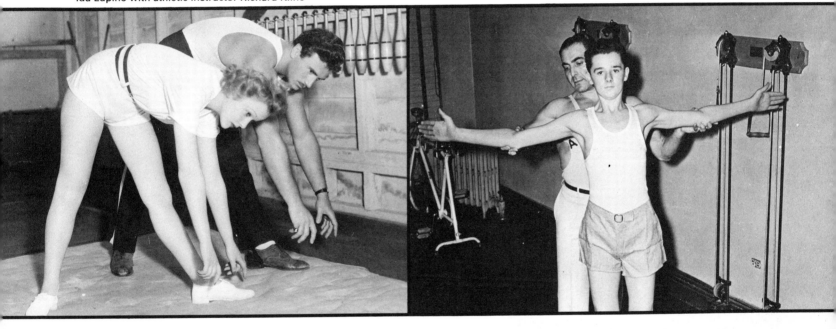

Raquel Torres has a turtle race with Leila Hyams across the MGM lot.

Paramount hopefuls James Ellison, Lee Bowman, John Payne, Richard Denning, James Craig, and Louise Campbell

More important than a budding star's physical transformation was the manner in which he or she took to the studio publicity machine. Tomorrow never came for hundreds of Stars of Tomorrow who failed to appreciate the value of seemingly mindless publicity stunts, like taking a sunbath on a cold winter's day with a few friends or racing turtles on the studio lawn.

Photo Session

Any girl can look glamorous,
all she has to do is stand still
and look stupid.

—Hedy Lamarr

The time spent in actual movie-making for a
new contract player was scant compared to that
devoted to packaging an image for the
media. Young actors and actresses
were expected to spend hours working
with the studio portrait photographers
to create whatever image—mystery,
glamour, wholesomeness—the publicity
department had conjured up for them.

Martha Raye thinks glamorous for photographer Eugene Richee.

Martha Raye *is* glamorous showing off
the latest in kitchen appliances.

Martha Vickers

Bette Davis

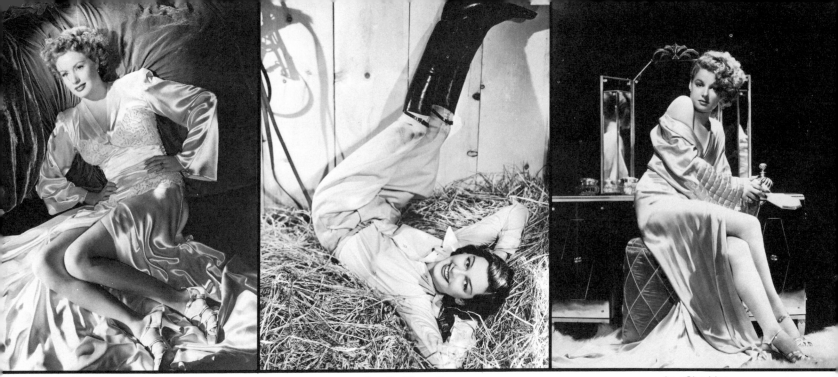

Mary Jane Harker

Rosalind Russell

Ann Sheridan

Anita Louise and Olivia De Havilland

Rosemary Lane

Andrea King is delighted with the results of her session with photographer Bert Six.

A Face in the Crowd

It was MGM boss Louis B. Mayer, who first decreed that "the public makes the stars." Mayer and his young lieutenant, Irving Thalberg, measured star potential by casting a young actor in two or three pictures to see if he aroused any audience response (which was gauged with preview cards and fan mail). Any actor or actress to whom audiences didn't respond had his option dropped; most were never heard from again—like many who have graced the last several pages.

Here are a few newcomers working their way toward stardom. Do you recognize the face in the crowd?

LUCILLE BALL, Eddie Cantor and the Goldwyn Girls in *Kid Millions* (1934)

DOUGLAS FAIRBANKS JR. and unidentified player in *Stephen Steps Out* (1923)

SHELLEY WINTERS, Lee Bowman, Rita Hayworth, and Florence Bates in *Tonight and Every Night* (1945)

HUMPHREY BOGART, Edmund Lowe, and Victor McLaglen in
Women of All Nations (1931)

BARBARA STANWYCK and friends in *Broadway Nights* (1927)

VIRGINIA MAYO, the Goldwyn Girls, and Danny
Kaye in *Up in Arms* (1944)

DOROTHY MALONE, Adolphe Menjou, and friends in *Step Lively* (1944)

John Wayne, Ona Munson, and **DOROTHY DANDRIDGE** in *Lady From Louisiana* (1941)

Wayne Morris, Penny Singleton, and **CAROLE LANDIS** in *Men Are Such Fools* (1938)

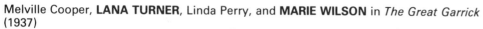

Melville Cooper, **LANA TURNER**, Linda Perry, and **MARIE WILSON** in *The Great Garrick* (1937)

Danny Kaye, **GWEN VERDON**, and friends in *On the Riviera* (1951)

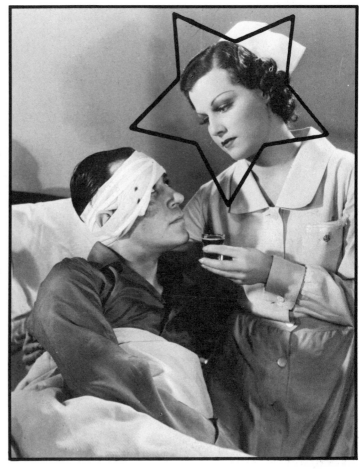

Robert Armstrong and **CAROLE LOMBARD**
in *Big News* (1929)

George Raft and **ANN SHERIDAN** in *The Glass Key* (1935)

William Boyd and **ROBERT MITCHUM** in *Hoppy Serves a Writ* (1943)

Anthony Bushell, George Arliss, and **JOAN BENNETT** in *Disraeli* (1929)

Julia Faye, **EVELYN KEYES**, Fredric March, and Margot Grahame in *The Buccaneer* (1938)

LUCILLE BALL, HARRIET HILLIARD, and **BETTY GRABLE** in *Follow the Fleet* (1935)

Gloria Delson, Paulette Goddard, unidentified player, and **GLORIA DE HAVEN** in *Modern Times* (1936)

Beryl Mercer, John T. Doyle, **BRIAN DONLEVY**, Helen Chandler, and Morton Downey in *Mother's Boy* (1929)

PAULETTE GODDARD and the Goldwyn Girls in *The Kid From Spain* (1932)

JUDY HOLLIDAY, Alvin Hammer, **BETTY COMDEN,** and **ADOLPH GREEN** in *Greenwich Village* (1944)

If enough preview cards mentioned a newcomer or if he got a surprising amount of fan mail, he was cast quickly in as many pictures as possible opposite the studio's established stars. Joan Crawford was one of the first stars to be created by the newly formed Metro-Goldwyn-Mayer.

Joan Crawford harvests a bumper crop of fan mail from her appearance in *Our Modern Maidens.*

Lana Turner prepares for her big break, a co-starring role with Clark Gable, by studying photos of some of his former film consorts.

Linda Darnell in *Star Dust*

Peter Falk makes no secret of his glass eye, but during the days of studio reign, great pains were taken to prevent audiences from realizing that certain stars weren't all they seemed. Harold Lloyd's missing fingers were always covered by gloves and drawn in in publicity photos. Directors attempted to keep Herbert Marshall's movements down to a minimum so as not to expose the fact that he wore an artificial leg (he'd lost his in combat during World War I).

A Nose by Any Other Name Dept.: Other young hopefuls who thought a change of nose was good for the soul were: Dean Martin, the Gabor sisters, Dana Wynter, Carolyn Jones, Peter O'Toole, Stefanie Powers, Suzanne Pleshette, Rita Moreno, George Hamilton, Joel Grey, Sissy Spacek, Carole Landis, Marie Wilson, Nanette Fabray, Joan Hacket, Jill St. John, Raquel Welch, Talia Shire, Marlo Thomas, Annette Funicello, and Barbara Eden. And there were the mid-career nose overhauls of Lee Grant, Dinah Shore, Vera-Ellen, Al Jolson, Cameron Mitchell, Bobby Van, Alan King, Mitzi Gaynor, Rhonda Fleming, Juliette Greco, Jan Sterling, Fanny Brice, and Milton Berle.

Harold Lloyd

It took only one look at Clark Gable's floppy ears for Samuel Goldwyn to know that the kid obviously had no future in films. Two of Hollywood's most popular heartthrobs also had their share of problems conforming to the industry's standards of ear fashion. George Raft flattened his unsightly protuberances via plastic surgery shortly after his arrival in Hollywood at the behest of the studio image-makers. Bing Crosby's receding hairline could be camouflaged for the screen with one of Perc Westmore's scalp doilies, but his large ears made him look like a singing sugar bowl. Against his will, he submitted to a complex procedure which involved the application of spirit gum to his ears which were then held in place by an elastic pressure turban until the fixative hardened. The only trouble with this little scheme was that the heat from the studio lights eventually softened the glue. After the resounding thwop of Bing's ears snapping back to their natural position interrupted one take too many, he decided that the world would just have to get used to his ears as they were.

The fact that Harold Lloyd had lost the thumb and index finger on his right hand from a faulty explosive prop didn't prevent him from continuing to perform his daredevil stunts in front of the cameras. When a scene from *Professor Beware* called for him to disrobe down to his underwear, George Westmore invented prosthetic fingers from textured latex to cover his wound and take the place of his perennial gloves.

At the insistence of her then mentor, super-agent Johnny Hyde, Marilyn Monroe had her jaw remodeled and the tip of her nose bobbed at the age of twenty-three. Love hadn't blinded Hyde to the fact that even Monroe would have to improve on nature a bit before she would be ready for stardom.

Bing Crosby

Have you ever noticed that none of the stars, supporting players, or even extras in vintage Hollywood films seem to be plagued by baldness? Young, old, and in-between, each and every male had a healthy head of the stuff. Must have been all that fresh California air, you say. Well, we don't want to disillusion you, but a great deal of that glorious growth was about as natural as Astroturf. It's only recently that stars like **Jack Nicholson** have been allowed to lose their hair in public, just like real people. Most male stars were fitted with headwarmers as soon as their hairlines began to show the slightest signs of receding, like those of **Jimmy Stewart, Frank Sinatra** (Ol'Transplant), **John Beal, Lon McCallister, Burt Reynolds, Jack Benny, George Burns, Brian Aherne, Fred Astaire, Brian Donlevy, Bing Crosby, Ray Milland, Charles Boyer, Gary Cooper, David Niven, Charlton Heston, Laurence Olivier, Humphrey Bogart, Rex Harrison, Robert Montgomery, George Raft, Henry Fonda, Sean Connery, Fredric March, Lee J. Cobb, Peter Sellers, Franchot Tone, Van Heflin, Gene Kelly,** and **Fred MacMurray.**

Ray Milland's hair abandoned ship after being molested by the studio hairdresser's primitive version of electric hair rollers for *Reap the Wild Wind.* **Carol Channing**'s hair also took offense at the constant bleaching required to convert her into a light-headed blonde; she sticks to wigs these days. **Margaret Dumont,** the Marx Brothers' favorite straight lady, was as bald as a billiard ball; Harpo liked to steal her wig. **Ida Lupino** has hardly any hair to call her own owing to a case of diptheria in the late 30s; she's wearing wigs in all those Warner Brothers epics.

Having too much hair could cause as many problems as having too little: we get the impression that the young **Tyrone Power** looked something like the young J. Fred Muggs around the time he arrived in Hollywood. When Darryl Zanuck saw young Ty in his first screen test, he screeched that he looked like a monkey, but his female assistants knew better. Electrolysis separated Power's hairline from his eyebrows, as it would a few years later for **Robert Preston** and **Rita Hayworth. Barbara Stanwyck** waited until very late in her career to undergo a defoliation program, but **Ginger Rogers,** whose peach fuzz is a legend down Hollywood way, preferred to have her photos barbered instead of her face.

Remember back in the early seventies when **Faye Dunaway** posed for that lifesized *Vogue* spread with her bushy underarm growth exposed for all the world to see? Of course, we'd always suspected it was there; Faye's that kind of girl. In any case, her armpit's debut apparently had something to do with the new natural look for women—no makeup, undergarments, teased or colored hair, etc. We'd come a long way since the fifties, when almost everything, even body hair, was considered immoral.

Robert Mitchum created headaches for Howard Hughes when he became the first beefcake star to refuse to shave his chest for the screen. Since he took his shirt off in practically every movie (it must have been in his contract), this act of rebellion could have been disastrous for his career. And he didn't stop there; he even developed a potbelly in order to avoid posing for pinup shots. What a man.

Jeff Chandler

Jeff Chandler's body hair was so thick, it practically had to be mowed. He spent his career in itchy discomfort from the stubble that covered his entire body.

Mitchum having set an example, more and more stars attempted to break the hair barrier. But some just couldn't seem to make up their minds, and alternated between hairy and shaved chests from picture to picture. **William Holden**'s chest hair was snipped for *Love is a Many Splendored Thing,* but he went natural for *The Bridges of Toko-Ri* the same year.

Not only was body hair considered unrefined, but ungodly to boot! **Jeffrey Hunter** had to be completely sheared for his role as Jesus in *King of Kings,* including his underarms, for the Crucifixion scene.

In the good old days, Hollywood cinematographers went to the trouble of disguising the fact that stars like **Virginia Mayo** and **Norma Shearer** had eyes that were just the teensiest bit crossed. Moviemakers don't bother with this sort of thing today; unflattering camera angles are responsible for often making stars like **Karen Black** look like Ben Turpin on screen.

Don't Want No Short People Round Here Dept.: Doesn't everyone know someone who knows someone who's seen Rock Hudson in the flesh and swears he's only 5′2″? For those who care—we know you're out there—here's a short list of masculine screen favorites who measure below the national average: **Steve McQueen, Robert Conrad, Richard Jaeckel, Fred Astaire, Al Pacino, Dustin Hoffman, Woody Allen, Peter Falk, Spencer Tracy, Sal Mineo, Jack Nicholson, John Garfield, James Cagney, Charlie Chaplin, Mickey Rooney, William Bendix, Charles Boyer, Gene Kelly, Humphrey Bogart, Edward G. Robinson, Bing Crosby, Peter Lorre, Brian Donlevy, Pat O'Brien, James Mason, Paul Muni, George Raft, Sammy Davis, Jr.,** and, last and probably least, **Alan Ladd.**

Remember the scene in *Sunset Boulevard* when the William Holden character first meets the aging silent star (Gloria Swanson) and says, "I remember you. . . . You're Norma Desmond. You used to be big." To which she responds, "I'm still big. It's the pictures that got small." Apparently, it's still a shock to see bigger-than-life screen queens in the flesh. **Raquel Welch** says that people are always disappointed that she's not the Amazon she appears to be in *One Million Years B.C.* in real life. If the fans are underwhelmed by Raquel's average 5′6″ frame, imagine how strange it must have been to see in person someone like **Norma Shearer,** who's just a smidgen over five feet tall. It was the surprisingly large number of diminutive leading men like Alan Ladd that created a demand for equally petite ladies, like **Veronica Lake,** who could melt in their arms without causing them physical injury. Other glamorous female munchkins who measure up at five feet or just over: **Gloria Swanson, Carole Lombard, Terry Moore, Elizabeth Taylor, Lana Turner, Judy Garland, June Haver, Lupe Velez, Ann Blyth, Joan Blondell,** and **Norma Talmadge.**

Glamour Is the Mother Of Dept.: **Marilyn Monroe** perfected a Vaseline-base lip gloss; **Carole Lombard** drew in a shadow along her natural cleavage line and lightened the top of her breasts to make them look bigger (**Kim Novak** adopted the same trick twenty years later); **Dietrich** pioneered facial contouring by means of makeup shadowing and used surgical tape to give a natural lift to her breasts; and **Alan Ladd** was able to reach co-stars like Sophia Loren for on-screen clinches by climbing elevated surfaces that were specially constructed to compensate for his diminutive size.

During the thirties, as mothers struggled vainly with their little girls' baby-fine tresses in an attempt to duplicate **Shirley Temple**'s celestial curls, they couldn't have known that Shirley's moptop was the product of Hollywood magic. Before Shirley filmed a scene, George Westmore affixed individual human-hair ringlets to her plebian growth, as he'd done a decade earlier for another screen sweetheart, **Mary Pickford.**

Shirley Temple

When **Elvis Presley** first arrived in Hollywood for his debut in *Love Me Tender,* he was a boyish blond with pouty good looks. But by the time he returned to the screen after his tour of duty in Germany, his hair color had gone from blond to bluish black, and he was sporting more mascara and pancake than his leading ladies. We can't account for the mascara and pancake, but Elvis's biographers have speculated that he dyed his hair to emulate his hero, rock singer Roy Orbison; Presley also insisted that his ward, the future Priscilla Presley, dye her hair the same color. Perhaps this was Elvis's way of conjuring up his beloved mother Gladys or even his first Hollywood crush—Debra Paget.

Did **Gloria Grahame,** "the girl with the novocaine lip," really stuff tissue under her upper lip to give it an even more exaggerated and sensuous pout?

For those fanatics who've pored over **Joan Crawford**'s photographs and spent hours in darkened theaters watching her films, it will come as no surprise that La Crawford's entire face and body were covered with freckles. She felt they marred her beauty and ordered that they be erased from all publicity stills by the studio retouching squad. Crawford's undersized and widely spaced teeth also had to be disguised with retouching. Her entire dental structure eventually underwent many painful renovations before acquiring the proper scale for her dramatically large features. This dental work contributed, along with her drastically overdrawn lipline, to her sensational new Sadie Thompson look in 1932.

Carole Lombard

Unfortunately, when screen gods and goddesses collide with the real world, they shatter just like mortals. Plastic surgery reconstructed the high-priced physiognomies of **Jason Robards, Mark Hamill, Edward G. Robinson, Merle Oberon, Carole Lombard,** and **Van Johnson** when their faces were disfigured in automobile accidents. Likewise **Ann-Margret,** after her fall from a scaffolding platform in Las Vegas. **Montgomery Clift** wasn't quite so lucky. A near-fatal automobile accident caused the loss of four teeth, a broken nose, a fractured jaw, and a monstrous cut from his nose down through his upper lip. Though he continued to make movies after his face was patched up, he'd lost his special beauty and he knew it. His self-consciousness showed on the screen; it almost seemed as if he were avoiding the camera. Fans claim to be able to spot the scenes with the before-and-after Monty in *Raintree County.*

Jack Palance's skull-like physiognomy has served him well during his career as a professional bad guy. But it seems that he began life with a regular-looking kisser before suffering facial wounds that necessitated extensive plastic surgery and skin grafting. It's difficult to pin down the circumstances that led to his injuries: one story has him surviving a plane crash during the war, while another holds that his face had to be rebuilt after years of being pulverized during his career as a professional fighter.

Simone Signoret says in her autobiography, *Nostalgia Isn't What It Used to Be,* that the **Marilyn Monroe** she came to know, during the time her husband Yves Montand worked with her on *Let's Make Love,* rarely wore makeup and preferred to spend her nonworking hours in a rayon dressing gown she'd purchased at a local Woolworth's. It seems that Monroe despised the process of getting into what she called her "Marilyn getup," an ordeal which took around three hours to accomplish. She outlined her imperfections in detail to her across-the-hall neighbor: "Look, they all think I've got beautiful long legs; I have knobby knees and my legs are too short." And Signoret says that the famous platinum blonde hair was Monroe's special nemesis: "Curiously, the roots of that hair, fluffy as the hair of a small child, didn't take the platinum dye as well as the rest of the hair on her blond head. The lock that fell over her eye so casually and so accidentally was produced by all that teasing, and it was a shield protecting those darker roots, which might be seen when the camera came in for close-ups. . . . In order to have platinum hair, and to kill her enemy the widow's peak, she sent for, and paid for, a very old lady who came all the way from San Diego. This old lady had once worked for Metro-Goldwyn-Mayer, and she now lived in retirement. She had been responsible for the platinum head of Jean Harlow throughout her short career—or so she said. . . . It was a kind of association through a third person between the Blonde Mark I and the Blonde she turned into. And in retrospect I think it was also a hand stretched out to someone who had been forgotten. . . ."

Makeup maestro George Masters says that **Raquel Welch** is plastic from the nose down. Amazing what they can do with the stuff nowadays, isn't it?

The dramatic transformations that stars underwent after arriving in Hollywood weren't always due to lighting or cosmetic tricks. Both **Joan Crawford** and **Marlene Dietrich** had their backmost molars, top and bottom, extracted to create their high-cheekboned beauty.

Spencer Tracy, Irene Dunne, and **Van Johnson** were filming *A Guy Named Joe* when Johnson sustained a fractured skull and numerous other injuries in a terrible motorcycle accident. Johnson hovered near death for days, and it seemed that there was nothing to do but replace him and continue filming. At this point, Spencer Tracy stepped in and wielded his influence to persuade L. B. Mayer to suspend production until Johnson was well enough to continue. Taking a gamble, Mayer agreed not to drop Johnson if Tracy would agree to lay off his lecherous pursuit of his co-star Irene Dunne. Tracy agreed. This story's happy ending comprises a chastened Tracy, a relieved Dunne, and a fixed-up Johnson, whose impact in *Joe* made him an undisputed star.

Van Johnson's skull was held together with a metal plate, and he still bears the extravagant scar from his repair job. But the scar isn't really noticeable in Johnson's subsequent films, thanks to slick camera work. It was almost always erased from studio publicity shots, unlike the one you see here.

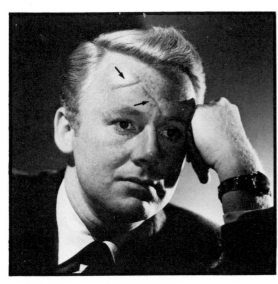

Van Johnson

For **Judy Garland,** coexistence with the high-priced beauty on the MGM lot was agony. Her imperfections were driven home relentlessly by the studio reconstruction experts, who tried everything possible to correct the irregularities in the face and body that boss L. B. Mayer despised. She was put on a diet of chicken soup and speed to control her wildly fluctuating weight; although her nose was well formed, it was given a detachable latex bridge because Mayer deemed it too pug; and since her work schedule couldn't possibly allow for time-consuming orthodontics, she was fitted with removable caps to cover the gaps created by her snaggleteeth.

Although it was a closely guarded secret, almost everyone on the MGM lot knew that **Clark Gable** sported dentures. It was his second wife, Ria Langham, who had staked the young actor to his first shiny new choppers. The fact that he was never really comfortable with them contributed to one of his most endearing mannerisms: when he appeared to be pursing his lips and pushing out his words at the beginning of sentences, he was actually trying, unconsciously, to press the alien presence into place. This involuntary gesture resulted in the dazzling display of dimples that has elicited female sighs for decades.

The famous dimple in **Kirk Douglas**'s chin is big enough to house a family of five to start with; in 35mm magnification, it looks like the Grand Canyon as seen from the air. After seeing the first rushes of the young newcomer, Paramount's Front Office quickly mobilized its team of makeup wizards to bridge the offending gap. Kirk told it to Andy Warhol like this in *Interview* Magazine: "They covered it all up with putty. And do you want to know something? When you cover this up you have no idea what the size of my chin is. You see, it breaks up the chin. Otherwise, I have the biggest chin in the world. Finally, it annoyed me. I said, 'What is this crap? For God sakes, I'm not a good-looking guy. This is what I am.' And that was the end of it."

Of course, everyone wants to know who has or hasn't in Hollywood...had a facelift, that is. For starters, there are the notoriously bad facelifts of **Gary Cooper** and **Mary Pickford.** The earlier attempts were primitive at best and often left the stars who took the gamble with masklike faces that looked grotesque on the screen. When **Merle Oberon** returned to films in the early seventies for *Interval*, critics reviewed her facelift instead of the film, saying that her lifts had made it impossible to discern her facial expressions, if in fact there were any. **Lana Turner**'s lift created more talk than her acting when she made her television series debut in "The Survivors." **Marlene Dietrich** refuses to own up to a facelift although she does admit to having had cosmetic surgery on her million-dollar legs (as well as Niehan's rejuvenative cell therapy). **Rita Hayworth** has made no secret of her facial renovation, while **Gloria Swanson** continues to deny having had any work. When last heard from, **Barbara Stanwyck** was still hesitant to undergo surgery, favoring instead a process used also by **Lucille Ball** for movie and television appearances, wherein loose skin is pulled back from the face with surgical tapes. Lifts have worked wonders for many male stars like **Henry Fonda, Jean-Pierre Aumont,** and **Dean Martin. Elvis Presley** had eye and temporal lifts a few years before he died. **Robert Taylor** professed to be thrilled with his facial lines after having endured three decades as a "pretty boy," but he eventually decided that those unsightly crow's-feet around his eyes had to go. Two successful facelifts helped **Joan Crawford** retain her amazing beauty well into late middle age.

Greta Garbo

Marilyn Monroe

Pardon My Past

The renovation process that could transform mere mortals into movie stars began with an inspired alliance between the Star of Tomorrow and the star's best friend—the makeup man. The Westmores and Dottie Ponedells were responsible for a very special element of screen fantasy. Along with the great fashion designers, cinematographers, and lighting technicians, they created a standard of beauty that will never again be duplicated.

In their never-ending quest for perfection, Hollywood makeup men invented lip gloss, false fingernails, hair sprays, setting lotions, toupees, body makeup, many hair dyes and lighteners, hair weaving, cold cream, skin freshener, and false eyelashes, not to mention various kinds of prostheses for augmenting body parts. Nose bobbing and cosmetic dentistry were the most common surgical reconstructions prescribed by the cosmetic masterminds. Many young stars submitted to hours of painful electrolysis to reshape hairlines and remove facial hair. The studios retained their own stable of plastic surgeons, who reshaped the noses of glamour girls like Carole Landis and musical comedy stars like Bobby Van. The heads of Robert Taylor, Leslie Howard, Jimmy Stewart, and Ray Milland were augmented by hair-thickening gels and permanented into glossy curls. Almost every star's face (even Shirley Temple's) was pulled up and back with surgical adhesive tape hidden under the hairline above the ears. Close-ups were usually shot through

Marilyn Monroe

Marlene Dietrich

gauze and enhanced by lighting techniques which smoothed away facial lines and imperfections while shadowing unflattering thickness.

Even Hedy Lamarr wasn't the glamour queen American audiences would come to know when she first arrived in Hollywood on the arm of Louis B. Mayer. Cinematographer James Wong Howe remembers, "She was bewildered and possessed of all the physical defects the average girl has, on her arrival at the film factory. Hollywood intended to transform her into a million-dollar asset and she had been put into *Algiers* to start the transformation. I was told: 'Make Hedy a glamour girl.'

"Hedy's black hair and ivory skin posed a problem. Black hair absorbs light and so I aimed strong lights at her chin to create a shadow which chiseled the chin more clearly. And other things had to be added. When it comes to glamour, the eyes have it, so I shot her just off full face and used a baby spot at a 35-degree angle above the eyes, in order to blend forehead and hair, and, more importantly, to concentrate on the eyes and mouth."

As the studio beauty machine worked its magic, the images of the most glamorous stars underwent several significant transformations over the years. Just as Picasso had his blue period, Joan Crawford had her blonde period, and so on. What follows are a few examples of Hollywood's handiwork...stars before, after, and during.

1928

Joan Crawford

1930

Elvis Presley
1956

The Thomases: Danny, Rose, Terry,
and **Marlo** , circa 1955.

Lana Turner 1937

Marlo Thomas
circa 1972

40

1938

1960

1933

Joan Crawford

circa 1942

Rita Hayworth 1938

Diahann Carroll 1953

1945

1967

41

Inspiration

Mae Murray

Rudolph Valentino

Jean Harlow

Lipstick, peroxide, and shoulder pads. The fashion innovations with the biggest impact were those that were the cheapest and most accessible. These were the smart

Ladies of the screen were forced to emulate Mae Murray's bee-stung lips during the twenties even if the tiny cupid's bow shape had to be drawn into more generous contours.

It took Hedy Lamarr's sensational American debut in *Algiers* to counter the fad for plantinum blondes which had begun with Harlow. Harlow's peroxide-blond tresses were so much a part of her persona that there was even a rumor that her untimely death had been the result of brain damage from peroxide poisoning.

For years women shaved their natural eyebrows and substituted an exaggerated penciled arch in an attempt to copy Jean Harlow and her screen imitators. Lana Turner's eyebrows were shaved during her grooming period as a starlet; they never grew back.

Even Joan Crawford copied the bee-stung lips of screen goddess Mae Murray before she shook up the world with her drastically overdrawn lipline as Sadie Thompson in *Rain*. Millions of women copied the look, but the French fashion magazine *Marie-Clare* advised its readers to refrain from imitating the Crawford mouth unless they had her "hippopotamus eyes" to balance it.

In addition to his dimples and protruding ears, Gable was known for his tousled hair and adorable forehead curl, but even he affected Valentino's brilliantined head in his first films. Patent-leather hair was kept in style for years after Valentino's death by screen sophisticates like Fred Astaire and Robert Montgomery, who found their hair pieces could fake it more convincingly than the natural look.

When Perc Westmore created Claudette Colbert's perky bangs, millions of admiring American women followed suit. Claudette still wears the coif today, forty years later.

Joan Crawford

Claudette Colbert

Ingrid Bergman

Gina Lollobrigida

touches that could be acquired for pennies at the dimestore or accomplished with a snip of the scissors.

In 1939, David O. Selznick memoed an associate: "Ann Rutherford, whom I saw on the train, told me something which might be the basis of some excellent publicity, which is that all the girls she knows are letting their eyebrows grow in as a result of Bergman's unplucked eyebrows [in *Intermezzo*]. So apparently our decision about Miss Bergman's eyebrows, based upon this studio's feeling that the public was sick and tired of the monstrosities inflicted on them by most of Hollywood's glamour girls, is going to have a national reaction."

Fashion-conscious American women weren't the only film fans to copy Audrey Hepburn's blond streaks in *Breakfast at Tiffany's.* Another trendsetter, Gloria Steinem, affected the style well into her liberated look of the seventies.

Insiders say that Gina Lollobrigida's poodle cut in *Trapeze* was the work of a wigmaster. But even if the Italian import isn't really as hirsute as we've believed all these years, she managed to inspire loads of teenaged girls to trade in their pony tails for poodles, back in the fifties.

Had it not been for an unexpected pregnancy, Cyd Charisse would have been Gene Kelly's dancing partner in *An American in Paris,* instead of newcomer Leslie Caron. And American girls would've had to wait until the sixties for waiflike Mia Farrow to provide the inspiration for the gamine cut.

Elizabeth Taylor deserves the credit, along with Italian street-gang girls, for the heavily lined eye and pearlized lipstick look of the late fifties and early sixties. Remember all those paparazzi shots of Liz in her Cleopatra eyes and fur hats, sneaking around Rome with Dicky?

Leslie Caron

Audrey Hepburn

Elizabeth Taylor

Stolen Face

Imitation is the sincerest form of plagiarism. It wasn't only matinee ladies who copied the cosmetic trademarks of their favorites; stars aped other stars. Look at an early Alice Faye and you will see an *hommage* to Harlow. For a time, even a reluctant Bette Davis sported platinum hair and plucked eyebrows. Dolores Del Rio took a cue from Crawford and exaggerated her eyes, which improved her look dramatically. Crawford, in turn, was heavily influenced by Gloria Swanson. Over at Columbia, everybody was given the Hayworth mane: Ann Miller, Jinx Falkenburg, Adele Jergens, Evelyn Keyes, and even a budding starlet named Marilyn Monroe. The hairdo of Hedy Lamarr altered the course of Joan Bennett's career. When the script of *Trade Winds* called for a dye job halfway through the film, Bennett startled moviegoers as an exotic brunette (a wig). Nothing new for those who'd seen *Algiers*. Hedy cattily attributed Bennett's new look to an ongoing romance with one of her old mentors, Walter Wanger. Cole Porter immortalized it in "Let's Not Talk About Love" by asking the musical question, "Let's speak of Lamarr, that Hedy so fair, why does she let Joan Bennett wear all her old hair?"

Rita Hayworth

Lana Turner

Jean Harlow

Alice Faye

Dolores Del Rio

Joan Crawford

Evelyn Keyes

Liza Minnelli

Rita Hayworth

Louise Brooks

Marlene Dietrich

Hedy Lamarr 1940

Joan Bennett
circa 1935

Joan Bennett
1942

Carole Lombard

45

Between the Lines

Every publicity photo of a star issued by the studios—and there were hundreds weekly during Hollywood's heyday—was the product of a collaboration involving an amazingly large group of people. First came the studio beauty machine: the makeup, coiffeur, and costume wizards who conjured up the heavenly bodies. Their handiwork was passed on to the talented still photographers who chronicled the film industry and ballyhooed its product; theirs was an art form that flaunted drama and artifice, a set of photographic conventions that became passé during the organic sixties. They could supply character and beauty where none existed and eliminate unflattering defects with shadow and light. Which brings up the subject of this section's *hommage:* the final component of Hollywood's legendary glamour photography, the studio retouching squad. These unsung heroes pored over the photographer's work in search of facial and figure flaws that couldn't be camouflaged even by the elaborate packaging of the beauty machine. They then spent untold hours using a multitude of sophisticated techniques to erase from the negative the physical imperfections that were considered unforgivable in a star.

The studio retouchers applied to their work their own aesthetic interpretation of physical perfection (based on doctrine handed down from the Front Office, of course). When a star laughed, smiled, or raised his eyebrows in a questioning glance, his facial contours seemed to remain at rest, smooth and lineless. Women's legs were contoured, wrinkles in clothing smoothed away, skin texture washed clean, veins and boniness removed from hands, wisps of flyaway hair etched out, waistlines reduced, and, until well into the fifties, cleavage erased, even if it necessitated drawing in new necklines for costumes to disguise the deletion.

One unhappy side effect of the studio's tendency to tamper with nature was the disappointment some stars encountered when they met the public in the flesh. Even the most beautiful ended up as Dorian Grays in reverse: they aged but their photographs didn't. When they made the transition from Hollywood's helpful embellishment to the stark lighting and photography of television, we were shocked. They seemed to have metamorphosed overnight from beautiful youth into aging mockeries of themselves.

We took the negatives for the shots you see here to our special photo lab and made the unusual request that one set be printed with the retouching as is, and one set with the retoucher's alterations "washed." When we returned, we were startled by the difference in the before and after faces and bodies. But the technician who removed the studio's alterations assured us that only a small portion of the retouching had been removed; the rest was "etched" directly on the negative. This is a time-consuming process that actually carves out tiny flaws like facial hair, pores, freckles, and the like. He further informed us that the meticulous work on these photos was the finest artistry he'd ever encountered, and that it would be impossible to find anyone capable of executing it today.

———— ☆ ————

Of course, most of the retouching applied to publicity photos was employed to counteract the onslaught of age. But even the photos of the young Barbara Stanwyck underwent a significant transformation before they were released for publication.

Barbara Stanwyck

Bette Davis

Ronald Colman

Claire Trevor

Adolphe Menjou

Claudette Colbert

Although this shot of Claudette Colbert was taken many years after her days as a *femme fatale,* she seems to have required little in the way of camouflage from the skillful hands of the studio retouchers. However, they did make one very interesting change. If you'll notice, a chunk of Claudette's shoulder has been painted out of the picture, thus creating the impression that she has a bit more neck than the original. Perhaps they'd heard about the time Noel Coward threatened Claudette, "I'd wring your neck, if you had one."

RANDOLPH
SCOTT
Paramount

A few Hollywood photographers, among them the great Hurrell, handled their own retouching chores, since they were well versed in the desires of their subjects. Hurrell recalls Bogart as a rarity, who instructed him to "leave in the lines. I'm proud of them." But Marlene Dietrich supervised every detail of the manner in which she was to be posed, lit, and retouched.

Hurrell worked with Dietrich for many years, and out of their alliance came some of the most memorable glamour shots of the era. He recently reminisced about their last collaboration:

Years later, when she was performing in nightclubs, I did a sitting with Dietrich. She was the same polite, concerned woman. Her bone structure still took the light as it had in the old days. But when she returned the proofs to me, they were marked all over with fine lines, indicating what should be removed by the retoucher. She shook her head sadly. "You don't take pictures like you used to, George." "But Marlene," I said, and also shook my head sadly, "I'm fifteen years older!"

THE GIRL CAN'T HELP IT

IT'S GOT THE HEAT! AND THE BEAT!

20th CENTURY-FOX presents

TOM EWELL · JAYNE MANSFIELD · EDMOND O'BRIEN

It may come as a shock to those of you out there who still think that Russ Meyer invented cleavage to discover that a great many of the popular films of the twenties and thirties had more in common with *Return of the Cheerleaders* than with *Orphans of the Storm*. America wasn't nearly so straitlaced in the old days as grandma would have you think. Frontal nudity wasn't exactly a staple of the silents and early talkies, but it was hardly unheard of either. As late as 1933, screen bosoms were slipping into something more comfortable (like a filmy negligee), bobbing perkily in sunken baths, and meandering unencumbered under clinging gowns. But by 1934, the party was over.

The film industry was given an ultimatum by those wonderful people who brought you Prohibition: either Hollywood doused the conflagration of flesh and freewheeling sex on the screen, or they—the American Legion and various women's groups—would see to it that public boycotts did. Hollywood knuckled under to the pressure groups' priggish demands. The Hays Office, the

THE GIRL CAN'T HELP IT

industry's censorship board, instituted the A___ ___ Law of 1934 (really) which officially blackli___ from the screen, thus stopping their career ___

For most of the thirties, the bosom was fo___ sanctuary abroad. The late, great Howard Hu___ expedite the bosom's return to the American screen with *The Outlaw* in 1943, but the country's wartime consciousness had become so self-righteous that warrants were immediately issued for its arrest. (A Baltimore judge observed that Jane Russell's bosom hung over the film like a "thunderstorm over a landscape.") It seemed advisable for the bosom to limit its exposure to foreign films and pinup work at the Front until things cooled off.

When cleavage came marching home in 1945, the moral climate of America had changed considerably. Sex was still a dirty word, mind you, but that's what made it so much fun. As usual, Hollywood was in the forefront of the culture's sexual chic, and, by its calculations, the bosom was due for a comeback. It was off with the sensible man-tailored suits and *Swing Shift Maisie* drabs of the war years for dames and doyennes alike and into the structured brassiere (affectionately referred to as the "bullet tit").

Almost single-handedly, Howard Hughes spread mammary madness throughout the country via the screen. Most of the homegrown Amazons and bosomy imports that monopolized the media during the fifties were signed exclusively to him. He might have failed at getting his Spruce Goose campaign off the ground with the public, but he got the nation by the libido when he revived *The Outlaw* in 1946.

The Outlaw had become a household word in America, even though it had been shut down almost immediately when it first opened in 1943. Three years later the film board still refused to grant its seal of approval unless generous portions of Jane Russell's cleavage were relegated to the cutting room floor. The Wizard of Hype compensated for the massive cuts by revving up the film's buildup with catchy slogans ("What are the two biggest reasons for Jane Russell's success?") and peddling a trumped-up story that he himself had invented an

___lywood everything it need___ the beginning of a new ___ America. But more impor___ the threshold of assuming ___

In the fifties, Hollywo___ context for exposed fles___ there could be no doubt t___ were on the move. Cleavage started showing up in women's prison movies, the kind that starred Cleo Moore, and films of the *Bosom and Sand* variety à la Yvonne De Carlo. Jayne Mansfield's endowments were glorified in *The Girl Can't Help It* by director Frank Tashlin, whose philosophy turned the bosom into one big joke. "There's nothin' more hysterical to me than big-breasted women—like leaning Towers of Pisa." In 1957, Jayne gave the bosom another thrust forward by becoming the first sort-of-big star to disrobe for *Playboy*, beginning what would be a long association between that magazine and Hollywood. And it was Jayne, of course, who broke the long-standing taboo forbidding big names to display their aggregate charms on the screen. *Promises, Promises* may have wrecked Jayne's career, but it was her unselfish act that paved the way for other serious actresses like Jane Fonda, Diane Keaton, and Faye Dunaway to give their all for their art.

Join us now for a cavalcade of cleavage, starring bosoms we have all known and loved. This category will test your cleavage IQ. If the size and shape don't ring a bell, then perhaps a costume will. There might be some cheesecake in the line that's unfamiliar to you; it's been included as a reminder that plunging necklines and cleavage chic aren't always limited to sexy types. As a built-in handicap, we give you the work of the studio retouching squad who airbrushed out cleavage in publicity shots of the thirties and forties, and drew it in from the fifties on.

1.

Her plush curves served as the inspiration for Hays Office censorship and life preservers.

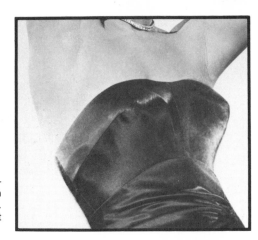

2.

She was Columbia boss Harry Cohn's greatest invention, but her rocky romances made them both miserable. "Men always expect me to be Gilda . . . they're disappointed when they find out I'm just me."

4.

America's first sex star, the former Theodoshia Goodwin of Chillicothe, Ohio, was the screen's exotic Egyptian vamp of the twenties.

5.

Although she was famous for her bosom, the Front Office would never have okayed this kind of exposure for its studio publicity. This shot is part of a series by master photographer George Hurrell for the risqué men's magazine, *Esquire.*

6.

She was ashamed of her bountiful bosom and was forever trying to hide it with tulle and lace. The camouflage worked with ordinary projection, but audiences ducked when she turned profile to front in the 3-D musical, *Kiss Me Kate.*

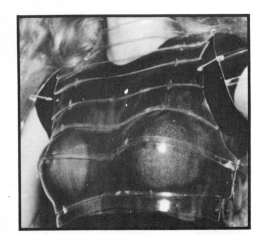

7.

She traded her plastic chest protector for suburban cleavage when she became a politician's wife.

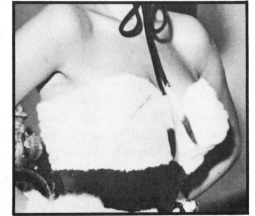

8.

Her career began to sag after she got into trouble with Uncle Sam in Korea. When she showed up for a USO show in an abbreviated ermine bathing suit, the Army brass sent her packing, saying it just wasn't healthy for lonely boys to see "that kind of girl" in that kind of act.

9.

When collectors purchased her bathing suits at the MGM auction, they were startled to find portions of her voluptuous anatomy still sewn inside.

10.

Fox's campaign for *The Tall Men* described her by saying, "They Don't Come Any Bigger!" George S. Kaufman had described her debut a few years earlier in *The Outlaw* as "The Sale of Two Titties."

11.

Uncle Walt demanded that she turn in her Mouseka-ears when she outgrew her Mouseketeer T-shirt. She traded Anything Can Happen Day for *Beach Blanket Bingo.*

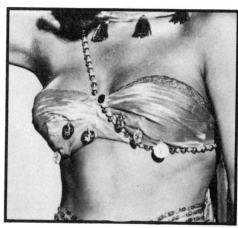

12.

In the fifties, she was Sweden's answer to Jayne Mansfield. These days, she's Sweden's answer to Kate Smith.

13.

In the fifties, she was Britain's answer to Jayne Mansfield. These days, she's Britain's answer to Anita Ekberg.

14.

She was discovered by Norma Shearer, but it took Howard Hughes to package her special talents properly. It was those very talents that earned her the Golden Bust Award from a brassiere manufacturer back in 1962.

15.

In *They Drive by Night,* the truck drivers made cracks about her "headlights."

16.

When asked if he intended to see the sensational, *Samson and Delilah,* Groucho Marx replied, "I never see movies where the man's tits are bigger than the woman's."

17.

She wasn't the first choice for the role of Maggie in *Cat on a Hot Tin Roof.* That's right, if Grace Kelly hadn't traded Hollywood for Monaco, it would've been *her* royal orbs, rather than those you see exhibited here on display in the movie version of the Broadway hit.

18.

This bombshell's cantilevered brassiere may have been the height of style back in the fifties, but it must have been impractical for dancing cheek-to-cheek.

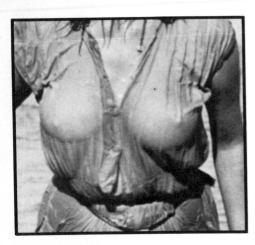

19.

"I was just a fifteen year-old kid with a bosom and a backside strolling across the screen" (in *They Won't Forget).* But the legend that she'd been discovered having a soda at Schwab's Drugstore was studio puffery invented to sell her first film.

20.

Her motto: "If you have physical attractiveness, you don't have to act."

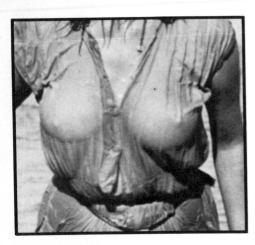

21.

She started out in pictures "the way Marilyn Monroe did—in my birthday suit. But there are some differences. I'm not ashamed of my bare-bottomed beginnings" (in Italian skin flicks).

22.

She was usually lost in a harem in hokum adventures, but that made no difference to her. "When I see myself on the screen, I am so beautiful that I scream for joy."

23.

Rave magazine said that "In 1947 her lollos were as little known as her name, but when she became Miss Italia, she caught the eye of a Mr. Hughes who flew her to Hollywood for a screen test."

24.

While filming *The Spanish Main,* she confessed her secret for foiling the censors to her costume designer. After undergoing a cleavage check before a scene, she pushed down her waistband and took a deep breath till her breasts almost popped out of her peasant blouse.

24. Maureen O'Hara　　　**25. Evelyn Keyes**　　　**26. Jayne Mansfield**

27. Joan Blondell　　　**28. Lupe Velez**　　　**29. Natalie Wood**

30. Judy Holliday　　　**31. Marie Wilson**　　　**32. Dame Edith Evans**

59

GOING HOLLYWOOD

Ida Lupino next to the hillside pool of her new Hollywood home.

t the height of the Depression, while socialist rhetoric exhorted the masses to cast out the demons of economic tyranny, the pages of *Photoplay* featured Joan Crawford's proclamation of her duty as patriot and star to fend off economic disaster by investing her movie star wages in furs and jewels. "I, Joan Crawford, I Believe in the Dollar. Every Dollar I Earn I Spend!" After all, didn't she owe it to her downtrodden fans to act the part of movie star to the hilt? And to the country to keep her earnings in circulation? No sacrifice was too great for our Joan.

Curiously, the citizenry did not rise up to demand the heads of those movie stars who flaunted their wealth as the rest of the country fought to free itself from the Depression's grasp. Maybe that's because most of us had heard that Joan Crawford herself used to sling hash before she went French Provincial, or that Clara Bow had paid her dues in a Brooklyn tenement before she could afford a mansion to flap in. Exotics and Britishers notwithstanding, screen fame seemed to have little to do with worldliness or education, and was ostensibly within anyone's reach.

These gods and goddesses had origins of clay and we knew it. The more stark our own worlds, the more necessary it became to keep alive these symbols of the American Dream. Stardom was bestowed by popular mandate; it was our hard-earned quarters that sanctioned a star's excess. The stars who survived were the ones who understood that what the fans gave, they could just as easily take away.

Taxes were still nominal, and Hollywood's kings and queens lived far more luxuriously than most of the reigning families in Europe. Most of them tossed their money around as though they manufactured it themselves in the cellar. They went in for solid gold bathtubs, chauffeur-driven Rolls Royces, champagne for breakfast and caviar every fifteen minutes. It was the kind of luxury that today only exists...for the sons of a few Latin American dictators.

—Groucho Marx

Smart stars like Joan Crawford and Constance Bennett alternated between socialites and shopgirls on screen in order to keep their images from becoming too highfalutin' for their straphanging fans. No matter how regal ("Gloria Swanson was a vision in sables and sapphires"), the stars were expected to have the common touch ("Myrna Loy admitted to us recently that she envies those Los Angeles secretaries who have the leisure time to shop on their lunch hours").

The stars were like public corporations with each fan owning a share; not only were they required to be constantly accessible on the screen, but they also were obliged to provide a public accounting of their newfound wealth on demand. Their marble chateaux, Moorish moderne haciendas, yachts, and fantasy automobiles were packaged for the fanzines right along with their families, love lives, and most embarrassing moments.

Beverly Hills was the enclave of the chosen, so exclusive that Douglas Fairbanks once seriously suggested that it be enclosed by a wall. Noisy sightseeing buses filled with slackjawed tourists made daily pilgrimages to the stylish encampment, the guides tossing off inaccurate data about the homes of the stars. (For years, the Bel Air Country Club was pointed out as Jean Harlow's home..."where champagne flows and anything goes.") *Nouveau riche* screen royalty aped the life styles of the *nouveau riche* robber barons of the East (who struggled to impress castle *riche* European nobility). The race to keep up with the Fairbankses resulted in some of the most outlandish cannibalizations of period and style to be seen this side of a studio backlot. Cape Cod and adobe collided head on with Oriental and ranch-style; pseudo-Tudor felt perfectly at home nestled in a grove of palm trees. Interiors were often designed by studio art directors who created an elegant if overstated translation of a star's image in his home surroundings. (See the Gary Cooper House.) Several transplants from the East like Fanny Brice and Miriam Hopkins were clever enough to decorate professionally, but if left to their own tastes, most stars tended to festoon their new digs in early Stella Dallas. Back East society snobs got a kick out of telling the one about the movie star who fired her decorator for blowing her moolah on that statue with the broken arms.

Studio administrators were often responsible for situating a promising new contract player in a lush Beverly Hills pad or for bestowing a snappy new roadster on a young star who was too busy to know what he or she couldn't live without. This proved to be a convenient arrangement, since the stars tended to be more docile when the old homestead was mortgaged to the company store.

Too much of a good thing is wonderful, and extravagance can be addictive. Many an unsuspecting Cinderella squandered her fortune on champagne and caviar, unaware that stardom can disappear practically overnight. Silent queen Mae Murray was deserted by MGM as well as her Italian count when her delusions of grandeur became too overbearing for the fans. One of the most spectacularly profligate of all the twenties stars, she was destitute a scant number of years after her reign came to an end. Veronica Lake got along by waiting tables when the public grew cold. And Mickey Rooney and Betty Hutton, who'd earned tens of millions for their respective studios, ended up making their most publicized appearances in bankruptcy court.

Expensive tastes, multiple marriages, and career misfires bounced the stars from hacienda to hacienda. The various Beverly Hills mansions, yachts, and custom-made autos passed through so many famous hands that Hollywood society could chronicle the ups and downs of a star's fortunes in terms of whose possessions he or she was renting at the time.

Today most of the fabled showplaces have been razed to make way for shopping centers and freeways, but a Beverly Hills home with a star-studded pedigree continues to be *de rigueur* for the glamour trade (and the pedigree is worth concocting should none exist). Nowadays, however, the hallowed halls of the few remaining movie star mansions resound with the jangle of rock-and-roll money. Elton John parks his feather boas and platforms in the mountainside mansion that once belonged to John Gilbert and later to David Selznick and his new wife, Jennifer Jones. Liberace can still be found at the address with the candelabra-shaped swimming pool, but things just haven't been the same since Ringo Starr painted Jayne Mansfield's all-pink dreamhouse white.

"Most appliance bulbs are brighter than Shelley Winters."
—Michael O'Donoghue

Al Jolson

Clara Bow

Carole Lombard

Gary Cooper's dining room

Claire Trevor outside her home

The Hollywood home of **Gloria Swanson**

The trophy room in the home of **Gary Cooper**

On screen Harold Lloyd was the personification of get-up-and-go for countless numbers of movie fans. It was his real-life application of this energy that made him millions in the movie business. No expense was spared in building Greenacres, his sixteen-acre Beverly Hills estate. Four years of work (beginning in 1924) and two and a half million dollars made it an architectural marvel. Surrounding the forty-four-room Italian Renaissance palace were an English cottage, formal gardens, and full athletic facilities. Anyone doubting that movie stars were America's answer to European nobility should survey His Majesty Harold's kingdom.

The children's garden—chute the chutes

The game room

The Grand Foyer

View of the front entrance to the main house

A rear view of the house and gardens

The master bedroom

The Olympic size pool

The Lagoon

When the cost of maintaining Greenacres became a burden to Harold Lloyd's heirs, they suggested to the California state legislature that it be acquired by the state and made available for tours like the Hearst castle. But the neighbors didn't want all those out-of-towners with their Hawaiian shirts and binoculars cluttering up their stylish community. So Greenacres was leveled in 1975 to be replaced by apartment houses.

Movie star homes weren't usually encumbered by the prevailing standards of good taste.. Flamboyant life styles demanded flamboyant environments. Hollywood manses existed in another realm—a never-never land in which styles could be madly mixed or carried to absurd extremes. Lilies were not only gilded, but fertilized with diamond nuggets.

In the same spirit of eclecticism and showmanship, we have combined these fragments of bygone Hollywood lifestyle into the ultimate movie star home.

John Barrymore in his study

Tom Mix's bedroom

Glenda Farrell in her living room

Marlene Dietrich in her private sitting room

The living room in the home of **Jean Harlow**

Dorothy Lamour in her dressing room

Elissa Landi at her bar

Cecil B. De Mille in his screening room

The sun porch in the home of **Ray Milland**

Pat O'Brien in his library

Adolphe Menjou and Mrs. Menjou
in their music room

Martha Raye in her rec room

Jean Arthur

HOW TO WIN AN OSCAR

Every spring, as Oscar time rolls around, the country's presiding culture mavens manage to work themselves into a colossal snit at the very thought of the impending ritual. They accuse the awards and the people who pick and package them of having about as much class as the Miss America Pageant. And every year Hollywood manages to prove them right. Oscar tackiness has run the gamut from the impromptu proselytizing of Marlon Brando's proxy, ersatz Indian Princess Sasheen Little Feather, to the most recent embarrassment—the revelation that the group of "deaf" children who accompanied Debby Boone's rendition of the 1978 Oscar-winning song, "You Light Up My Life," with sign language weren't really deaf students from the John Tracy Clinic as announced, but professional child actors specially coached for the telecast.

Oscar's reputation first became tarnished during the fifties with the decline of the studio system and with what, some say, was the quality of motion pictures themselves. Up until then, aside from a tendency to be overly impressed with the film performances of stars primarily known for their work on the legitimate stage (these were the Mr. and Miss So-and-So's like "Mr." George Arliss and "Miss" Helen Hayes whom the studios tended to showcase in heavy drama or plodding epics), it's difficult to find fault with the Academy's choices. Most of the great films and talents of the period were given their due, except for a few unforgivable oversights . . . like Cary Grant, Rosalind Russell, and Irene Dunne, not to mention Edward G. Robinson, who was never even nominated. But after the war, the country became mesmerized by its small screens at home, and Hollywood responded by making its product even bigger and more expensive than before via star-studded casts, Technicolor, and projection gimmicks like Cinerama and Todd-A O. Instead of movies, it gave us "history making events" like *Around the World in Eighty Days* and *Ben Hur* with casts of thousands and costs of millions. And for some years hence when it came time for Hollywood and Oscar to salute cinematic excellence, it was spectacle not quality that carried the day. But then, Hollywood has always had a tendency to fall for its own hype.

It was also during the fifties that rumors began to be bounced around by the press and various Hollywood watchers to the effect that Oscar's affections could be bought. *Confidential* magazine even went so far as to suggest that the annual presentation of the Academy Awards would be more aptly titled "The Price Is Right." From around this time on, the public's skepticism about the integrity of the awards has never really been dispelled. Only recently *Oui* magazine called Oscar a "symbol of totally irrelevant accomplishment," observing that "if Oscar were a real person, instead of a thirteen-inch bowling trophy, he'd be doing hard time at Folsom Prison right now" on a bunko rap.

But our answer is that, of course, the awards are

baloney...and yes, Virginia, there *is* more to winning one of those lovely little gold-plated statuettes than talent. But then, no one ever said that all the profiteering and narcissism that accompanies the Academy Awards is at odds with the ideals on which the Academy was founded, now did they? The fact is that politicking and power games happen to coincide beautifully with the spirit in which the Academy was conceived.

It all started back in the twenties, when MGM boss Louis B. Mayer made the astute observation that the film industry had the affection of the country, but not its respect. Using a rationale that sounded something like Frank Morgan's final speech as the Wizard of Oz (in which he deduced that the only thing keeping the scarecrow from having a brain was a diploma) Mayer reasoned that Hollywood had only to shower itself with public praise, to become praiseworthy in the public eye. The fact that there might be a potential conflict of interest, since said praise would be doled out by a congress of judges composed of business associates and potential competitors, was immaterial. In any case, he wasn't going to wait around for a commemorative stamp.

Mayer and his co-conspirators had hatched the idea for the Academy Awards while the film industry was still feeling the sting of pressure groups' demands that Hollywood curb the scandalous off-screen behavior of its stars and the prurient nature of much of its product. It's no coincidence that the creation of the Academy was masterminded by the same crew that had hurriedly created the industry's self-policing censorship board a few years earlier. Both institutions were part of an ingenious propaganda campaign contrived to clean up Hollywood's image with the public. The founding fathers intended to convince the public that movie-making was an art, not a hustle.

Officially the Academy was to be an autonomous non-profit organization devoted to technical research and the exchange of artistic ideas. But that was for later. In the meantime, the primary function of the Academy, underneath all that lofty rhetoric, was to conduct the awards ceremony.

Taking a cue from its own suspense thrillers, the Academy announced nominees months in advance of the ceremony, amidst tons of Hollywood hoopla. The ceremony itself evolved into a dazzling mixture of a gala movie premiere, the Pulitzer Prize announcements, and a company picnic. Millions of Americans attended the ceremonies via radio broadcasts and newsreels during the first years, and television audiences for the event would eventually number as high as 300,000,000 in the years following its first televised broadcast in 1953.

All that Tinseltown pomp and show biz circumstance have worked like a charm over the years to confer prestige and dignity on the most unlikely candidates. Take *The Exorcist,* for example . . . a lavishly appointed horror show whose bag of tricks included a little girl masturbating with a crucifix while shouting obscenities at her mother. It earned several Academy Awards as well as receiving nominations for Best Picture and Best Supporting Actress (the little girl). The millions spent on the production of *The Exorcist,* as well as the gratifying box office returns, absolved the film, screenwriter William Peter Blatty, director William Friedkin, and each and every one of the Brothers Warner (R.I.P.) of the taint of obscenity for purposes of crass exploitation. (Guest appearances by two Jesuit priests helped to win the film an R rating.)

It's no secret that Oscar is keenly aware of the debt owed an expensive production like *The Exorcist* which keeps hundreds of high-priced actors and technicians employed. But for those of little faith who insist that Academy members vote with their Swiss bank accounts, not their heads, we submit that when it comes to acting kudos, Oscar is a sucker for certain rarely publicized gambits that have nothing to do with payola.

For instance, there's nothing that inspires the gentleman's respect more than when one of the screen's elite has the guts to tousle his hair or forsake his makeup, corsets, and specially designed wardrobe in the name of art. This approach is particularly effective if utilized while portraying an idiot, drunk, nut case, or aging Southern belle. And Oscar adores flashy thespian conceits like those in which an actor goes from childhood to senility in the time it takes to finish a box of Dots.

Yes, there are all of these and more. And they're just a few of the paths that lead to Oscar's door. So if you're out to win the affection of Hollywood's most sought-after male, you'll do well to remember that surprise and sentiment pull more weight with our boy than genius and gelt combined.

In fact, if someone will hand us the envelope, please . . . we'll show you just exactly how it's done.

Sandra Dee's real name is Alexandra Zuck.

BE DESERVING THE YEAR BEFORE . . .

Joan Fontaine for *Suspicion (Rebecca)*

Right:
Glenda Jackson for *A Touch of Class (Sunday Bloody Sunday)*

BE HOLLYWOOD'S ANSWER
TO JACKIE ROBINSON . . .

Sidney Poitier for *Lilies of the Field*

IF YOU'RE AN ACTOR'S ACTOR,
TAKE OUT YOUR TEETH . .

WEAR A FUNNY NOSE . . .

Walter Huston
for *The Treasure of the Sierra Madre*

Lee Marvin for *Cat Ballou*

José Ferrer for *Cyrano de Bergerac*

BE A PERSONAL FRIEND OF GOD'S . . .

Jennifer Jones
for *The Song of Bernadette*

Bing Crosby and **Barry Fitzgerald**
for *Going My Way*

IF YOU'RE A TOUGH GUY, DUST OFF YOUR TAP SHOES . . .

James Cagney for *Yankee Doodle Dandy*

IF YOU'RE A FUNNYMAN, PLAY IT STRAIGHT . . .

Jack Lemmon for *Days of Wine and Roses*

Red Buttons for *Sayonara*

IF YOU'RE A GLAMOUR GIRL,
SHOW YOUR AGE . . .

Vivien Leigh for *A Streetcar Named Desire*

MUSS YOUR HAIR AND
LET IT ALL HANG OUT . . .

LET YOUR EYEBROWS GROW IN . . .

Elizabeth Taylor for
Who's Afraid of Virginia Woolf?

Jane Wyman for *Johnny Belinda*

Olivia De Havilland for
The Heiress

TEAR YOUR DRESS . . .

Sophia Loren for *Two Women*

TRADE YOUR DIORS FOR SEAR'S CATALOGUE CHIC . . .

Grace Kelly for *The Country Girl*

Patricia Neal for *Hud*

IF YOU'RE A GOOD GIRL, PLAY A BAD GIRL . . .

Donna Reed for *From Here to Eternity*

Shirley Jones for *Elmer Gantry*

IF YOU'RE A BON VIVANT, PLAY A LUSH . . .   **OR A NERD . . .**

Ray Milland for *The Lost Weekend*

David Niven for *Separate Tables*

WASHED UP? MAKE A COMEBACK . . .

Frank Sinatra for *From Here to Eternity*

Ingrid Bergman for *Anastasia*

Joan Crawford for *Mildred Pierce*

BE AN UNDERDOG . . .

Julie Andrews
for *Mary Poppins*

CHEAT DEATH . . .

Elizabeth Taylor for *Butterfield 8*

GIVE YOUR RIGHT ARM
FOR YOUR COUNTRY . . .

Harold Russell for
The Best Years of Our Lives

HANG ARO[UND]

Margaret Rutherford for *The V.I.P.'s*

John Wayne for *True Grit*

George Burns for *The Sunshine Boys*

Ruth Gordon for *Rosemary's Baby*

EXPIRE . . .

Peter Finch for *Network*

81

Robert Montgomery and Carole Lombard in *Mr. and Mrs. Smith*

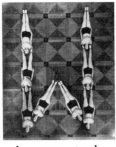

When it came to love among the stars, official studio policy went something like this: it was perfectly acceptable for the stars to be photographed together in a passionate embrace on the set of their newest; or to travel cross-country together to ballyhoo their latest; or to be seen together after hours holding hands at a stylish watering hole. But under no circumstances was all this togetherness to lead to copulation. Of course, it rarely led to anything else.

But who could blame them? There they were, the most beautiful, the most desirable, the most tantalizing creatures that ever set foot on the planet, the *crème de la crème* of humankind, thrown together for hours on end, speaking the words of love, miming the motions of desire. Who could blame them if they couldn't slow down the emotional momentum simply because the cameras stopped rolling? Not us, certainly. Though there must have been a few hapless Hollywood spouses who could blame them plenty. But, apparently, even they understood that the rules of love were different for the stars; and besides, there was usually never any real cause for alarm, seeing as these little infatuations had a way of going up in smoke once a picture was in the can. It was as if the co-stars had an unspoken agreement that whatever the ailment was they were suffering from—be it love, lust, or the tunafish salad they'd had for lunch—convalescence was just for the length of shooting time.

Between us, even the studios approved of this arrangement. Their unofficial position on the subject was that an affair between co-stars or a director and his leading lady was good for a picture. For, besides promoting a sense of mutual trust between co-workers in what is potentially one of the most tension filled atmospheres imaginable, the sparks that fly when lovers play lovers gives off a discernible heat on the screen. When a star had that "special glow" in the rushes, studio insiders spoke knowingly of the "inspiration" she was getting from her leading man.

And then there were those liaisons between the powerful and the meek that could be so beneficial to a newcomer's career and so uplifting to a mogul's morale. Clearly, the friendships of Marilyn Monroe with Joseph Schenck, Ingrid Bergman with David O. Selznick, Lana Turner with Mervyn Le Roy, and practically every starlet in Hollywood with Howard Hughes didn't do their careers any harm. Surely everyone knows by now that a starlet didn't really have any choice if she expected to get anywhere in the movies. Joan Collins recalls in her memoirs that when she first arrived at Fox, she was cornered by boss Darryl Zanuck who pressed her against a wall and informed her by way of introduction, "You've had nothing until you've had me. I am the biggest and the best. I can go all night and all day." Joan says she declined Zanuck's offer, but more ambitious newcomers didn't dare take the chance. And as far as affairs between directors and their leading ladies go, as Otto Preminger explained to Dorothy

Dandridge on the first day of *Carmen Jones,* "It's the accepted practice." Frank Capra says it like this: "It's true that directors often fall in love with their leading ladies, at least while they're making a film together. They come to know each other so intimately—more so than married couples—and their relationship is so close emotionally, so charged creatively, it can easily drift into a Pygmalion-and-Galatea affinity." Yup, that ol' creatively charged air will do it every time.

However, the same air that can bring on an incipient case of the hots might then again prove too turbulent for Cupid's darts. Elvis Presley, for instance, was absolutely crazy for Ann-Margret while they were making *Viva Las Vegas* together till one of the film's directorial assistants became so smitten with the lady himself that he ended up virtually cutting Elvis out of the movie. Elvis eventually warmed up to his co-star again once the Colonel had the lovesick assistant canned. Today power tussles like studio romances have a way of vanishing once a picture is, as we show biz folk say, "wrapped" with the former combatants pledging their eternal friendship (usually for the benefit of the tv cameras). The ill will that pervaded the set of the recent Streisand-Peters production of *A Star Is Born* was so heavy that Kris Kristofferson ended up blowing his cool in front of a gaggle of reporters. He informed producer Jon Peters that, "If I need some shit from you, I'll squeeze your head!" But as soon as the picture was ready for release, the bad feelings between Kris, Barbra, and Jon had disappeared as if by magic, and all three got together for the premiere and lots of kissy photos. Director Frank Pierson was a most visible exception. He vented his wrath against Barbra and Peters with a hot behind-the-scenes account of the filming in *New York* magazine. Apparently once the principals had gotten away from the turmoil of the set and had a chance to cool off, they'd decided to bury their grievances for the welfare of the picture. They had little choice, since in order for *Star* to sell, audiences were going to have to buy Kris and Barbra as lovers.

During the years of studio indenture, however, if a star had a rivalry going with a fellow contract player for roles or for the attentions of a member of the opposite sex, the antagonism was constantly aggravated by the nature of the studio setup. Just like any office or factory worker, the stars rubbed elbows with their enemies daily at work, in the commissary, and in social situations. And if that weren't bad enough, the studios fostered these feuds and rivalries by pitting star against star. Disciplining an uppity actor who refused to do a particular script by threatening to give the part to a despised competitor was an excellent way of keeping him in line. And in terms of publicity value, there was nothing like a public airing of a feud between stars like, say, Bette Davis and Miriam Hopkins to fuel the adversary relationship they had on the screen. It was no coincidence, for instance, when Jack Warner teamed off-screen rivals Edward G. Robinson and George Raft as the friendly enemies of *Manpower*. These long-standing conflicts eventually became almost as legendary as the stars themselves. George Raft despised Edward G. Robinson who detested his *Barbary Coast* co-star Miriam Hopkins who made life miserable for Bette Davis who slugged her *Elizabeth and Essex* leading man Errol Flynn who put a dead snake in the unmentionables of Olivia De Havilland who couldn't stand her sister Joan Fontaine who couldn't abide Cary Grant and.... Well, we could go on all day.

And just as the power game between the men in command and their stars could quite naturally segue into a sexual tango, so could it just as easily explode in rebellion and temper tantrums over matters of ambition or artistic interpretation. Bette Davis fled to England to escape Jack Warner's second-class scripts and first-class bullying; Lee Marvin showered his contempt on *Paint Your Wagon* director Josh Logan by urinating on his shoes; and director Michael Curtiz found working with Joan Crawford on *Mildred Pierce* so frustrating that he literally ripped the shoulder pads out of her dress.

Some of Hollywood's romantic couplings (Tracy and Hepburn, Garbo and Gilbert) and star wars (Fields and West, Davis and Hopkins) have become so familiar, they're practically a part of the national heritage. However, you won't find the juicy details in that handy little tv-movie guide that you keep next to the bed. And let's face it, what you'd really like to know about all those movies that perambulate the Late Show isn't who gets the girl at the end of the movie, but who made the girl while the picture was being shot. Or who clobbered his co-star when she got in the way of his close-up. So, with that thought in mind, we've put together our very own handy little guide to Hollywood's four-star feuds and flirtations, an index to who made it and who didn't in Tinseltown.

We give you Hollywood with Love and Hisses...

Cyd Charisse's real name is Tula Finklea.

1. **Ryan O'Neal** and **Ali MacGraw** in *Love Story*

2. **Steve McQueen** and **Ali MacGraw** in *The Getaway*

3. **Marlene Dietrich** and **Gary Cooper** in *Morocco*

4. **Marilyn Monroe** and **Yves Montand** in *Let's Make Love*

5. **Gary Cooper** and **Clara Bow**

6. **Marlene Dietrich** and **James Stewart** in *Destry Rides Again*

7. **Marion Davies** and **Dick Powell** in *Hearts Divided*

8. **Joan Crawford** and **David Brian** in *Flamingo Road*

9. **Joan Crawford** and **Richard Egan** in *The Damned Don't Cry*

10. **Ann Sheridan** and **Jack Benny** in *George Washington Slept Here*

11. **Elvis Presley** and **Ann-Margret** in *Viva Las Vegas*

Love . . .

Producer Robert Evans decided to look the other way when Ryan O'Neal and his wife Ali MacGraw got together for some unscheduled love scenes while filming *Love Story.* But he couldn't exactly look the other way when Ali ran off and married Steve McQueen, her co-star in *The Getaway,* now could he?

Hedda Hopper was still a struggling actress when she became friendly with Clara Bow during the making of *Children of Divorce.* One day during a break she asked Clara how she was getting along with boyfriend Gary Cooper. "Well, I'll tell you this," Clara confided, and then proceeded to describe Cooper's lovemaking equipment by comparing it to that of his horse.

Mary Benny was well aware that she had problems with her boy Jack when she married him; believe it or not, Jack was a real ladies' man. The former Saddie Marks had landed the "Aristocrat of Humor" on the rebound and had had to keep a tight rein from then on. When Mary got the word that Jack was starting to get serious about Ann Sheridan during the making of *George Washington Slept Here,* she decided she'd better grab the Oomph Girl by the snood. She confronted Sheridan at a party and told her, "Miss Sheridan, Jack wouldn't trade my little finger for your whole body." When she told Jack about the confrontation, he assured her in hushed tones, "That's right, doll."

Simone Signoret says in her memoirs, "I was thoroughly enjoying the Roman spring and my return to Europe and my dinners with the film crew in the old Trattorie. I spent three delicious months in Rome...and that keeps me, even today, from judging what may have happened during my weeks in Rome and [Arthur] Miller's weeks in New York between a man, my husband, and a woman, my pal [Monroe] who were working together, living under the same roof and consequently sharing their solitudes, their fears, their moods and their recollections of childhood poverty."

Rumors of an affair between Marlene Dietrich and Gary Cooper had begun while they were filming *Morocco* together. They started up again while Dietrich was living with silent star John Gilbert. Dietrich had been instrumental in getting the lead in her film *Desire* for Gilbert with the hope that it would reverse the downward spiral his career had taken since his disastrous talkie debut. She'd helped him prepare for the role, even devised lighting techniques to help hide his wrinkles and creases, and guided him through the tests and photo sessions. But heavy drinking and mental stress brought on a heart attack which caused Gilbert to be struck from the picture. Dietrich continued to nurse Gilbert, until one day when his former lover Greta Garbo suddenly appeared at the door and Gilbert rushed out to her car and spoke animatedly with her for an hour. Dietrich was humiliated and immediately fled. After this incident, she took up with Cooper again. Gilbert's daughter Leatrice recalls, "Marlene was unable to resist Gary Cooper. The moment father found out, he went to pieces again, and didn't stop drinking until the day he died." One day after Cooper was announced for the leading role in *Desire,* John Gilbert died of a heart attack.

Joan Crawford had a number of younger male proteges during the fifties, but none of these relationships led to matrimony. Joan had already taken a stab at marriage with a younger man, Phil Terry, during the forties, which had ended miserably for both. Although she became very friendly with younger male stars like David Brian while making *Flamingo Road* and Richard Egan during *The Damned Don't Cry,* it appears that as Joan moved into middle age, she grew more and more reluctant to sacrifice her charm bracelets and Keene paintings to the California community property laws for a fling with a pretty face.

Producer Joseph Pasternak says that when Marlene Dietrich arrived at Universal to do *Destry Rides Again,* "She took one look at Jimmy Stewart and she began to rub her hands. She wanted him at once! He was just a simple guy; he loved Flash Gordon comics—that was all he would read. So she did something incredible, the most incredible thing I ever saw. She locked him in his dressing room and promised him a surprise. The surprise was that she presented him with a doll which she had had the studio art department come in over a weekend and make up for him—a life-size doll of Flash Gordon, correct in every detail! It started a romance!"

As she did with most of her male co-stars, Marion Davies developed a crush on Dick Powell while they were making the costumer *Hearts Divided.* Powell was all too happy to reciprocate, but the ever-present figure of William Randolph Hearst dampened his enthusiasm. In fact, Hearst became upset if mistress Marion so much as smiled at her leading men during the course of her acting duties. Some say that the ambitious young actor used Davies to further his career, but Hearst's biographer W. A. Swanberg quotes Powell as imploring the powerful publisher not to believe any stories he might have heard about a romance, assuring him that he need have no worries on that score. Hearst never answered Powell, he just laughed.

I want to roam, to soar, geographically, educationally, musically.
—Cybill Shepherd

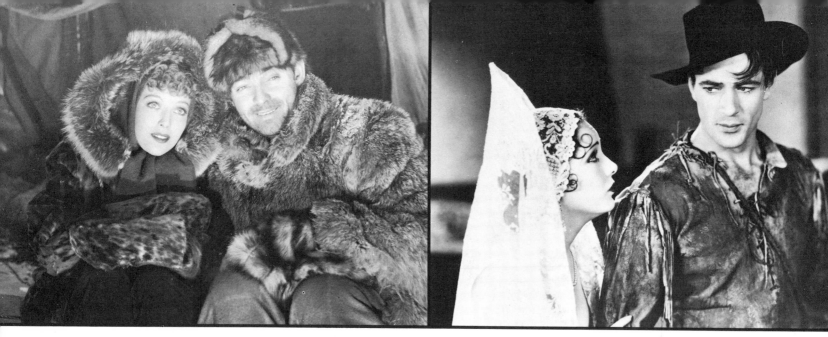

Loretta Young and **Clark Gable** in *The Call of the Wild*

Lupe Velez and **Gary Cooper** in *Wolf Song*

For probably the first time ever in his career, Clark Gable behaved unprofessionally while filming *The Call of the Wild* on location in Mount Baker, Washington. It seems that Gable couldn't concentrate on anything other than his co-star, the beautiful Loretta Young. Rumors eventually began to filter back to Hollywood and to Gable's wife Ria Langham that the expensive delays the film was suffering were due not to the weather, but to the fact that Clark and Loretta were playing house.

Clark Gable turned down a third party's offer of the services of one of the film colony's favorite party girls, Lupe Velez, but Gary Cooper wasn't so shy. Coop's reputation as a stud subsequently went up a few notches as Lupe sang his praises to the Hollywood heavens. Gable got back at his rival by ordering a custom-made Duesenberg—that was one foot longer than Coop's.

Robert Taylor and Eleanor Parker were both in the process of splitting up with their respective mates when they got together both on screen and off for some torrid lovemaking. Although MGM kept their affair a closely

guarded secret and the press called their "friendship" a matter of "mutual admiration and professional devotion," the fact is that Taylor was so smitten with Parker that he almost proposed marriage. But he apparently got cold feet because Parker was so much like his first wife, Barbara Stanwyck, somewhat domineering and a little flighty. Bob's only comment was, "She makes me nervous."

They say that the only time devout Catholic Spencer Tracy ever really considered getting a divorce from his wife (to whom he stayed married until the day he died), was when he fell in love with the twenty-year-old Loretta Young while making *Man's Castle*. Loretta eventually announced to the public that she and Tracy would not marry since both were devout Catholics and would suffer excommunication.

The director of *Seven Sinners,* Tay Garnett described the way Marlene Dietrich became involved with John Wayne like this: "We had a problem. Our plot was *Madame Butterfly* with a twist. A singer fell for a naval lieutenant; then, realizing she would ruin his future, she left him. We

Eleanor Parker and **Robert Taylor** in *Above and Beyond*

Loretta Young and **Spencer Tracy** in *Man's Castle*

John Wayne and **Marlene Dietrich** in *The Spoilers*

Clark Gable and **Joan Crawford** in *Love on the Run*

needed a tough he-man type who could use his fists, and decided to borrow him from Republic. His name was John Wayne. Marlene had the choice of all her leading men. I decided not to mention Wayne to her, but simply to place him in the Universal commissary where she couldn't miss seeing him. He stood between us and our table as we walked in for lunch, chatting with a couple of actresses I had set up. She swept past him, then swiveled on her heel and looked him up and down as though he were a prime rib at Chasen's. As we sat down, she whispered right in my ear, 'Daddy, buy me that!' I said, 'Honey, it's settled. You got him.' Then, at a prearranged signal, Wayne came to the table. If you didn't know what was gonna happen you'd be as blind as a pit pony. Their relationship got off like a fireworks display. They were crazy about each other, but every man on the picture wanted her. I did, but she wouldn't lay.''

When interviewer David Frost queried Joan Crawford on his tv show as to who was the sexiest actor in Hollywood, part of Crawford's answer had to be bleeped from the air. Without a moment's hesitation, she responded that the most exciting man ever to set foot in Hollywood was Clark Gable. But it was her straightforward assessment of what made his presence

so charismatic both on-screen and off that got Frost in trouble. It consisted of one word: ''Balls!''

Donald Sutherland had become somewhat radicalized by his activist wife Shirley, but his affair with Jane Fonda during the making of *Klute* turned him into a full-fledged revolutionary. This was rather ironic, since Shirley Sutherland had been one of the first to interest Jane in radical politics.

The parents of the teenage Mary Astor were so strict with their daughter that they ''practically required complete chaperonage just to go to the corner to mail a letter.'' They made an exception, however, when it came to the great John Barrymore. The young Mary was allowed to spend afternoons with the actor while making *Don Juan*, so that he might mold her into a great actress. When Mary wondered out loud to Barrymore at the contradictory nature of her parent's rules, he threw back his head and guffawed, ''They are damn foxy, you know. They are shutting their eyes to what is really between us. It's their way of letting you out on a rope but keeping you feeling guilty.'' At first Mary defended her parents, but then she remembered her father telling her, ''that many European fathers took their sons to an older woman, a whore, for their sexual education.''

Donald Sutherland and **Jane Fonda** in *Klute*

John Barrymore and **Mary Astor** in *Don Juan*

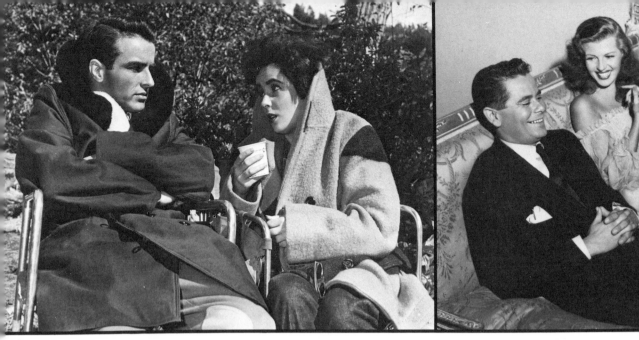

Montgomery Clift and **Elizabeth Taylor** on the set of *A Place in the Sun*

Glenn Ford and **Rita Hayworth** in *Gilda*

Elizabeth Taylor knew there was something different about Monty Clift, something separate and mysterious, but she couldn't avoid falling madly in love with him while they were filming *A Place in the Sun.* Monty's friends remember that he was attracted to Taylor in a way that he'd never been to a woman before. He often effused that they were so much alike that Liz was practically his "other half." They spoke of marriage, and Monty told everyone that that was what he wanted, that and children. But when Liz challenged him to dissuade her from marrying both her first husband, Nicky Hilton, and her second, Michael Wilding, he backed down.

Columbia boss Harry Cohn was so annoyed by the friendship that was building between Glenn Ford and Rita Hayworth during the making of *Gilda* that he made Rita promise that she would put an end to the intimate little tête-à-têtes she'd been having with Glenn during filming breaks. He had her dressing room bugged to make sure she kept her word.

The on-again-off-again love affair of director Peter Bogdanovich and Cybill Shepherd has left them both sad and confused. Seems it's been a

little sticky since Peter has children by his first wife, screenwriter-art director Polly Platt. Cybill recently complained, "I don't see what the big deal is if a man wants to have a wife and mistress too."

Maybe director Otto Preminger is explaining to actress Dorothy Dandridge that affairs between directors and their leading ladies are the accepted practice, in this photo taken between scenes during the filming of *Carmen Jones.* Maybe not. But in any case, Otto and Dorothy did hit it off rather well together. Although it was hushed up by the press for years, their romance developed into a long-term relationship. Preminger was especially discreet about keeping their friendship under wraps since he was still married (although separated from his wife) while involved with Dandridge.

Well, we can't exactly say that Robert Taylor didn't get along with his co-star in *The Conspirator*, seventeen-year-old Elizabeth Taylor, but he *did* have his problems with her. Supposedly it was one of the few times in his life when the lady-killer was able to control his attraction for a woman,

Peter Bogdanovich directing **Cybill Shepherd** in *The Last Picture Show*

Otto Preminger directing **Dorothy Dandridge** in *Carmen Jones*

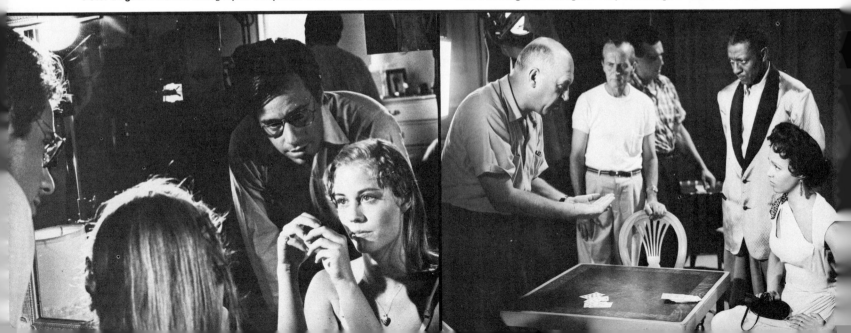

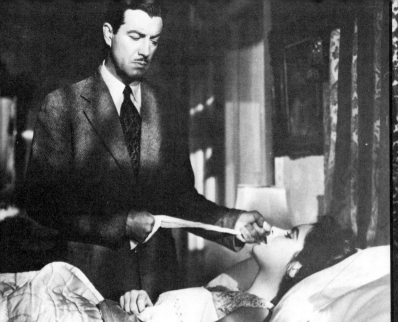

Robert Taylor and **Elizabeth Taylor** in *The Conspirator*

Katharine Hepburn and **John Barrymore** in *A Bill of Divorcement*

but unfortunately, "not from the waist down." He explained his physical condition to the cameramen, who agreed to focus the camera on him above the waist.

Katharine Hepburn wasn't quite the tough cookie she became when she first arrived in Hollywood, according to Garson Kanin in *Tracy and Hepburn*. Like many other starlets, the unwitting Hepburn fell prey to John Barrymore's advances while they were making *A Bill of Divorcement* together. Barrymore told Kanin:

"I gave her the eye a few times, then I stopped till *she* gave *me* the eye. After a few more days, we gave each *other* the eye. So I knew the time was ready. I'm *never* wrong about such things. I never *have* been. I said to her, 'How about lunch?' She said, 'Fine.' We went over to my dressing room. I locked the door and took my clothes off. She just stood there looking at me, and finally I said, 'Well, come on. What're you *waiting* for? We don't have all day. Cukor's one of those finickers who goes into a *spin* if you're five minutes late.' She didn't move, so I did and started to grab her, but she backed away and practically plastered herself against the wall, by God. I

said, 'What's the *matter*?' And she said, 'I *cahn't!*' I said, 'Never mind, I'll show you how.' She started babbling, 'No, no. Please. It's impossible. I *cahn't!*' I've never *been* so damned flabbergasted. I said to her, 'Why *not*?' And what do you think she said?"

"I've no idea."

He saved his uncanny imitation of Kate for his punch line.

"She said, 'My father doesn't want me to have any babies!' "

Elvis Presley got a king-size crush on his first screen leading lady, Debra Paget, while they were filming *Love Me Tender* together, but Debra didn't even know Old Swivelhips was alive. But then, of course she didn't. She was dating Howard Hughes at the time.

In 1953, Mrs. John Wayne named actress Gail Russell as correspondent in her divorce suit against the Duke. Both Wayne and Russell denied the charges, but the scandal drove Russell into a sanitorium.

Richard Egan, Debra Paget, and **Elvis Presley** while filming *Love Me Tender*

Gail Russell and **John Wayne** on the set of *Angel and the Badman*

George Raft and **Edward G. Robinson** in *Manpower*

Bud Abbott and **Lou Costello** in *Rio Rita*

The next time you catch George Raft and Edward G. Robinson in *Manpower* on the late show, keep this little piece of behind-the-scenes prattle in mind. Raft and Robinson were rivals for the choice tough-guy roles at Warners though they were of totally different temperaments off screen. Robinson was considered an intellectual and a homebody, while Raft was a sleek hustler who made the Hollywood scene with some of the most desirable women in town. But, temperament notwithstanding, they quite simply detested each other. With perverse delight, Jack Warner cast the rivals in Raoul Walsh's *Manpower* as hard-bitten power linemen battling for the affections of "cafe hostess" Marlene Dietrich. As if things weren't bad enough, both Raft and Robinson decided they had eyes for their co-star. There was no question as to who would win the affections of Dietrich either on or off screen, but that didn't keep Eddie from trying. During one rehearsal, a knock-down-drag-out ensued between the two stars which was caught by a photographer from *Life* magazine. Since both Robinson and Dietrich were married, Warners had to pull strings to keep feud and photo under wraps.

For months, Clark Gable adamantly refused to team up with America's new singing sweetheart, Jeanette MacDonald, for *San Francisco*. It seems that the King couldn't stand the thought of dimpling for minutes on end while Jeanette batted her lashes and trilled opera in his face. He relented,

however, when he heard that she'd given up her own salary to get him. Even so, he avoided her like the plague on the set, causing her to shed torrents of hysterical tears. Friends say that Jeanette and Greer Garson are the only females Gable ever really disliked. He especially detested the slogan that MGM had thought up to announce his return from the war and subsequent starring role with Greer in *Adventure*. He flinched every time he was reminded that he was back and Garson had him. But then everybody knows that Gable liked down-to-earth women like his late wife Carole Lombard and his other co-star in *Adventure,* Joan Blondell; you could have your Queen-of-the-May types with the carrot-Technicolored hair.

Abbott and Costello's comedy partnership began in 1930 at a bump-and-grind palace. Lou Costello pulled ticket clerk Bud Abbott into the act when his straight man stood him up. Friends say that Costello complained on occasion about "carrying" Abbott during their years as Top Ten movie draws, but they seemed friendly enough off-screen. However, when Costello's heart was broken by the death of his adopted son in a drowning accident, his grief led him to drink; he became embittered and hostile, especially toward his partner. By the late fifties, the public seemed to have tired of their kind of comedy, and both were feeling the pinch. Lou Costello was suing Abbott for $222,000 in unpaid royalties when he died of a heart attack in 1959.

Greer Garson, Clark Gable, and **Joan Blondell** in *Adventure*

Edward G. Robinson and **Miriam Hopkins** in *Barbary Coast*

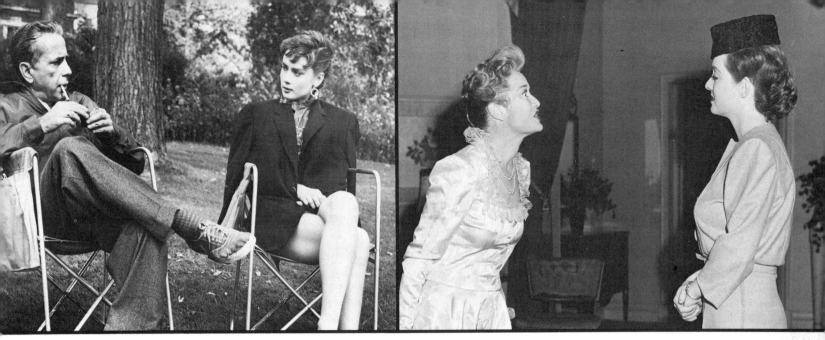

Humphrey Bogart and **Audrey Hepburn** on the set of *Sabrina*

Miriam Hopkins and **Bette Davis** in *Old Acquaintance*

Edward G. Robinson didn't fall for Miriam Hopkins's southern belle act for a minute when they worked together on *Barbary Coast.* He thought her "puerile and silly and snobbish." But then who could blame him? In addition to being pouty and temperamental, she'd refused, for no particular reason, to alter her elaborate costumes (which made the tiny Robinson look even tinier), insisting instead that he stand on a box for their scenes together. Robinson finally got some fun out of his work when the script called for him to deliver a healthy slap to his antagonist. The entire crew burst into applause when he knocked Hopkins sprawling with a right uppercut to the jaw.

Humphrey Bogart was extremely uncomfortable in the part of the debonair Wall Street broker of *Sabrina,* a role that had originally been intended for the urbane Cary Grant. And, in addition to having to co-star with William Holden, whom he considered an overripe juvenile, he was forced to endure the screen's newest sensation, Audrey Hepburn, who was "awright…if you don't mind a dozen takes." His oversize ego was further bruised when the critics suggested that he was a little long in the tooth to win the girl from Bill.

Next to the Bette Davis–Miriam Hopkins brawls during the making of *Old Acquaintance,* the most famous movieland feud of the war years involved Paulette Goddard, Veronica Lake, and Claudette Colbert. When an interviewer asked Goddard which of her *So Proudly We Hail* co-stars she preferred, Colbert or Veronica Lake, she answered: "Veronica, I think. After all, we are closer in age." Colbert exploded. All three women fought over the film's photography, since lighting which was flattering to one was harsh for the other. And you thought all the fighting went on overseas.

Marlene Dietrich spent several weeks in the gypsy encampments outside of Paris to research the role of the seductive gypsy in *Golden Earrings.* She hadn't made an American film in three years, but there were still a few twicks left in the old girl yet. It must have been a shock to return to Hollywood and rumors that co-star Ray Milland had threatened to walk out on his contract rather than play love scenes with an "old bag" like Marlene. (At forty-five she was two years older than Milland, but she might as well have been Dame May Whitty, as far as Ray was concerned.) Cast and crew were miserable as Milland and Marlene battled it out between making it on the screen. The hostilities climaxed well into the filming when Marlene, still in character, showed her contempt for the boorish Milland gypsy-style. Director Mitchell Leisen recalls, "When we were shooting the scene where he first meets her as she's stirring the stew, Marlene stuck a fishead into her mouth, sucked the eye out, and then pulled out the rest of the head. Then, after I yelled cut, she stuck her finger down her throat to make herself throw up. The whole performance made Ray violently ill."

Veronica Lake and **Claudette Colbert** in *So Proudly We Hail*

Marlene Dietrich and **Ray Milland** in *Golden Earrings*

Clark Gable and **Vivien Leigh** in *Gone With the Wind*

Humphrey Bogart and **Ida Lupino** in *High Sierra*

Ever fearful of offending, Vivien Leigh was impeccable in her hygiene. Consequently, she refused to continue filming the love scenes in *Gone With the Wind* unless Clark Gable remedied the foul odor produced by his dentures. The same off-screen drama was reenacted many years later when Lee Marvin forced his affections on Viv as a part of his acting chores on board the *Ship of Fools.* Only this time it was liquor, not choppers, that gave Viv a case of the vapors.

Fans thrilled to the dreamy love scenes between Tyrone Power and Kim Novak in *The Eddy Duchin Story.* Off screen however, Power testily reported to the press that the Lavender Lady had a tendency to confuse bad manners with temperament. Of course, this was hardly the first time that stars made love on screen and war off. Joan Fontaine muttered curses between clinches in her love scenes with Cary Grant during the filming of *Suspicion.* Nothing serious—she just found him to be an incredible boor. Ida Lupino was so annoyed by Humphrey Bogart's continual sarcasm and needling while they were doing *High Sierra* that she refused to be reteamed with him for *Out of the Fog.* Bette Davis made no secret of her irritation over Robert Montgomery's upstaging tactics on the set of *June Bride.* Apparently Bob just wouldn't roll over and play dead like dear old George Brent while Bette stole the show.

Rumor has it that Vivien Leigh found Marlon Brando to be every bit as brutish as his screen alter ego Stanley Kowalski when they made *A Streetcar Named Desire* together. Of course, Brando reveled in the fact that the genteel actress found him so repulsive and went to great pains to do things like grunt or belch whenever she was around. Viv spent most of her time in her dressing room, pressing her gloves.

Peter Fonda so resented Warren Beatty's insensitive behavior toward the fatally ill director, Robert Rossen, during the filming of *Lilith* that as soon as the picture was wrapped, he rounded up a posse to teach him some manners. Jean Seberg, Warren's romantic interest in the film, wasn't exactly a fan either; she simply wasn't amused when he entertained himself by flicking the contents of his nose at her during filming breaks.

It was Vivien Leigh's success in *Gone With the Wind* that kept her from starring opposite her roomate, Laurence Olivier, in *Rebecca.* For, besides

Cary Grant and **Joan Fontaine** in *Suspicion*

Marlon Brando and **Vivien Leigh** in *A Streetcar Named Desire*

Jean Seberg and **Warren Beatty** in *Lilith*

Joan Fontaine and **Laurence Olivier** in *Rebecca*

feeling that there would be damaging publicity if the real-life lovers made love on the screen while still married to others, David O. Selznick felt the public would never buy the tempestuous Scarlett as the drab, demure girl of *Rebecca.* His lovelife thwarted, Larry vented his frustration on the little milquetoast who'd been cast opposite him by whispering obscenities in her ear during their screen clinches. Director Alfred Hitchcock was aware of the tension, but he made no attempt to clear the air since Joan Fontaine's dazed reaction to Olivier's abuse imbued her with just the kind of timorous vulnerability he wanted to see in the second Mrs. deWinter.

By the time Errol Flynn and Olivia De Havilland were reteamed for *The Charge of the Light Brigade* after their success in *Captain Blood,* Flynn was sure he was in love with his demure leading lady, although he was still very much married to Lily Damita. Flynn showered Olivia with attention in the form of grade school pranks, like leaving a dead snake in her panties. De Havilland, who always made an effort to exhibit in her personal life the same ladylike restraint she evinced on the screen, was repelled by her co-star's bumbling attempts to break the ice. Decades later, Olivia's friend, Bette Davis, theorized in her memoirs that "it was Olivia De Havilland

whom Flynn truly adored and who evaded him successfully in the end. I really believe that he was deeply in love with her."

Speaking of Flynn and Davis, do you remember the famous off-screen battles between the co-stars of *The Private Lives of Elizabeth and Essex*? Bette had pleaded with Jack Warner to cast Laurence Olivier as Essex, but Warner refused to pay Olivier's price since he had a perfectly good Essex under contract in Errol Flynn. He even had a British accent—sort of. (Flynn was Australian.) Bette thought Flynn would be disastrous in the part; she saw him as just another pretty face, trying to coast on her steam. Flynn later speculated that it was jealousy over his salary ($6000 to her $5000), not artistic conscience that had Bette off her feed. Things got off to a bad start immediately when the two stars met for their first scripted exchange. Perhaps Bette was still preoccupied with dreams of Olivier when she delivered what was supposed to be a stage slap, since in so doing she almost knocked the six-foot-four Flynn out cold. His timid request that she cool it sent her into a tirade about her "art" and Flynn to his dressing room to throw up. Despite the subsequent success of the film and their rapport on screen, Flynn never gained Bette's good graces, though he tried off and on for years.

Olivia De Havilland and **Errol Flynn** in *They Died With Their Boots On*

Bette Davis and **Errol Flynn** in *The Private Lives of Elizabeth and Essex*

Spencer Tracy, Irene Dunne, and **Van Johnson** in *A Guy Named Joe*

Spencer Tracy, Clark Gable, and **Myrna Loy** in *Test Pilot*

Fans tended to think of Spencer Tracy as Father Flanagan, the perennial good guy, noble and self-effacing (and nonsexual). However, the real Tracy was one of Hollywood's best-kept secrets. He was a sourpuss with a strong affection for the bottle and for most of his leading ladies. Although he remained married to the same patient woman all his life, he regularly indulged his passion for starchy, unobtainable types like Loretta Young and Katharine Hepburn. Consequently, it came as no surprise when he developed a severe case of the hots for Irene Dunne, his prim leading lady in *A Guy Named Joe.* But when Tracy regaled Irene with whispered blow-by-blow descriptions of his plans for a romantic interlude, her carefully lacquered coif stood straight on end. Filming was brought to an abrupt halt when the indignant Irene adamantly refused to continue filming unless L.B. Mayer replaced her amorous co-star. (For the heartwarming conclusion to this story, see "Cosmetic Rumors.")

Joan Crawford and Loretta Young referred to them as "inseparable" and

"as close as brothers," and yet, however willing Spencer Tracy might have been to defer to Gable on the screen, he was consumed with jealousy of the King's charisma and natural grace, especially with the ladies. Gable, on the other hand, both admired and was intimidated by Tracy's reputation as an actor's actor; he was always leery of being upstaged by Tracy's classy histrionics. Though they roughhoused and kidded their way through four phenomenally successful buddy films, Tracy eventually tired of walking into the sunset without Myrna Loy. His demands for top billing put an end to their collaboration.

Although Raquel Welch's dislike for her *100 Rifles* co-star Jim Brown was little more than skin-deep, he took it very personally. During a lunch break, however, Jim suggested that perhaps Raquel might grant him a temporary truce and pass the salt, since, after all, "*it* wasn't black."

Raquel Welch and **Jim Brown** in *100 Rifles*

Tatum O'Neal and **Burt Reynolds** in *Nickelodeon*

Maurice Chevalier and **Jeanette MacDonald** in *The Merry Widow*

Nelson Eddy and **Jeanette MacDonald** in *Sweethearts*

Peter Bogdanovich knew he had a gold mine in Ryan O'Neal's little girl, Tatum, but that didn't make it any easier to work with an inexperienced child; he says that their first film together, *Paper Moon,* was "one of the most miserable experiences of my life." Things went a little more smoothly for Bogdanovich a couple of years later with the older, more self-assured Tatum when they filmed *Nickelodeon,* but not for her co-star Burt Reynolds. He explained it like this: "I like children. But she ain't no kid."

Clark Gable wasn't the only male star who had an aversion to Jeanette MacDonald. Maurice Chevalier thought her a bloodless prima donna whose apple-pie image sapped his screen sex appeal. And though there are rumors that she and Nelson Eddy fought because he was constantly on the make, it's more likely that Eddy resented her merciless scene-stealing tactics during his big musical numbers. As for MacDonald, she considered his talent marginal at best and certainly not comparable to hers; she was

dismayed by the overwhelming public demand for more of their screen duets.

Dirk Bogarde decided to overlook the flaws in the script of *I Could Go On Singing* since it presented him with the opportunity to work with one of his longtime idols, Judy Garland. And, as he expected, he and Judy hit it off beautifully—in the beginning. She called him "darling" and he called her "Miss Garland." But after weeks and weeks of Judy's Dexedrine dithers, tantrums, and tardiness, Dirk ended up referring to her as "it."

According to director Frank Pierson, Kris Kristofferson dealt with the lunacy that prevailed on the set of *A Star Is Born* and his co-star, Barbra Streisand's temperament by staying soused from sunup to sundown.

Dirk Bogarde and **Judy Garland** in *I Could Go On Singing*

Kris Kristofferson and **Barbra Streisand** in *A Star Is Born*

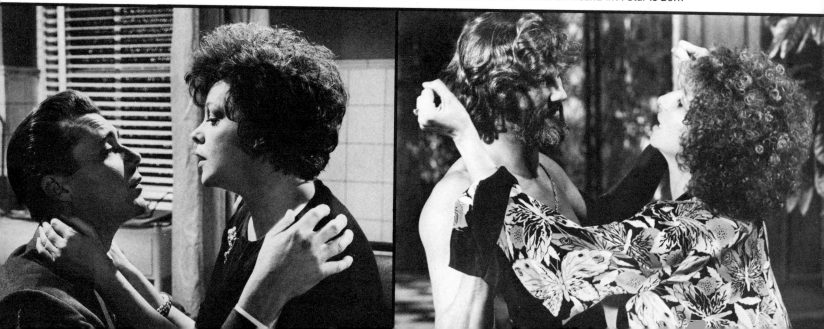

Ginger Rogers and **Fred Astaire** in *Swing Time*

Mae West and **W.C. Fields** in *My Little Chickadee*

She said "Neether" and he said "Nyther" but, fortunately for us, Fred and Ginger didn't call the whole thing off. The aristocratic Astaire was rather irritated, however, when the public demanded more of his collaboration with Ginger Rogers after their surprise success together in *Flying Down to Rio*. Ginger tried hard to be the perfectionist he was, but though Fred called her a "hard worker," he found her to be a bit on the floozyish side. She would show up for their screen *pas de deux* wearing feathers and doodads which invariably got caught in his cuff and stuck to his nose. But, like a trouper, he bravely endured her brassiness for nine all-singing, all-dancing hits. To this day he discreetly brushes aside rumors of dissension between them, and yet he did refuse to be reunited with her recently at a Lincoln Center tribute. Though Ginger made light of his absence by kissing a top hat for photographers, she probably agrees with Helen Lawrenson's *Esquire* article that, "It's Best Just to Remember Fred."

Mae West clashed with W. C. Fields when he insisted on improvising his gags instead of collaborating with her on the script of *My Little Chickadee*. After filming was completed, she allowed as how "There's no one quite like Bill in the world…Thank God!" Her clashes with Raquel Welch while filming *Myra Breckenridge* thirty years later were a bit more basic. Raquel sent flowers at first, but then threw down the gauntlet by appearing for their

first scene in a black dress with a white ruffle—the color scheme West had demanded exclusively for herself in her contract. Raquel lost the ensuing battle with the brass and disappeared for three days. When she reappeared it was in a black dress with a blue ruffle—but the blue was so pale it might as well have been white.

Despite the fact that Bette Davis and Joan Crawford had been bitter rivals for years, Jack Warner managed to get them to agree to co-star in his upcoming thriller, *What Ever Happened to Baby Jane?* The press predicted that all hell would break loose when the girls got together, but director Robert Aldrich, keenly aware that his budget couldn't afford costly delays, kept the girls apart as much as possible when they weren't working. When the two screen queens were reteamed for *Hush, Hush, Sweet Charlotte*, however, the predicted fireworks became a reality. Riding high as a result of the earlier film's success, Bette and Joan apparently felt they could afford to engage in some impromptu histrionics for *Charlotte*'s cast and crew.

The hostilities ceased when Crawford became ill. After doctors told her that she would have to bow out, Crawford cried for three days in her hospital bed. When she read that Olivia De Havilland was to replace her, Crawford announced that she was happy for Olivia since she "needed the

Mae West and **Raquel Welch** in *Myra Breckenridge*

Bette Davis, Jack Warner, and **Joan Crawford** before *What Ever Happened to Baby Jane?* commenced shooting

Ethel Waters, Eddie "Rochester" Anderson, John Bubbles, and **Lena Horne** in *Cabin in the Sky*

Elizabeth Taylor, Richard Burton, Sue Lyon, and **John Huston** on the set of *Night of the Iguana*

sure that neither she nor Clift would be called for retakes or any other little last-minute business. After Mankiewicz assured her that that was right, Hepburn ceremoniously spat in his face.

Ethel Waters insisted that it was her strong religious convictions that caused all the feuding and fighting during the filming of *Cabin in the Sky*. You see, her conscience just couldn't abide the flippant way religion was treated in the film's script. At least that's what she says in her autobiography, *His Eye on the Sparrow*. Probably more to the point was Waters' fear that her first starring role was being stolen by director Vincente Minnelli's girlfriend, a new girl named Lena Horne.

The steamy climate of Mexico's eastern coast provided the perfect setting for Tennessee Williams' *Night of the Iguana* and for the variegated ensemble of actors who comprised its cast. Elizabeth Taylor stuck close to Richard Burton to make sure his contact with Ava Gardner remained strictly platonic. She needn't have worried, since Ava was otherwise engaged, zipping up and down the beach in her Ferrari with the local beach boys. Screen nymphet Sue Lyon was accompanied by her mother as well as her fiancé and his current wife. The rest of the company consisted of a rare

assemblage of mutual ex-wives, ex-husbands, continuing liaisons, and feuds. Creepy John Huston soothed the egos of his gang of neurotics by buying each one a gun.

When Barbra Streisand made her film debut in *Funny Girl*, she wasn't exactly an unknown, but the twenty million bucks Hollywood had budgeted for her first film was unprecedented, even in Elizabeth Taylor's hometown. Who can blame her for putting on airs and refusing to follow veteran William Wyler's direction? Producer Ray Stark told Wyler not to take the whole thing seriously since, "after all, this *is* the first film Barbra's ever directed."

Most actors keep their complaints about the way a film is handled to themselves until the final grosses have been counted. But after completing *Such Good Friends,* Dyan Cannon wasted no time in telling anyone and everyone that she'd give up her career rather than work with director Otto Preminger again. Lee Marvin couldn't seem to get along with director Josh Logan either, but his method of expression was a little more direct. When Logan blamed Marvin's drunken antics for the expensive delays on *Paint Your Wagon* (the third most expensive film ever made), Lee showed his vexation by urinating on Josh's shoes.

William Wyler and **Barbra Streisand** during the making of *Funny Girl*

Joshua Logan and **Lee Marvin** on location with *Paint Your Wagon*

Edward Judson — **WMT** — Rita Hayworth — **WMT** — Aly Khan — **?** — Gene Tierney — **WMT** — Oleg Cassini

BROTHE

Rita Hayworth — **WMT** — Orson Welles — **WMT** — Virginia Welles

Dick Haymes — **WMT** — Joanne Dru — **WMT** — John Ireland

Dick Haymes — **WMT** — Nora Eddington

Igor Cassini

William Randolph Hearst, Jr. — **IMT** — Austine Hearst

Nora Eddington — **WMT** — Erroll Flynn — **WMT** — Lily Damita

Patrice Wymore — **WMT** — Erroll Flynn

WMT means "Was Married To"
IMT means "Is Married To"

Hollywood's Craz

Jack Whiting

Buddy Rogers — **IMT** — Mary Pickford — **WMT** — Douglas Fairbanks — **WMT** — Sylvia Ashley — **WMT** — Clark Gable — **WMT** — Carole Lombard

Douglas Fairbanks — **WMT** — Beth Sully

FATHER OF

Douglas Fairbanks, Jr. — **IMT** — Mary Epping

Huntington Hartford, Jr.

Carole Lombard — **WMT** — William Powell — **IMT** — Diana Lewis

Alfred Steele

Beth Sully — **WMT** — Joan Crawford

Phil Terry — **WMT** — Patricia Knight

Cornel Wilde — **IMT** — Jean Wallace

Joan Crawford — **WMT** — Franchot Tone — **WMT** — Barbara Payton — **WMT** — Tom Neal

Huntington Hartford, Jr. — **WMT** — Marjorie Hartford

Marriage Tangle

Irene Dunne in *Together Again*

he American film industry gave birth to a whole new kind of journalistic star gazing, yellow journalism and purple prose that fed off the budding celebrity of screen stars. Press coverage of the Hollywood scene has splintered in hundreds of directions since it first appeared in the early 1900s. But one thing seems true of all the varying manifestations of Hollywood reportage—they're rarely plagued with accuracy. Like the illusory world they purport to portray, they're filled with invention and bias.

Each genre has been allowed to establish its own axioms: Hollywood can be Camelot-by-the-Pacific or Babylon reborn. It's been up to the consumer to pick his own brand of movie star mythology, the gospel according to *Photoplay, Screenland, Silver Screen,* Louella, Hedda, *Confidential, Hush-Hush, Vice Squad, Tattle, Midnight, The Star, The National Enquirer,* or *People.* More than any other social phenomenon of the Twentieth Century, Hollywood history is enmeshed in legend. We'll never know the truth.

The millions of words written by Hollywood columnists and fan magazine writers have, for the most part, been supportive of the industry and its stars. It was the penny journalism of tabloids like the *Daily Graphic* and Hearst's San Francisco and Los Angeles *Examiner*s whose headlines gleefully trumpeted the latest Lotus Land scuttlebutt. During the twenties freelance reporters and correspondents from these journals scoured Hollywood like bounty hunters for evidence of sin and debauchery. If there was none to be found, the more unscrupulous invented it. They didn't have to look very far, however. The film colony seemed only too happy to oblige with a smorgasbord of scandals like the drug overdoses of silent stars Wallace Reid, Alma Rubens, and Barbara La Marr; Fatty Arbuckle's party etiquette; and the murder of William Desmond Taylor, which remains an unsolved mystery to this day.

The coverage of the Taylor case included tantalizing accounts of the fifty-year-old director's involvement with drugs and illicit sex in the company of two of the screen's most popular stars, teenaged Mary Miles Minter and comedienne Mabel Normand. The public's hunger for more revelations concerning the crime eventually led members of the Hollywood press to attempt to solve it themselves. One reporter, Florabel Muir, a correspondent for the *New York Daily News,* and her managing editor, Al Weinshank, were so sure that Taylor's homosexual black butler, Henry Peavey, was the culprit that they conspired to kidnap Peavey and scare him into confessing. While Muir and an accomplice drove the blindfolded Peavey to the graveyard where Taylor was buried, Weinshank, covered by a sheet, waited crouched behind the murdered man's tombstone. When the three arrived, Peavey's blindfold was removed, and Weinshank leapt out from his hiding place yelling, "I am the ghost of William Desmond Taylor. You murdered me! Confess, Peavey!" However, instead of the intended reaction, Peavey began to shake, not with fear, but with gales of uncontrollable laughter. Besides looking ridiculous in his ghost's getup, Weinshank had delivered the accusations in his heavy Chicago twang, whereas Peavey's former employer had spoken with a British accent. The kidnappers ended up apologizing sheepishly to their victim and escorting him safely home. Over the years, more than three hundred people confessed to the crime, but the Los Angeles police eventually dismissed them all as crackpots.

Jazz babies and midtown toilers were enthralled by these tales of debauchery and the terrible price of fame. But women's groups and the American Legion were not amused. By 1922, Hollywood could no longer ignore the threat of public boycott. Studio heads quickly mobilized to counteract impending government censure by forming their own moral police squad, referred to as the Hays Office (after its president, Will Hays). Hollywood's newfound propriety was given a noisy send-up in the press.

At the behest of Hays, the studio brass set out to make sure that the lifestyles of their stars measured up to the propaganda by inserting morality clauses into their con-

munity of fun-loving, wholesome young people, working and playing in the California sun. These highminded youngsters understood that the lascivious high life of the good old days was dead. But that didn't rule out a little good, dirty fun, if you knew how to do business with Hedda and Louella.

At that time there were two reigning queens in Hollywood, both female, each with a daily column in the two leading newspapers and a weekly radio show. They were pandered to and fawned upon to an incredible degree, and for all intents and purposes, they ran the town. One of them was Louella Parsons, top columnist for Hollywood goings-on for the Hearst press and apparently a newspaperwoman from the year zero. By comparison with her rival she was rather kindly and seemingly vague, though with a mind like a bear trap. She never forgot a thing and, by the same token, never forgave anyone who crossed her. But she was never vicious. The other one was Hedda Hopper, top Hollywood columnist for the L.A. *Times* and an unmitigated bitch. She was venomous, vicious, a pathological liar, and quite stupid. . . . Wise Hollywood hostesses never invited columnists to their parties, because once you did you could never leave them off your list for future parties or they would crucify you.

—Ray Milland,
Wide-Eyed in Babylon

Perhaps crucify is not quite the word to describe the way in which columnists chastised the stars and the studio bigwigs. The tone set by the most influential during the twenties through the forties was more that of small-town gossips whose mission in life it was to watchdog the high jinks of exuberant youth. There's no doubt that they could be devastatingly cruel, but with a clucking it's-for-your-own-good posture. ("Aren't all those late night revels taking their toll on Constance Bennett's beauty?") On the occasions when Hedda or Louella did get on their broomsticks to cash in on a movieland scandal, it was usually after, not before, the whistle was blown. But once the charges of a drunken-driving arrest, an act of violence, or a morals charge crossed the police blotter, they were a matter of public record, which meant they would be splashed across the tabloids within hours. Naturally, the pros had no intention of being upstaged in their home territory, but they rarely brought out the heavy artillery until public revelation was a *fait accompli*. Hedda and Louella did get carried away on occasion however. One striking example occurred when Hedda wrote in her book *The Whole Truth and Nothing But* that she had tried to dissuade Elizabeth Taylor from marrying Michael Wilding because he had had a homosexual relationship with Stewart Granger. The injured parties subsequently sued

tracts. According to restrictions, a performer was obligated to conduct himself "with due regard to public conventions and morals" and must do nothing to bring himself "into public hatred, contempt, scorn, or ridicule, or tending to shock, insult, or offend the community or outrage public morals and decency." To make sure that the stars were honoring the clause, Hayes hired private detectives to infiltrate Hollywood's decadent after-hours scene. The resultant blacklist—the Doom Book—signaled the end of the game for many.

Hays was also responsible for establishing a method for persuading the press to write favorably about Hollywood. This approach involved flattering the reporters and editorial writers who'd been responsible for the defamatory coverage by courting them with luncheons, interviews, and studio tours with the stars and their bosses. If a newsman wrote approvingly of what he saw, Hays sent him a personal thank-you along with an update on the latest efforts being made to clean up the town. Hays also had the brilliant idea of hiring newsmen away from their jobs to become public relations experts for the studios. So, ultimately, the same group that had been responsible for vilifying Hollywood ended up rebuilding its reputation. The publicity people sequestered the stars behind the safety of the studio walls. If a reporter intended to write about Hollywood on a regular basis, he was expected to treat his subject with discretion or his supply of information would be turned off.

Propaganda machines were thrust into full gear, cranking out fanciful publicity picturing Hollywood as a com-

her for $3,000,000. Their reputations were repaired by a hefty out-of-court settlement and an apology from Hedda.

The resident tongue-waggers were privy to most of the skeletons in Hollywood's walk-in closets. They had informers everywhere—manicurists, janitors, doormen. But the more serious dirt was generally stockpiled for future reference. Scooping the competition meant being the first to announce role castings, marriages, and divorces. Innocuous gossip and industry news were far better suited to Hedda and Louella's breakfast-table readership than the lurid details of adultery, alcoholism, or mental breakdown that were the realities of life in Tinseltown.

A typical Louella exclusive was her announcement that "one of the world's greatest living psychoanalysts," Sigmund Freud, was going to act as technical advisor on the Bette Davis picture *Now Voyager*. (Unfortunately, Siggy was unavailable for comment; he was busy being dead at the time.) And in Hedda's very first column, she perpetrated a lulu to the effect that Greta Garbo, who was soon, she said, to marry Leopold Stokowski, had undergone inspection by Stokowski's patrician Philadelphia relatives. Not only did the romance turn out to be nonexistent but so did Stokowski's Philadelphia relatives. A rudimentary instinct for checking sources would have spared Hedda that blooper. Hedda's non-show-business observations were even more whimsical. She once reverently intoned that, "For more than 2,000 years, Jews and Christians all over the world have tried to follow in the footsteps of our Saviour." Fortunately for Hedda, she knew how to turn even the most outrageous mistakes into a joke. But the main reason that both Louella and Hedda could get away with printing what they did was that they knew still fancier stuff about their subjects that the mail would not carry. The machinations by which Hedda and Louella used this information to procure an exclusive has been recreated in this imaginary scenario by David Niven in *Bring on the Empty Horses:*

COLUMNIST: *Who was that girl you were nuzzling in that little bar in the San Fernando Valley at three o'clock this morning?*
ACTOR: *I was with my mother. . . .*
COLUMNIST: *According to my information, you had one of her bosoms in your hand.*
ACTOR: *It fell out of her dress. . . . I was just helping her put it back in.*
COLUMNIST: *Rubbish! . . . But I won't print it because I don't want to make trouble for you.*
ACTOR: *Bless you—you're a doll.*
COLUMNIST: *Got any news for me?*
ACTOR: *Afraid I haven't right now.*

COLUMNIST: *Call me when you hear anything, dear.*
ACTOR: *(wiping brow) You bet I will.*

And he would, too.

A columnist may have known about a married star's involvement in a clandestine affair, but she kept it under her hat if she knew what was good for her. However, if the star's jealous husband shot the wife's lover, as did Joan Bennett's husband, producer Walter Wanger (who was convicted of shooting Bennett's agent Jennings Lang in the groin) then a columnist like Hedda could unleash all her indignation in print. Especially if she felt she'd been slighted by the star and her husband while playing a supporting role in one of their film collaborations. Most columnists were politically astute at echoing public sentiment pro or con a transgressor. When Louella jumped in to take a few parting shots at Frances Farmer after her grotesque mental breakdown, she was swinging at a star already unpopular with the public and co-workers, and a pinko to boot. But Hollywood was a company town, and if too many had been blackballed, the press would have been cutting its own lifeline. If anything, Hedda and Louella acted as apologists for the erratic and irrational behavior of the studio properties. For example, indiscriminate mating was described as "dating"; Lana's stable of studs were called "beaus." A whole new kind of euphemistic lingo was invented to chronicle the escapades of the favored and to reprimand the errant.

The Confidential

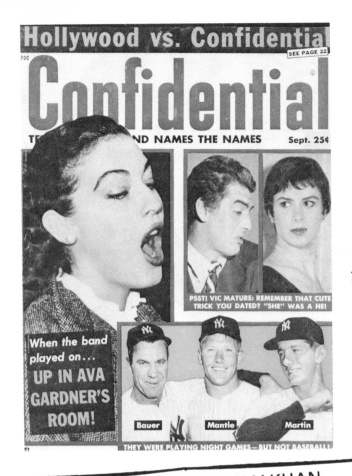

The decline of studio power which began in the fifties paved the way for the *Confidential* magazine reign of terror. In the past, the studio head was the first to be called if a star was involved in an incursion of the law. (MGM boss L.B.Mayer was on the scene of the "suicide" of Jean Harlow's husband Paul Bern two hours before the police were summoned. And it was Mayer, not Harlow, who surrendered the suicide note purportedly written by Bern, and who suppressed the uneven findings of the coroner's inquest.)Without the protection of the studio, a star's only recourse against the scandal sheets was to ransom his privacy with hush money. The blackmail business turned out to

ERROL FLYNN AND HIS TWO-WAY MIRROR
Pheasant under glass isn't the only dish he served at his posh address on Mulholland Drive. Some of the other entrées made guests shriek and head to the nearest bar for a quick bracer!

HOW MENTAL SADIST ALY KHAN LOUSED UP GENE TIERNEY'S PSYCHE
The Playboy Prince's refusal to marry her so shocked and humiliated the exotic beauty, she took refuge in a rest home.

WHEN THE BAND PLAYED ON . . . UP IN AVA GARDNER'S ROOM

LIZABETH SCOTT IN THE CALL GIRL'S CALL BOOK
Just a routine check ma'am and out popped....The vice cops expected to find a few big name customers when they grabbed the date book of a trio of Hollywood Jezebels, but even their cast-iron nerves got a jolt when they got to the S's! In recent years Scotty's almost nonexistent career has allowed her to roam farther afield. In one jaunt to Europe she headed straight for Paris and the left bank where she took up with Frede, the city's most notorious lesbian queen and operator of a nightclub devoted exclusively to entertaining deviates just like herself!

EDDIE FISHER AND THE 3 CHIPPIES

BOY BOOZER AT 11: EDWARD G. ROBINSON, JR.

BING'S BRATS: BOOZE! BABES! BRAWLS!

MARIO LANZA, THE STOMACH THAT WALKS LIKE A TENOR!

WILL SEXCESS SPOIL NATALIE WOOD?

WHY GEORGE RAFT CAN'T USE LEO DUROCHER'S APARTMENT ANYMOF

Reign of Terror

be as lucrative as publishing for *Confidential*'s publisher, Robert Harrison, and his henchmen.

Essentially, *Confidential* and its imitators attacked Hollywood's free-swinging life style. Their specialties were allegations of homosexuality, misogyny, nasty profiles, and the usual nightcourt scene—celebrity drunks, brawls, etc. The self-righteous tone of *Confidential*'s attacks had the same ring as the HUAC harrassment of Hollywood. Its scandal-sheet prose, a style inherited from Harrison's alma mater the *Daily Graphic,* had the macho thrust of men's adventure pulps; its methods and morality were couched in *Police Gazette* vernacular.

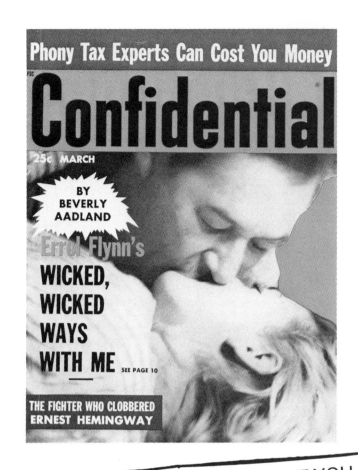

Phony Tax Experts Can Cost You Money

Confidential

25¢ MARCH

BY BEVERLY AADLAND

Errol Flynn's
WICKED, WICKED WAYS WITH ME — SEE PAGE 10

THE FIGHTER WHO CLOBBERED ERNEST HEMINGWAY

FRANK SINATRA . . . THE TARZAN OF THE BOUDOIR
The poor girl got practically no sleep for days. . . . Frankie was flying high on his Wheaties.

MEMO TO BARDOT: CORK THAT SEX

MISSING PERSON'S BUREAU: HAVE YOU FOUND JACKIE GLEASON'S FATHER?

WAS ZSA ZSA OFF HER ROCKER? THEN WHY DID SHE SPEND SIX WEEKS IN THE BOOBY HATCH? HUBBY, CONRAD HILTON SAID SHE LOST HER BUTTONS
It took a stretch in a swank sanitarium for the Hungarian playgirl to prove she wasn't nutty as a fruitcake. Or was she?

WHAT MARY PICKFORD'S AUTOBIOGRAPHY DIDN'T DARE TELL!
America's sweetheart was just like any other woman scorned when she lost Doug Fairbanks, Sr. to Sylvia Ashley. Mary made a fortune playing "little girl" roles, but handled her love life as cooly as a seasoned courtesan. Mary's been off the screen since '33, and her evident aging has made a joke of comeback plans.

GLORIA DEHAVEN . . . REMEMBER WHEN YOU WERE MISBEHAVIN' WITH JEFF CHANDLER?

HARLEM AND HOLLYWOOD . . . CAN MIXED MARRIAGE SUCCEED?
Both Pearl Bailey and Lena Horne have crossed the color barrier. What are their chances for happiness?

IT HAPPENED ONE NIGHT: THE SIZZLING STORY OF "WHY DEANNA DURBIN WON'T COME BACK"
The beautiful young girl who sang her way into the hearts of millions on film, sang her swan song one moonlit night in a lonely canyon, on a car seat.

WHY GIRLS CALL SONNY TUFTS A CANNIBAL
He was such a dedicated chow hound he ate his way right out of the movies . . . but his chomping molars didn't get him in trouble until he started nibbling on strip queens on the bur-le-que runways.

WHY DESI ARNAZ TOOK THAT TRAMP ABROAD

JANE FONDA: HOLLYWOOD'S WILDEST POT-SMOKING REBEL

HOW MICKEY ROONEY GOT THE GOODS ON HIS WIFE. HE TUNED IN ON MAMA AND HEARD HER CALL HIM "THAT LITTLE JERK"

WHAT HAPPENED WHEN . . . THE BOSTON TYCOON RAN OUT ON GLORIA SWANSON
And what's the deep, dark secret that drove her mentor out of Hollywood?

KIM NOVAK AND SAMMY DAVIS, JR.

Who broke up their romance? Exclusive! Boy meets girl, boy gets girl. . . . It's a Hollywood movie plot no more. Here's how Hollywood broke Sammy's spirit on the rocks. It's the tragic love story of the century. In *Romeo and Juliet* the lovers could only be reunited in death . . . when their parents wouldn't let them marry. In real life a king gives up his throne for the woman he loves and gives up a five million dollar bank account. In this case SAMMY DAVIS, JR. WOULDN'T GIVE UP THE NEGRO RACE! Kim Novak wouldn't give up the white race! Of course, there was the fact that his skin was black and her skin was white, but in Hollywood there's no such thing as a color line.

Harry Cohn, the volatile head of Columbia took Sammy aside and said, "Do you realize this girl is worth twenty million dollars to me? Have a fling for a few months but don't get married."A dramatic decision had to be made. . . . Sammy made it. He married a colored girl. Maybe his marriage had something to do with the visit Sammy received from two of Cohn's thugs who said to Sammy, "YOU HAVE ONE EYE NOW. WANT TO TRY FOR NONE? WELL THAT'S THE WAY THE FUTURE LOOKS IF YOU DON'T MARRY A COLORED GIRL WITHIN THREE DAYS OR ELSE!" A few months later Cohn himself was dead. Rumors going around Columbia said that [Kim and Sammy's] romance had killed Harry.

HOW HEDY LAMARR FIBBED TO THE LIE DETECTOR
The "*Ecstasy* girl" couldn't face the naked truth.

THE WILD PARTY THAT ALMOST LANDED WALTER PIDGEON IN THE COOP

EVA BARTOK: DID PRINCE PHILIP'S PAL FATHER HER CHILD?

KNOCK, KNOCK. WHY DID JOHNNIE RAY TRY TO BREAK DOWN PAUL DOUGLAS' DOOR?
It was just 3:00 a.m. in the swank Dorchester Hotel when the slim, handsome boy slipped out of room 420 in his birthday suit and sashayed over to room 417.

SHOCKING NEWS FROM BRITAIN: "EVERY TENTH ENGLISHMAN IS A FAG" —SAYS BRITISH MEDICAL ASSOCIATION.

NEVER TOLD BEFORE . . . THE INSIDE STORY OF DEAN MARTIN AND JERRY LEWIS

Broadway's five million dollar brush-off! Broke and scared Jerry cried like a baby and begged for a job. Once he and Dean teamed up they tied a can to the man who gave them their start. Dean's agent arranged for his nose job and then lost Dean, nose and all.

. . . . HOW TERRY MOORE BECAME A TURKISH DELIGHT

They all gasped when Terry sat down to pose . . . here's the shot heard round the world and the facts the papers only whispered about. . . .

LANA TURNER AND AVA GARDNER

No males in sight, but the girls had their hair down.

WHEN TYRONE POWER CAUGHT A CHILL FROM EKBERG, THE ICEBERG

TUESDAY WELD: TOO HEP AT 16— THE STARTLING INSIDE STORY

WHEN TARZAN OF THE APES LEX BARKER MET THAT PRETTY SCANTIES MODEL HIS THOUGHTS TURNED TO MONKEY BUSINESS

Not long after, the lord of the jungle was running from the stork.

HAVE TUX WILL TRAVEL AND THAT'S WHAT BOB HOPE DID WITH THAT BLONDE

Bob Hope is always zooming around the country. . . . The liveliest tour of his life began when saucy Barbara Payton came for cocktails and stayed for capers.

WHEN LIZ TOOK OFF FOR TEXAS, MIKE WAS HEADED FOR STRIP CITY

Jenny Lee, bouncy bazoom girl came along for the swim. . . .

"SORRY—WRONG NUMBER."

What happened when thousands of fans called bosomy Anita Ekberg— and got the Swedish Ministry of Church Affairs!

MONTGOMERY CLIFT . . . THE WOMAN HE LOVES [LIBBY HOLMAN] WAS ONCE CHARGED WITH MURDER!

Until the underdogs mobilized to silence the monster (individual slander suits were brought by Liberace, Errol Flynn, Dorothy Dandridge, Maureen O'Hara, and Lizabeth Scott), *Confidential* had plenty of ammo with which to terrorize a community not known for its restraint. Although most of the suits were settled out of court, Harrison eventually cooled his attack. Lurid headlines still screamed from its cover, but aside from rehashing old, worn-out stories like Robert Mitchum's pot bust or Rory Calhoun's past prison record, the exposés inside were fakes. Eventually the stars themselves would be responsible for putting the scandal sheets out of business by merchandising their troubles in biographies, exploitation films, and television talk shows.

111

The Movie Magazines

While the tabloids flaunted Hollywood's crimes and the columnists chastened its children, about the most shocking piece of information a movie magazine had to offer was that "Myrna Loy's mother wishes she'd become a nurse instead of an actress" or something equally hair-raising. From the beginning the fanzines wrote about Hollywood and its stars in hushed, idolatrous tones. Until the scandal sheet mentality of the fifties began to creep into their pages, the fanzines generally pictured the stars either as hard-working kids like you and me or mythical gods and goddesses who were immune to the laws of mere mortals. Under-the-hair-dryer entertainment, their formulas were similar to those of the romance pulps: recipes, hair-styling hints, fashion advice, confessions, and contests. Because they were prepared months in advance, they couldn't really hope to scoop the daily columnists. (Especially since most Hollywood romances didn't last the time it took to prepare them for press.) So they concentrated instead on movie reviews ("No matter what the critics write, the audience has the final word."), letters from fans, and prettified reporting usually taken verbatim from studio press releases.

SHIRLEY TEMPLE'S LAST LETTER TO SANTA

Mrs. Temple says that Shirley is "on the edge" in her belief in Santa. This is probably the last Christmas she will ever write to him and we are proud to present her letter.

TO MY SCREEN BOOK FRIENDS

"I regret more than I can say that my marriage with Hal Rosson did not work out. Believe me, this is no frivolous matter—but the only way out for both of us. We are uncongenial and while there is no ill feeling between us, we realize that it is best for us to separate." JEAN HARLOW

Unlike their competitors, fanzines maintained, well into the fifties, an intensely protective stance when writing about the stars.

IT COULDN'T BE, THEY SAID. THE MARRIAGE OF FERNANDO LAMAS AND ARLENE DAHL WAS DOOMED, THEY SAID. THAT WAS UMPTEEN YEARS AGO—AND SEE HOW HAPPY THEY LOOK NOW!

TONY PERKINS: YOU'D TAKE HIM HOME TO MOTHER!

ELVIS PRESLEY: HE DOESN'T DRINK OR SMOKE, HIS BIG VICE IS DROPPING COINS IN JUKEBOXES.

The fanzines of the sixties and seventies, however, have learned a few tricks from *Confidential* as far as provocative cover come-ons are concerned. Their primary chore seems to be getting Jackie O. and Elizabeth Taylor in the same cover line.

LIZ CAUGHT WITH NUDE YOUNG MAN . . . HOW SHE EXPLAINED TO HER CHILDREN

[Liz attends an Academy Award Ceremony at which a streaker appeared onstage.]

ROBERT REDFORD'S WIFE KIDNAPPED! HOW THEY KEPT THE STORY OUT OF THE PAPERS!

[Redford takes a day off from a busy schedule to pick up his wife and sneak away for some time alone with her.]

EXCLUSIVE . . . SHE'S GOING TO BE A MOTHER AGAIN . . . ONE NIGHT OUT WITH JACKIE'S HUSBAND MAKES LIZ'S DREAM COME TRUE . . . AND WHY JACKIE CAME CRYING HOME TO HER FAMILY

[Photo of Jacqueline Kennedy Onassis weeping at the grave of her slain husband. Liz invents a fictitious date with Onassis in order to make Richard Burton jealous, so that he will allow her to adopt yet another child.]

THE WHOLE CHILLING STORY: LIZA MINNELLI FEARS JUDY'S GHOST WANTS HER NEWBORN BABY: "MAMA NEVER LEAVES US ALONE" SHE CRIES!

[Liza thinks Judy would have wanted a grandchild.]

MARTIN MARRIAGE COLLAPSES . . . DEAN ADMITS THE ONE-YEAR OLD BABY IN HIS HOUSE IS ANOTHER WOMAN'S!

[The baby is his grandchild, Martin's wife protests babysitting chores.]

Aside from *People* magazine (a bloodless but respectable fan magazine that throws in a few heart surgeons and a woman jockey now and then to disguise its fan-mag status), movie magazines have changed very little in their sixty-seven-year span. Today a star's fear of dread disease (unfounded) and the heartbreak of psoriasis continue to be a winning formula with the checkout-counter-contingent, just as in decades past.

When a scandal involving a major Hollywood personality was willingly handed over to the media by the studio bosses, there was good reason to believe that the transgressor was being used as a scapegoat. Kenneth Anger says that Errol Flynn's trial for rape would never have been brought to court had it not been for the "concealed pressure" brought to bear on the studios by "corrupt Los Angeles politicians who had decided that the studios were making a fortune with wartime escapist entertainment movies and were not coming across with juicy enough kickbacks." Another example of a star serving as an inadvertent sacrificial lamb was the marijuana bust of Robert Mitchum in 1948. Mitchum was just one of several stars that narcotics agents had been watching in Hollywood during the years following the war. (Judy Garland was another.) Though Mitchum was still a relative newcomer, he'd been branded a rebel by the industry troubleshooters and was considered to be a highly disposable commodity. Consequently, the studio big shots decided that he could be forfeited in order to buy time from the authorities for other more important stars. That the bust would spell the end of Mitchum's career was a foregone conclusion. However, the public image of the sleepy-eyed Mitchum was hardly that of Dr. Kildare. Somehow the bust came across as a scene from one of his movies. And, if anything, he was even stronger after his two-month sentence than before. Another pariah, Howard Hughes, lost no time in getting Mitchum back on the screen.

When it came to the public images of valuable stars, the studios could usually call the shots with the authorities. For several decades Hollywood was a tightly run company town, and it was relatively easy for studio arbiters to persuade the

——————— ☆ ———————

★ There are home movies of Hollywood orgies starring some of the biggest screen personalities of the thirties.

★ Paulette Goddard stooped to conquer Anatole Litvak's affections while under a table in Ciro's.

★ Clark Gable was with another woman when he received the news of wife Carole Lombard's death in an airplane crash.

★ Mae West is a female impersonator.

★ Clara Bow showed her "It" to the entire Thundering Herd (the U.C.L.A. football team) in a single night of revelry.

★ Shirley Temple is a midget.

★ Columbia boss Harry Cohn used his mob connections to convince Sammy Davis, Jr., that he wasn't the man for Kim Novak.

★ Jean Harlow died while trying to induce the abortion of a child fathered by her fiance William Powell.

★ James Dean is not really dead, but a vegetable kept alive by life-sustaining machines in a hospital in his home state of Indiana.

★ Jill St. John has an IQ of 172.

★ Clark Gable's love affair with Loretta Young during *The Call of the Wild* produced an offspring which was "adopted" by Loretta.

★ Dinah Shore and Kay Francis are of mixed ancestry.

★ Paul Bern was murdered by Jean Harlow's jealous gangster boyfriend, Longie Zwillman.

★ Louella Parsons witnessed the murder of film pioneer Thomas Ince by publisher William Randolph Hearst. The coveted job of Hearst's Hollywood correspondent was the reward for her silence.

★ Kirk Douglas carved the dimple in his chin.

★ Marilyn Monroe was murdered by the CIA because she knew too much about the Kennedy assassination.

★ Simone Simon was the illegitimate daughter of Marion Davies and William Randolph Hearst.

★ Milton Berle, John Ireland, Charlie Chaplin, and Frank Sinatra were four of the biggest pricks in Hollywood.

★ An outraged Frank Sinatra broke up Lana Turner and Ava Gardner during an intimate slumber party.

★ George Raft, Dean Martin, and Jerry Lewis were mob protégés.

★ Jean Harlow's second husband Paul Bern was murdered by his mistress of many years, the mentally unstable actress Dorothy Millette, who committed suicide the day after Bern's death.

★ Marlene Dietrich and Greta Garbo are gentlemen at heart.

local authorities not to press charges when a star got out of line. Yet even though the cops and the press corps could be silenced, there was no way to still the rumors of scandal that reverberated through the studios and local service trades. The lurid details of a shocker had a way of spreading via a network of hired help to Hollywood's netherworld of prostitutes and racketeers and on to the people who paid for that particular kind of information—private detectives, showbiz attorneys, or maybe Hedda and Louella. But even the most insignificant link in the chain of Hollywood gossip and innuendo understood that a star's image had to remain untarnished as far as the outside world was concerned. The facade of respectability was kept alive for decades, despite the fact that thousands of co-conspirators were privy to the truth.

We make no claims of veracity for the Great Hollywood Rumors that follow. In fact, we'll even admit that some might have been concoctions of scandalmongers like *Confidential*'s Robert Harrison ("Crunch, Crunch . . . 'Oh no,' moaned the beautiful blonde. It was Frankie in the kitchen eating his Wheaties again."). Maybe you yourself have an uncle in the movie business, and you know for a fact that those invitations to the "wedding" of Jim Nabors and Rock Hudson were the malicious contrivance of a group of gay Malibu pranksters. But no matter how many people you straighten out, the story seems to survive.

Fact or fantasy? What follows are rumors written in the indelible ink of hearsay, passed on from generation to generation by word of mouth. Once again, we remind you that we'll never know the truth.

———— ☆ ————

★ Hollywood's casting couch to stardom operates for men as well as women.

★ L. B. Mayer was more than a father to Judy Garland, Jeanette MacDonald, Myrna Loy, and Lena Horne.

★ Audrey Hepburn has to diet continuously to remain thin.

★ Merle Oberon's face had to be reassembled after a severe case of makeup poisoning.

★ Cary Grant and Randolph Scott played house when they shared a bachelor beach pad during the thirties.

★ Charlie Chaplin's favorite song was "Thank Heaven for Little Girls."

★ Hollywood stars gave information to *Confidential* magazine about themselves for so-called exposés.

★ Tony Curtis is Cornel Wilde's illegitimate son.

★ The involvement of highly placed French officials in a posh drug-and-sex community that included film stars and political figures kept Alain Delon's involvement in the murder of his bodyguard off the police blotter.

★ Judy, Elvis, and Clark kept their tendency toward obesity under control with Dexedrine.

★ Perry Como blew his movie career by singing "Fuck you, Mr. Mayer" instead of the final chorus of the Happy Birthday Song at the MGM boss's studio birthday party.

★ James Dean's unusual sexual preferences won him the nickname "the human ashtray."

★ The Kennedy boys were avid movie fans (even old Joe). Some of their favorites included Angie Dickinson, Gene Tierney, Hedy Lamarr, and Marilyn Monroe.

★ Joan Crawford and Marilyn Monroe starred in porno loops to pay the rent in their days as aspiring starlets.

★ John Cassavetes and Ben Gazzara are the same person.

★ Rudolph Valentino was the impotent plaything of two ambitious lesbians, Nazimova and Natasha Rambova.

★ Jayne Mansfield had an IQ of 164.

★ Leslie Howard, whose plane was shot down by the Germans on a flight from Lisbon to London, was used as a decoy by the British to divert attention away from Churchill who was also flying that day.

★ Sissy Spacek and Billy Mumy are the same person.

★ In accordance with his last wishes, Walt Disney's body was preserved cryonically so that he might be resurrected at such time that a cure for the cancer that felled him is discovered.

POSITIVELY
NO LOAFING

STUDIO
ENTRANCE

Stu Erwin in *Make Me a Star*

xcuse us, but wasn't that Troy Donahue working the burrito bar at that Taco Hut in Encino? And by the way, what ever happened to Sonny Tufts?

Where do they all go, those overnight sensations, those morning-after also-rans? They start out young, attractive, and greener than the freshly cut grass on a movie mogul's Bel Air estate. They're shot from the cannon of Hollywood hype into the public consciousness where they dazzle briefly, then flicker and fade into oblivion. Their names may remain vaguely familiar, but if we remember them at all, it's mostly as a bad joke.

Almost all that's left of the careers of Fatty Arbuckle and John Gilbert, for example, are the sad and sordid circumstances of their decline and fall; few recollect much of anything about their film work. Even Luise Rainer, an actress who managed to command two Academy Awards for Best Actress during her four-year film career, is remembered more for the mystery that surrounds her sudden disappearance from the screen than for her on-screen achievements.

There can be any number of reasons for a Hollywood light to fail. Some stars, like Frances Farmer, had built-in self-destruct mechanisms that sent their careers up in an all-too-public blaze of humiliation. (It should be noted that Farmer's disgrace and subsequent eight-year confinement in a state mental institution had as much to do with her unpopular political views and a predatory mother as with her anguished mental condition.)

Sociological factors may also play a key role in a star's untimely descent. During the war years, for instance, there was the "girl he left behind" cinema sorority—Joan Leslie, Teresa Wright, Marsha Hunt, etc. They represented Hollywood's version of the latest style in womanhood—girls, not women, all sweetness and innocence. This crop of fresh-faced maids was, by and large, a figment of Hollywood's imagination, one which said more about what wartime America wanted to believe about itself than about what the boys were dreaming of in their foxholes. When the boys came home, these celluloid virgins were promptly replaced with the inflatable sexpots of the late forties and fifties.

Since movies are meant to mirror and exploit particular cultural trends, they tend to be acted out by models who embody whatever's hip and desirable at the moment. Many a screen luminary has lost his hold on fame simply because he resisted the latest fad as something dangerous and subversive. During the fifties and sixties, for instance, those stars who decried the influx of the torn T-shirt contingent and clung to their limos and furs, were automatically relegated to Hollywood's old-timer's club.

When an ongoing career seems to dry up and blow away overnight, more than likely the luckless star has been defeated by some kind of underlying obsolescence factor. The child stars of the forties were particularly vulnerable to this problem; too many of the precious darlings grew awkward as they grew up. Peggy Ann Garner won a special Oscar for her performance in *A Tree Grows in Brooklyn*

"Every time someone tells me to watch a particular movie on tv, I forget the name every fucking time."
—Al Franken

117

back in 1942. At fourteen, she was one of the biggest stars on the Fox lot, receiving thousands of fan letters a week. But, unlike her contemporary and co-star in *Jane Eyre*, Elizabeth Taylor, Garner grew up to be a rather pallid looking young woman, lacking the social and sexual precocity of MGM's jewel. And so today while Liz bounces from one expensive flop to another, little Peggy Ann pays the rent by managing a used car dealership in Santa Monica.

The professional teenagers of the postwar years faced similar problems. Many an overnight sensation found fame as short-lived as youth itself. Stars like Sandra Dee, Sal Mineo, and Russ Tamblyn became so identified with the juvenile stereotypes they played that the public just couldn't accept their graduation into more mature roles. Other Hollywood ingenues of the same period, such as Diane Varsi and Millie Perkins, seem to have been done in by their own real life ingenuousness. With no sustained studio buildup to shape their careers, they didn't stand a chance in the Sammy Glick world that Hollywood had become by the fifties.

In fact, many of Hollywood's best known losers can blame their abortive careers on the simple fact of being born too late to enjoy the benefits of the paternalistic studio system. Though the film industry can still propel an aspiring newcomer to overnight fame as a part of the PR for a blockbuster movie package, Hollywood, as a rule, is no longer in the business of building careers. Today's would-be movie stars will never know what studio-created stardom could mean; what it is to be shielded from adverse publicity, to have defects, physical and mental, disguised by movie magic, and to be given just enough of the right kind of exposure so as to make fame a foregone conclusion.

Although the herd of white elephants that stampeded across the screen during the fifties can't be blamed exclusively on the demise of the studio system, it's no coincidence that the floperoos began to outnumber the stars with greater and greater regularity around the same time. A parlor game: list all the stars you can think of who were ensconced in Hollywood heavens during the heyday of studio reign; then try to come up with more than a dozen big names per decade whose fame has survived the post-star-factory years.

The fact is, there's so little room at the top in the movie biz today that most actors would be thrilled to get as far as has-been status. At least a has-been has been. That being the case, just where are all the new flash-in-the-pan celebs coming from these days? Television, of course. It's tv that's the new has-been factory. (Whatever happened to Vince Edwards?) The exposure achieved by even the biggest screen stars in the old days can't begin to compare with that of the star of, say, a weekly tv series, for instance. What with talk shows, variety show guest shots, endorsement, product spin-offs, and personal appearances, we barely have time to meet a tv star before we want a divorce. So, to get back to the pressing question of where all the bad show biz jokes of the future are being born, the answer is simple. Just turn on your tv. The Carroll Bakers of tomorrow are on "Charlie's Angels" tonight. Stay tuned.

CLARA BOW

How about Ann-Margret in *The Ann Miller Story*?

FATTY ARBUCKLE

One wonders whether the roly-poly comic, Roscoe "Fatty" Arbuckle, would be remembered today at all were it not for the charges of rape and manslaughter brought against him for the death of starlet Virginia Rappe back in the twenties. Arbuckle has the unfortunate distinction of being the first star to be offered up by Hollywood as a scapegoat for its own transgressions, as well as being the first to be victimized by tabloid sensationalism.

The press version of Rappe's last days was provided by her friend, actress Maude Delmont, who claimed that Rappe had made a "deathbed" accusation against Arbuckle to the effect that he had, during the course of a drunken party weekend in San Francisco, forced her into a bedroom, locked the door and raped her, causing her to suffer "internal" injuries. Delmont's account of the incident couldn't possibly have stood up in court (she was never called to testify) since the facts of the case showed that the cause of Rappe's death in a nursing home a few days after her weekend of revelry was, in fact, acute peritonitus. She was also pregnant and suffering from venereal disease at the time. These recent revelations (from the doctor treating Rappe at the time of her death and the coroner's report) would imply that Arbuckle was guilty of little more than drunkeness and lechery, but the truth has long been obscured by the leering embellishments supplied by the press and the fertile imagination of the public. The tabloids fanned readers' indignation with headlines like: *Hollywood Comic Star Takes Young Girl Into His Room and Rapes Her! Arbuckle Dances While Girl Is Dying! Arbuckle Cries, "I Have Waited for Five Years and Now I've Got You!"* Sob sisters and self-proclaimed saints painted the comedian as a villain incarnate, an obese barbarian of depraved appetites. Earl Rogers, a prominent San Francisco lawyer who was approached to defend Arbuckle, observed prophetically that, "Arbuckle's weight will damn him. He will become a monster to the public. They'll never convict him, but they will ruin him."

The Hollywood community, fearful of the damaging repercussions that the scandal could have for the industry, found it expedient to turn on Arbuckle along with the public. Almost every special interest group in Hollywood issued statements deploring the affair. Arbuckle's movies were yanked from the nation's theatres, and two others that had recently been completed were never released, costing Paramount an estimated one million dollars.

As for Arbuckle himself, he was eventually acquitted of the crime by the courts, though his name remained indelibly blackened. Just prior to Rappe's death, he'd signed a contract with Paramount for three million dollars, but almost everything he owned had gone to cover the massive legal costs incurred during the course of his three trials. Only thirty-six at the time of the scandal, he survived another decade, a lost and broken man. He attempted a comeback as a director (under another name) with one of his first assignments being to direct Marion Davies, the mistress of the man most responsible for his downfall, William Randolph Hearst. (Hearst had been heard to boast that Arbuckle had sold more newspapers than the sinking of the *Lusitania.*)

Sadly, death has brought Arbuckle an ignominious and undeserved immortality. Over half a century after his banishment from the screen, the mere mention of his name still elicits lewd allusions to Coke bottles and heavyweight sex. Shortly before his death, he spoke of the press and its coverage of the scandal: "I read what they printed about me in the newspapers. Reporters used words because they made their stories sound better, without stopping to think what they do to a man. After things are once printed, whether they are true or not, you can't change people's ideas. But it didn't seem as if it could be me they were talking about."

LOUISE BROOKS

JOHN GILBERT

Louise Brooks learned the hard way that the film industry neither forgives nor forgets. A "difficult" star, she angered the powers-that-be by quitting Paramount in 1929 and turning down other offers as well. When she returned to Hollywood in 1936, she desperately tried to reestablish her career by agreeing to do chorus work in a Grace Moore musical, *When You're in Love*, in return for a test for a leading role in another film. Columbia promoted the film by releasing stills captioned: "Louise Brooks, former star, who deserted Hollywood at the height of her career, has come back to resume her work in pictures. But seven years is too long for the public to remember, and Louise courageously begins again at the bottom."

P.S. She stayed at the bottom, forgotten, until film scholars rediscovered her European films two decades later.

Legend has it that John Gilbert's career was KO'd when his Minnie Mouse voice was greeted with howls of derisive laughter at his talkie debut. Rumor also has it that his career was sabotaged by L.B. Mayer, who despised the hot-tempered star. The truth is more complex. His voice was high but far from absurd. It was the florid dialogue of *His Glorious Night* ("I love you! I love you! I love you!") as much as his voice which caused the snickers. Gilbert's full-bodied romantic acting style was simply too fervent for sound pictures which called for a more naturalistic approach. Gilbert refused to allow MGM to buy him out of his contract, and was cast in more down-to-earth roles. However, by that point the public's interest was gone, as was Gilbert's interest in life. He drank himself to death at the age of thirty-nine.

ANNA STEN   LUISE RAINER

Accents have always had it tough in Tinseltown. For every Garbo and Dietrich there are dozens of Franciska Gaals from *The Bucaneer* and from Hungary. That faraway quality in their voices sent them far away after casting directors ran out of foreign outposts in which to station them. Goldwyn tried hard with Anna Sten, or Anna Stench, as she was known to his stockholders. He spent a fortune promoting Sten, but in glamorizing her he buried her natural beauty under doll-like makeup. She's remembered as a famous flop, Goldwyn's very own Edsel.

"The Viennese Teardrop" Luise Rainer was dropped by MGM after only four years of stardom, during which she had won Academy Awards for best actress for *The Great Ziegfeld* (1936) and *The Good Earth* (1937). Her fluttery mannerisms and tearful smiles must have worn thin with the popcorn eaters. Despite her Oscar victories, there were no mass demonstrations to get her back on the screen. Her artistic sensitivity, which manifested itself in temperamental outbursts, was her ruination. L.B. Mayer supposedly threatened her by saying that if he could make a star, he could also break a star. *Auf Wiedersehen.*

VERONICA LAKE

A tough yet torpid manner and an eye-obscuring coif made audiences sit up and take notice when Veronica Lake slithered onto the screen. Sultry was the adjective usually applied to Lake, especially when she was teamed with the equally insolent Alan Ladd. However, by the fifties she was thought of as an ex-novelty. Heavy drinking had taken its toll on her looks, which were not extraordinary sans her peekaboo curl. (She had shorn her shoulder length page boy at the request of the War Department because female munitions workers' copycat do's were getting caught in ma-

chinery.) But more to the point is the fact that Lake was so cantankerous that studio executives lost interest in her before the fans did. The public was shocked when in 1962 the press discovered her working as a waitress in a Manhattan cocktail lounge. She hit the headlines again by being arrested for drunkenness. The publication of her autobiography, *Veronica,* caused a momentary flurry of attention which helped her to land a few jobs in local theatre productions and a part in a Canadian cheapie, *Footsteps to Zero,* her last film. She died in 1973; her four marriages had ended in divorce.

PEGGY   BETTY

CUMMINS   HUTTON

Peggy Cummins got one of Darryl Zanuck's big buildups in anticipation of her starring role in *Forever Amber.* But after shooting a million dollars worth of footage, Zanuck decided that Peggy lacked sex appeal and replaced her with the more voluptuous Linda Darnell. Cummins stayed on at Fox, but her roles were not of the star-making caliber. Perhaps her innate intelligence made her difficult to cast. In any case, she returned to the British cinema, a dreary fate for any actress.

Betty Hutton (the "Incendiary Blonde") burnt herself out. Her manic, madcap personality was as much a part of the ethos of the forties as big band brassiness. She was still socko at the box office in the early fifties, but a king-size ego made her impossible to handle. Her movie career never recovered from her fall off Paramount's mountain; no other studio would touch her after she and her alma mater parted company. Eventually she slid from the pages of *Variety* to those of the *National Enquirer.*

GALE SONDERGAARD

The screen's sleekest purveyor of distaff villainy, Gale Sondergaard, was cast out of Hollywood by the blacklist. An Oscar for *The Life of Emile Zola* in 1937, the first awarded for a supporting role, could not ward off the evil spirits which swept through Filmland in the late forties.

ANNE REVERE

Anne Revere was another Oscar winner (for *National Velvet* in 1944) victimized by the Red Scare. Her careworn face and guttural voice made her ideal for peasanty mother roles. As a result of the blacklist, her role in *A Place in the Sun* was trimmed before the film's release. It was to be her last movie work for twenty years.

LARRY PARKS

Larry Parks, whose portrayal of Al Jolson was enjoyed by millions, also found every door in Hollywood closed to him during the blacklist. Hedda Hopper personally launched a campaign to have him barred from the studios. Recent dramatizations of HUAC hearings have recreated the mental torture to which Parks was subjected in order for the Committee to wring out his anguished testimony.

JOHN IRELAND

John Ireland never really climbed into the big star bracket although he came very close on several occasions. *Red River* could have been his big break, but his role was cut drastically during production. The film's screenwriter Borden Chase claimed that director Howard Hawks made the cuts to punish Ireland for rustling the film's leading lady, Joanne Dru, from his own corral. (Hawks was married to someone else at the time, so his revenge had to be meted out on the sly.) Chase says that he met John Wayne and Hawks for lunch one day during the shooting and when Hawks got up to go to the men's room, the Duke told him " 'We're dumping Cherry Valance [Ireland].' I said, 'What do you mean?' 'Well,' he said, 'he's fooling around with Howard's girl.' I said, 'What the hell has that got to do with making a picture! I don't care if he's fooling around with the Virgin Mary, you've got a picture to make and the guy is good!' 'Well,' he said, 'look, he's out. That's it.' " Hawks denied all of this, insisting that he was fed up with Ireland's unpreparedness on the set due to late night drinking and pot smoking. Whatever the reason, Ireland does disappear for long stretches of *Red River.* He surfaces again at the climax of the film for the sole purpose of being gunned down by the Duke. He and Dru were married shortly after completing the film.

PEGGY ANN GARNER

Peggy Ann Garner won a special Oscar for her performance in *A Tree Grows in Brooklyn* back in 1942. At fourteen, she was one of the biggest stars on the Fox lot, receiving thousands of fan letters a week. But, unlike her contemporary and co-star in *Jane Eyre,* Elizabeth Taylor, Garner grew up to be a rather pallid looking young woman, lacking the social and sexual precocity of MGM's jewel.

SAL MINEO

Sal Mineo was one of the last boy starlets to receive the full glamour treatment from Hollywood, complete with parties, premières, concocted love affairs, and fanzine adoration. However, as one studio exec prophetically observed, "either it works, or good-bye Sal." After several years as a child actor on the Broadway stage and a few low-budget movies, Mineo had been catapulted into stardom at the age of seventeen by his remarkable portrayal of Plato, the boy who loved James Dean in *Rebel Without a Cause.* Without the slightest hesitation, he plunged into an overblown star trip, recklessly throwing his money around on clothes, cars, and a $250,000 Long Island estate for his parents. By the time he was nominated for an Academy Award for *Rebel,* he was so cocky that he threw himself a huge celebration bash and covered the outside of his new Hollywood pad with banners wishing himself "Congratulations Sal" in honor of an Oscar he would not receive.

The movie mags wrote that Sal had been discovered by a talent scout in front of his Bronx home, but the fact is that the stage appearances and dancing classes which had been his springboard had evolved as an alternative to a stretch in reform school. A street gang member at eight, he'd had numerous run-ins with school and juvenile authorities and was generally considered to be a bad kid. He'd gone from street tough to star without once looking back, but the ride was over shortly after he reached the age of consent. Sal grew out of teenage parts soon after *Rebel,* but remained too small and sensitive looking to pull off romantic leads. His looks were cut from the punk style of the fifties; there just was no way for the kid with the waterfall hairdo to hang out with the muscled surfers and button-down types that dominated the screen during the sixties. As the offers for movie or tv parts became fewer and fewer, it must have become obvious to Sal that the game was over. Yet, he couldn't or wouldn't allow himself to settle into a straight non-show-biz existence. Loans from friends and a talent for skipping out on the rent in the middle of the night kept him solvent. The boyish looking man with the petulant face, the white suits, and Borsalino hats continued to be recognized in fashionable New York and Hollywood haunts, but his pretensions and flamboyant homosexuality made him an easy target for the chic set's derision. Although things weren't exactly on the upswing for Mineo's career, he did manage to get a couple of guest shots on tv cop shows in his last months. At the time of his brutal murder in the parking lot of his semi-swank apartment building, he was living alone with a few pieces of furniture and an expensively framed poster from *Rebel Without a Cause.*

RUSS TAMBLYN

MILLIE PERKINS

Like George Chakiris, Richard Beymer, and Rita Moreno, former child star Russ Tamblyn's career reached its zenith with his performance in the musical classic *West Side Story*. Although he'd shown a wide range of acting ability in dramas *(Retreat, Hell)* and in comedies *(Don't Go Near the Water)* in addition to a genius for acrobatic stunts *(Seven Brides for Seven Brothers)*, movie-going audiences were inclined to think of him only as the perennial wide-eyed boy, the leprachaun from *tom thumb*. Like his career, his personal life was full of ups and downs. Both his marriages, to beautiful actress Venetia Stevenson and to showgirl Elizabeth Kempton, ended in messy divorces. He went into semiretirement in 1965 after the *L.A. Times* attributed several public disturbances to his drunkenness. He was not seen professionally until 1969 when he returned to the screen for *Satan's Disciples,* a sickie-quickie based on the Manson murders. Today Russ keeps busy by painting, a hobby which has become a full-time interest. As a child, 35 percent of his earnings was socked away in a trust fund; presumably it's these earnings that keep him afloat today.

West Side Story's success was so overpowering—despite the critics' reservations about casting Natalie Wood as a Puerto Rican and the cherubic Tamblyn and WASPy Beymer as street toughs—that there was simply no place for its stars' careers to go but down. The demise of the movie musical didn't help matters much either.

Rita Moreno has managed to carve a niche for herself via children's television ("The Electric Company"), but she still complains that producers see her only in terms of ethnic parts. Typecasting has also plagued her co-star George Chakiris, whose Oscar for *WWS* got him almost nowhere in Hollywood. He's filmed only two movies in the States since then and those were little more than variations on the Bernardo role (as Yvette Mimieux's Hawaiian boyfriend in *Diamond Head* and a Mayan prince in *Kings of the Sun*). Like so many others, he ended up doing films and tv work in Europe, most recently in the BBC serialization of the life of George Sand, "Notorious Woman,"

Richard Beymer landed a few juicy leads after *WWS*—*The Adventures of a Young Man, The Stripper*—but somehow his personality just never clicked on the screen. He's been out of the public eye for years. Today he leads a quiet life, teaching Transcendental Meditation in L.A.

In 1958 Millie Perkins, a twenty-year-old model with no acting experience, won out over 10,000 competitors for the title role in *The Diary of Anne Frank.* Many reviews for the film dubbed her debut "dazzling," yet the best offers she got following *Anne* were a ditzy war comedy and an Elvis Presley movie. Eventually she ran away from that feeling of "success and failure" which had been smothering her in Hollywood, to start a new life in Oregon.

Consider the differences between Perkins and Jean Seberg, another small-town girl foisted on the public by a Hollywood talent search. Like Perkins, Seberg was largely untutored in the art of acting, but unlike Perkins, she'd had a disastrous film debut. The critics had used her performance as a pretext to attack director Otto Preminger's presumed egomania in pitting an inexperienced girl against Shaw in *Saint Joan.* But Seberg's Iowa pluck surfaced after her Hollywood fiasco. She picked herself up and went to France where she connected with Jean-Luc Godard who was about to stun the film world with his anti-cinema cinema. *Breathless,* his first film and the first to carry the appelation "nouvelle vague," became a modern-day classic, due in no small degree to a Hollywood flop named Seberg. Not only did she survive, but she survived with class, even deigning to return to America on occasion for other, sometimes memorable (*Lilith*) films.

DOLORES HART

Plenty of flash-in-the-pan movie names have fled the Hollywood rat race, but no one ever ran as far away from the Tinseltown way of life as Dolores Hart. It seems she got religion once her career began to fade. (Maybe all those good-girl roles went to her head.) They don't ask Sister Dolores *Where the Boys Are* anymore.

GEORGE NADER

Like Steve Reeves, Lex Barker, and many others, it took cheapie European adventure flicks to provide George Nader with the stardom that had eluded him in Tinseltown. Nader was almost a decade older than the leading pretty boys of the period when he first broke into the movies, but he managed to hold his own very nicely on the pages of beefcake and fan magazines. However, with very few exceptions, Universal gave him little to do in films like *Congo Crossing* other than display his impressive biceps. After only a handful of films, his screen career took a turn for the worse. (There are rumors to the effect that Nader was blackballed by his own studio, which had made a deal with *Confidential* magazine to buy that publication's silence on the subject of the sexual proclivities of another of its biggest male stars in return for a Nader exposé.) Nader made one last play for the spotlight in the early sixties with a couple of tv series, but the times and the styles, they were a changin'. So he packed up his muscle shirts and headed for Europe, Germany to be exact, where for a time he became its number one box office attraction in ersatz James Bond thrillers. But when the spy genre fizzled, Nader's career fizzled with it. He has since returned home to Hollywood to rest comfortably on his European-earned laurels.

FAITH DOMERGUE

Legend has it that Howard Hughes stashed Faith Domergue in a Hollywood hideaway and almost forgot where he'd left her. True or not, he *did* keep her waiting around for years while he fashioned the ideal launching pad for her talents. But unlike Hughes's greatest hype, *The Outlaw* with Jane Russell, Faith's premier effort, *Vendetta*, was the victim of its own massive publicity campaign. She ended up in *Planet of the Prehistoric Women* and worse. If Faith is remembered at all, it will be as another of Hughes's Follies, his celluloid Spruce Goose.

JEAN PETERS

Nobody kisses Hollywood good-bye while still on top. Stardom is too intoxicating a drug to kick cold turkey. About the only dropouts who weren't dropped first were Jean Peters and Grace Kelly, both of whom quit in the mid-fifties. But it took a billion bucks and a kingdom to lure them away. Ms. Peters is sorely missed. She was no dainty ingenue on the screen, but a woman with guts capable of holding her own in a man's world. In *Apache* she fought side by side with her man, Burt Lancaster, while in *Niagara* she tussled with Joseph Cotten over the rapids. What a waste it is that she agreed to sign a document drawn up by Howard Hughes wherein she consented not to make movies for the duration of their marriage.

CARROLL BAKER

TAB HUNTER

TROY DONAHUE

Remember Carroll Baker? She was the Girl-Most-Likely to take up where Monroe left off, if you believed her publicity. While most sex stars begged to be accepted for their talent, Baker, who'd shown real potential as a serious actress, sought fame as a sex symbol. And for a time it actually looked as if she might pull it off. She caught the public's eye in *Giant,* then knocked them for a loop as the pouty, perverse *Baby Doll.* Almost overnight, her career was on fire. However, her next few films—*The Miracle, But Not for Me,* etc.—were duds, and she was back where she started. It was around this time that her new husband, sometime director Jack Garfein, came to the conclusion that Carroll would have to sell sex if she wanted to climb back up to her *Baby Doll* notoriety. So all of a sudden a brand new Carroll Baker began showing up on the cover of every fanzine and tabloid in the country, complete with a glossy new look—furs, transparent gowns, and platinum blond page boy. About the only one in Hollywood who paid the least bit of attention to this spectacle was fledgling producer Joseph E. Levine, who decided to cast her as the wisecracking tramp of his first American production, *The Carpetbaggers.* The film itself drew critical jeers, but it yielded a bonanza at the box office and once again Carroll was back on top. Levine and Paramount signed her to a seven-picture contract. As the Baker ballyhoo reached its most fevered pitch, it was announced that Levine had purchased *Harlow,* the trashy Shulman bio, to exploit the success Carroll had had as a Harlow-style actress in their first film together. But the film and the hype were a disaster. There'd been all sorts of problems with the script and a rival production starring Carol Lynley, but the main problem was that Carroll's PTA prettiness and clipped delivery just didn't meld with her concocted image. She felt awkward in the role and her discomfort showed on screen. Perhaps even more to the point is the fact that cultural styles were rapidly metamorphosing when the film was released and the public simply wasn't in the market for a platinum blond bombshell in 1965. After *Harlow,* her much publicized legal hassles with Paramount left Hollywood leery of her temperament (it was already doubtful of her drawing power). Depressed and jobless, she divorced Garfein and fled to Rome to join its colony of Hollywood expatriates. She returned to America in 1977 to be exploited again in Andy Warhol's aptly titled *Bad.*

Tab Hunter may have had a muscled surfer look long before the phrase was coined, but pinup boys are a highly disposable commodity in Hollywood. "That Sigh Guy" committed career suicide when he suddenly pulled out of his contract with Warners, who had given him an extensive and longwinded publicity buildup, saying only that he wanted "better scripts." They quickly replaced him with another Siegfried who alienated the affections of Tab's fickle fans. Though Troy Donahue's acting ability was just as limited, he filled out a windbreaker magnificently—and isn't that what really counts? Troy's place in the sun was to be snuffed out in the mid-sixties when bodies and hair became stringier. The comatose "Male Jayne Mansfield" became obsolete in post-Beatle America.

MICHAEL PARKS

CHRISTOPHER JONES

Michael Parks found out that it takes more than fumbling line readings and brooding good looks to make a new James Dean. Christopher Jones was also labeled as a new Dean, for a few minutes anyway. But, as with Parks, his reputation for refusing to take direction eventually stymied his career.

JEFFREY HUNTER

The blame for Jeffrey Hunter's decline can't be laid merely to his casting as Christ in *King of Kings,* or, as some critics called it, *I Was a Teenage Jesus.* He was never really a big star. His blue-eyed earnestness made him popular with teenyboppers, but he never possessed the authority to become a major leading man. Even when his hair turned gray, he came across as a juvenile.

IMITATION OF LIFE

Why all the fuss? After all, I just played myself.
—Errol Flynn in response to the rave reviews
for his performance in The Sun Also Rises

t was not uncommon during Hollywood's heyday for stars to allow themselves to be seduced into acting out their personal lives on the screen. They gave their souls to the public even if it meant throwing in scraps of painful personal history in the bargain. Like tightrope walkers, they challenged us not to look away as film fantasy skirted precariously close to the truth. Their screen swagger made them dangerous and exciting to us—a timid public that found life difficult enough without exposing our own dirty linen to the world.

Studio exploitation of star personae was especially prevalent during the fifties, when the movie business would try anything to pull the public's attention away from their television sets. The results were usually embarrassing for both the stars and their fans, but still audiences couldn't seem to stay away. The noise generated by Lana Turner's portrayal of an ambitious actress whose career is destroying her daughter, coming as it did only months after the murder of Lana's lover by her daughter Cheryl Crane, created a veritable landslide of publicity for the film. The media might be titillated or appalled by this kind of vulgarity, but it was never uninterested.

Exploitation films were often so successful that stars ended up paying the bills for their own real life *tsouris* by reenacting it for the public over and over again. Lana Turner remains financially solvent today thanks to her income from *Imitation of Life*, a film which willfully milked her domestic and romantic hardship. But as she would remark years later, she knew of no other way to earn a living; the screen was her life.

Image exploitation, on the other hand, could be as innocuous as a star's sharing a little joke on himself with the fans, like Victor Mature's hilarious aging matinee idol in *After the Fox,* or MGM's teaming of the famous pair of off-screen lovers Garbo and Gilbert for *Love.* However, audiences weren't always aware of the truth that masqueraded as fantasy when a star acted out the more unsavory aspects of his own private life, as with Bing Crosby's portrayal of an alcoholic singer in *The Country Girl.*

Excluding Woody Allen's own special brand of purgatorial screen therapy, cinema psychodrama seems to have gone the way of Smell-O-Vision and 3-D. Images and personality quirks may be exploited now and then, and scripted love scenes still have a tendency to linger on after filming has ceased, but as a rule today's New Breed likes to cloak itself in Garboesque mystery. Most refuse to give personal interviews, let alone act out their private lives on screen. Perhaps they're haunted by the specter of unwitting Hollywood greats who ended up imitating their own celluloid caricatures in real life.

Is Benji the only happy star in Show Business?

Ted Healy and Joan Crawford in *Dancing Lady*

Joan Crawford and Lionel Barrymore in *Grand Hotel*

Let me explain something about people raised in films. We learned a lot from acting. I learned to read by reading scripts. I learned how to react—learned strength and humor—from parts I played. I would rehearse lines I had in a picture and use them for myself, let them become a part of me. I think Clark Gable took the humor and sex from the characters he played. We all did it, but not consciously, believe me. Hepburn is still part *African Queen*, part *Philadelphia Story*. . . . We didn't know it, but we grew through the years, playing characters.

—Joan Crawford

Is it masochism or exhibitionism that entices a star to act out his own life's ups and down on screen? We tend to associate this kind of self-exploitation with the downslide of fame. We forget that the films of studio creations like Joan Crawford and Lana Turner have almost always been autobiographical. It's just that the ride to the top isn't quite so painful to watch.

Millions of shopgirls identified with Joan Crawford when she acted out her own rags-to-riches saga during the thirties. In *Dancing Lady*, Joan is a dancer in a burlesque house who makes it in the big time on Broadway. Despite the sleazy atmosphere of her surroundings, she has managed to keep herself decent for the man she'll come to love, Clark Gable. In *Grand Hotel*, Joan is a stenographer who foregoes wealth and luxury for the love of a good man. If Joan didn't start out wealthy in her early films, she always ended up that way or in love, or both. (And a star.)

Joan Crawford in *Torch Song*

Lana Turner and Artie Shaw in *Dancing Co-Ed*

During the forties, Lana Turner inherited Crawford's Cinderella stories in films like *Dancing Co-Ed*, in which she was the quintessential jitterbug as Joan had been the ultimate flapper, and *Rich Man, Poor Girl,* which more or less sums up the genre. In *Week-End at the Waldorf,* a remake of *Grand Hotel,* Lana played Joan's part as the stenographer on the make. These screen roles portrayed ambition, and they were played by actresses who the public knew had struggled to pull themselves up from the lower class backgrounds.

But Cinderella stories were not without hardship. Fanzine readers knew that the real-life Crawford and Turner successes hadn't brought them the love for which they sacrificed everything in the movies. Their marriages had been as brief as their liaisons on screen. For generations brought up on Hollywood morality, success could mean nothing without love; consequently, aging Cinderellas like Joan and Lana often found themselves locked in the screen clichés of their youth, forced to act out the ugly consequences of ambition again and again.

For instance, in *Torch Song* Crawford is Jenny Stewart, a ruthlessly ambitious musical comedy star, who makes life miserable for everyone around her. Director Charles Walters has acknowledged that he filled the film with Crawfordisms such as her compulsive stubbing out of cigarettes and her insistence on perfection of detail that bordered on the neurotic.

And, since millions had turned out to watch Lana Turner's re-enactment of her own domestic woes in *Imitation of Life,* exploitation specialists like producer Ross Hunter kept the ball rolling by casting her as a sexy matron involved with murder in *Madame X* and *Portrait in Black.*

Lana Turner and Van Johnson in *Week-End at the Waldorf*

Sandra Dee and Lana Turner in *Imitation of Life*

How fortunate we are in this age of technology to be able to eavesdrop unobserved while legendary symbols of insatiable lust demonstrate their prowess on screen.

Moviegoers were titillated by the sight of the screen's fabled swordsman, Errol Flynn, playing the world's greatest lover in *The Loves of Don Juan* just a few short years after his headline-making trial for the rape of Peggy Saterlee.

Errol Flynn in *Adventures of Don Juan*

Audiences knew that Ava Gardner's role as *The Barefoot Contessa* was based on the tempestuous life of Rita Hayworth, but they weren't unaware of the parallels between Ava herself and the sexually aggressive Maria Vargas. She continued to exploit her international playgirl image in addition to her well-known appetite for male flesh in *The Sun Also Rises.*

Ava Gardner and Humphrey Bogart in *The Barefoot Contessa*

Julie Christie and Warren Beatty in *Shampoo*

It's heartwarming to know that if someday our grandchildren want to know what made Warren Beatty such a big deal, they need only replay one of those dusty old videotape cassettes in the attic to catch Warren's act in *Shampoo.*

Who needs Rock and Doris when we can watch celebrated romances being acted out for our viewing pleasure on the screen? Seventies audiences were just as aroused by watching real-life lovers Diane Keaton and Woody Allen making love in *Annie Hall* as fans had been decades before when MGM exploited the off-screen couplings of Garbo and Gilbert and Taylor and Stanwyck.

John Gilbert and Greta Garbo in *Love*

Robert Taylor and Barbara Stanwyck in *This Is My Affair*

Woody Allen and Diane Keaton in *Annie H*

Eddie Fisher and Debbie Reynolds in *Bundle of Joy*

Eddie and Debbie were the public's very own Ken and Barbie during the fifties. Things were so thick between America's sweethearts and their adoring fans that the Fishers even made a movie about the unexpected arrival of a baby into the lives of a young couple, just a few months after Debbie had given birth to her very own *Bundle of Joy.*

Is it any wonder the fans had such a proprietary air of indignation when Elizabeth Taylor stole Eddie from Tammy? And not a year after her own husband's death! Besides, Liz was practically one of the nation's family too. Hadn't the public turned out by the millions to watch her screen wedding in *Father of the Bride,* which MGM had released to coincide with her own real-life nuptials to hotel heir Nicky Hilton? Perhaps if Liz had been a good little girl and played the long-suffering martyr, she might have ended up playing *The Singing Nun.* But instead, Hollywood responded to her naughtiness by casting her as the high-priced call girl of *Butterfield 8* and the most tantalizing femme fatale of them all, *Cleopatra.*

The fans decided that anyone who could demolish Eddie Fisher couldn't be all bad. So poor Eddie ended up acting in real life the role of the shadowy milquetoast that Liz had insisted he play in *Butterfield 8* .

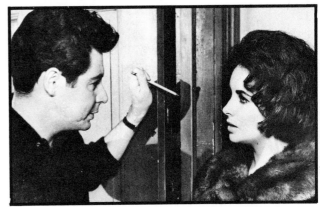

Eddie Fisher and Elizabeth Taylor in *Butterfield 8*

The world went absolutely wild when it got wind of the off-camera love scenes between Cleo and Tony while director Joseph Mankiewicz cooled his heels waiting for the lovers to get down to business. When *Cleopatra* became "the most talked about film ever made," MGM rereleased *Cat on a Hot Tin Roof* and *Butterfield 8* with the come-on, "See the films that gave Liz her reputation." You know the rest. . . .

Liz and Burton recreated their struggle against temptation for a million big ones in *The Sandpiper,* which wound up ranking number twenty on MGM's list of all-time moneymakers. In it Burton plays a man of the cloth married to the kind but plain Eva Marie Saint; Liz is a naturalist painter, devoted mother, and lover of little animals who lives in sumptuous seclusion with no visible means of support. Throughout the film the principled clergyman and the bohemian child-woman make a Herculean effort to refrain from violating the ninth commandment. In fact, their intentions are so honorable that it's difficult to stay awake. But we come to understand that our Liz is a prisoner of love, a free spirit who can't be judged by man's law—or God's, for that matter. Hopefully, their real-life adultery was not quite so uplifting.

It wasn't long, time flying the way it does, before Taylor and Burton had become the Lunt and Fontanne of the extravagant flop. Perhaps if Liz and Dick's scripts had been a little meatier, the public wouldn't have tired of their marriage before they did. Now that the Burtons have split the sheets, Liz has to make the turkeys all by herself.

Yes, there's a new sadder-but-wiser Liz on display nowadays. But not to worry. You can count on seeing lots and lots of Liz just the way you love her best, in her latest and most exciting role to date—*Mrs. Smith Goes to Washington.*

Richard Burton and Elizabeth Taylor in *Cleopatra*

Richard Burton and Elizabeth Taylor in *The Sandpiper*

Reality weaves in and out of films in which performers play performers. The public loves to speculate about the parallels past and present that exist between the drama on screen and a star's personal life.

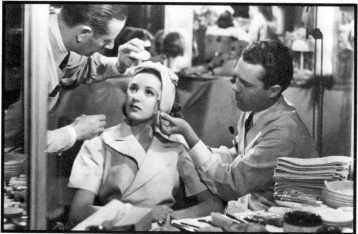

Linda Darnell in *Star Dust*

Only a few years after Darryl Zanuck had sent her back to Dallas to do some more growing up, Linda Darnell basically just played herself as an eager young girl being groomed for stardom in *Star Dust*.

Movie audiences weren't always aware of the parallels in a performer's screen role and his own private life.

Billie Dove and Marion Davies in *Blondie of the Follies*

In *Blondie of the Follies,* real-life Follies grad Marion Davies and Billie Dove (off-screen girlfriend of tycoon Howard Hughes) played Ziegfeld showgirls who are kept by repugnant but wealthy sugar daddies. The film was produced by Davies's very own sugar daddy, William Randolph Hearst.

When Jean Harlow portrayed a sex symbol who is manipulated by family and studio in *Bombshell*, audiences were unaware of her mother's willfull squandering of her earnings. Friends and public alike were stunned a few years later when it was revealed that Harlow's estate amounted to little more than $25,000 at her death.

Franchot Tone and Jean Harlow in *Bombshell*

Jennifer Jones is said to have suffered considerable distress during the filming of *Madame Bovary,* in which she played an ambitious woman who abandons her husband to pursue romantic folly. In 1949, the year of the film's release, she married her powerful mentor of many years, David O. Selznick, after having divorced the ill-fated actor, Robert Walker.

Jennifer Jones in *Madame Bovary*

After his happy second marriage to actress Kathryn Grant, Bing Crosby apparently felt secure enough to admit in interviews that he had suffered from long-term alcoholism in the past, just like the singer on the skids he'd portrayed with such feeling in *The Country Girl.*

Bing Crosby in *The Country Girl*

Jack Lemmon has revealed that he was suffering from alcoholism at the time of his first dramatic starring role in *Days of Wine and Roses.* His realistic portrayal won him an Academy Award.

Jack Lemmon in *Days of Wine and Roses*

Whirlpool exploited Gene Tierney's star persona as well as her real-life traumas. In it she portrayed a socialite whose sedate manner masks emotional turmoil. The role was tailored to Tierney's image: a trancelike expression combined with nervously intense gestures and hints of madness in her voice and eyes. The film also used Tierney's troubled life as raw material. *Whirlpool*'s heroine, like Tierney, is the victim of an overprotective father. (Tierney's real father sued her when she broke away to marry Oleg Cassini.) Although Tierney's major breakdown was to come six years after *Whirlpool,* she was mentally unstable throughout the forties. It must have been eerie for an actress attempting to hide emotional stress to play the role of a woman trying to do the same.

Gene Tierney in *Whirlpool*

Some films exploit the physical debilitation or mental anguish of their stars.

The public was very much aware of the mysterious suicide of Jean Harlow's husband, Paul Bern, when she played the role of an actress who becomes embroiled in a messy scandal after her emotionally disturbed husband commits suicide in *Reckless*.

In *I Could Go On Singing,* Judy Garland plays a world-famous singer who has traded her private life for a cult following. Her backstage agonies are rendered in documentary fashion as she waits to perform before a real concert audience. When she's told that her audience is waiting, an emotionally spent Garland speaks words that could have been taken from her own life: "To hell with them. I can't be spread thin like a pastry . . . so everybody can take a big bite out of me!"

Directors who are romantically involved with stars have been known to use strips of film as clotheslines to air their grievances. *The Lady From Shanghai* can be read as a "kiss-off" by director Orson Welles to Rita Hayworth. Their marriage was in trouble ("She bores me.") when the movie was shot, and there seemed to be a real effort on Welles's part to destroy his estranged wife's image. He cast her as a poisonous manipulator of men and himself as her chief victim. Josef von Sternberg did the same thing as his partnership with Marlene Dietrich was waning, having Dietrich portray a heartless femme fatale who bedevils Lionel Atwill (made up to resemble Sternberg). Neither *The Devil Is a Woman* nor *Lady From Shanghai* was popular with audiences, due to the coldness of their central female roles. Was it malice which prompted Welles to cut off Hayworth's trademark, her flowing tresses, and dye what remained a hard yellow? And what about those hints of sadomasochism in *The Devil Is a Woman?*

Orson Welles and Rita Hayworth in *The Lady From Shanghai*

Marlene Dietrich and Lionel Atwill in *The Devil Is a Woman*

On a few memorable occasions, stars have lampooned their trademarks or vices on screen . . .

Dean Martin was Dino, a boozy crooner who wakes up in the morning with a headache if he hasn't had any sexual action the night before in *Kiss Me, Stupid.*

Dean Martin and showgirls in *Kiss Me, Stupid*

The Band Wagon begins with an auction of mementos belonging to Tony Hunter (Fred Astaire), which includes a top hat and cane used by Tony in *Flying Down to Costa Rica.* Like Tony Hunter's, Astaire's own career at the time. of *The Band Wagon* wasn't exactly in high gear. Once again, Hollywood presents us with the double-exposure image of a performer making a comeback playing a performer making a comeback.

Cyd Charisse and Fred Astaire in *The Band Wagon*

In *After the Fox,* Victor Mature plays an ex-Hollywood hunk named Tony Powell trying to make a comeback in a spaghetti spy film and suffering a middle-aged short circuit.

Jayne Mansfield may have been called Rita Marlowe in *Will Success Spoil Rock Hunter,* but she was quite obviously playing herself. Lest we fail to notice the similarities between Jayne and her screen alter ego, director Frank Tashlin shows Rita starring in a Mansfield opus, *The Wayward Bus,* in addition to casting her husband, muscle man Mickey Hargitay, as her boyfriend, Bobo Branigansky, the tv Jungle Man.

Victor Mature and Martin Balsam in *After the Fox*

Tony Randall and Jayne Mansfield in *Will Success Spoil Rock Hunter*

Victims of the fifties Red Scare have occasionally used the cinema as a medium for overt social comment.

In *A King in New York,* Charlie Chaplin mocks the climate of political persecution generated by the House Un-American Activities Committee that exiled him to Europe.

Van Johnson, as a television star trying to survive the scandal sheet disclosure of a past prison record, mounted an impassioned protest against the burgeoning power of the exposé racket in *Slander.* If his anguish looks real, it could be, since he himself had been the victim of an ugly smear campaign by *Confidential* magazine.

Almost everyone involved in the making of *The Front* had been blacklisted at some point in their careers. One such casualty, Zero Mostel, portrays an overbearing comic who becomes the scapegoat for political opportunists. The role combines elements of his own career's nose dive during the blacklist and that of the tragic J. Edward Bromberg, a Hollywood character actor, whose suicide was attributed to the Committee's harassment.

Age does not rest gracefully either on screen or off for stars who are haunted by the long-playing images of their youth on The Late Movie. Stars in the throes of middle age portraying stars on the decline make fascinating subjects for the wrinkle-watching brigade.

Gloria Swanson in *Sunset Boulevard*

Gloria Swanson, as the former silent star Norma Desmond in *Sunset Boulevard,* was surrounded with Swanson memorabilia from her own days as Queen of the Silents. In addition to making little in-jokes like the uncredited guest appearances of other silent greats like Buster Keaton and Anna O. Nilsson, director Billy Wilder wove screen fiction from Hollywood's past by having Norma Desmond screen *Queen Kelly,* an unfinished film starring the real Swanson and directed by Erich von Stroheim, who also appeared in the film as Norma Desmond's former director-husband.

Vivien Leigh and Warren Beatty in *The Roman Spring of Mrs. Stone*

Tennessee Williams wanted the lead in *The Roman Spring of Mrs. Stone* to go to Katharine Hepburn, after seeing her performance as the scheming mother in *Suddenly Last Summer.* But Hepburn, who resented the way her advancing years had been treated in that film, had no intention of inviting comparison between herself and the lonely middle-aged actress who buys the attentions of a male hustler. Although the public was intrigued by rumors of an off-screen liaison between the film's subsequent stars, Vivien Leigh and Warren Beatty, *Spring* was a disappointment at the box office. It seems that audiences were uncomfortable with the film's depressing theme, and with the painful similarities between the lives of Vivien Leigh and the mentally unstable Mrs. Stone.

Errol Flynn, constantly on the run from lawyers and bill collectors during the last years of his life, allowed Darryl Zanuck and Jack Warner to showcase his physical and mental deterioration by casting him as melancholy drunks in *The Sun Also Rises, The Roots of Heaven,* and as John Barrymore (in real life Flynn's beloved drinking companion) in *Too Much, Too Soon.*

Mel Ferrer and Errol Flynn in *The Sun Also Rises*

Dorothy Malone and Errol Flynn in *Too Much, Too Soon*

Flynn's impersonation of Barrymore was much less cruel than Barrymore's of himself as *The Great Profile*. In it he burlesqued his recent Broadway run in the play *My Dear Children,* an unfunny comedy kept alive by curiosity-seekers who had turned out in droves to watch his drunken stage shenanigans. His tempestuous marriage to demi-actress Elaine Barrie was also thrown in, in the person of an irritating groupie played by Mary Beth Hughes.

Mary Beth Hughes and John Barrymore in *The Great Profile*

Consider the stark contrast between Barrymore's devastating self-mockery and John Wayne's eulogistic tribute to John Wayne in *The Shootist.* As the last of the great gunfighters, Wayne's sentimental reminiscences present the cinematic equivalent of Sinatra singing "My Way."

John Wayne in *The Shootist*

Ad shot for Bette Davis in *The Star*

Two-time Academy Award winner Bette Davis played an actress who discovers that her Oscar can't keep her warm at night in *The Star.*

Hedy Lamarr underscored her own decline by appearing as an aging movie star in Universal's tacky *The Female Animal.* Another refugee from the greener pastures of MGM, Jane Powell, played her daughter. The screenplay called for the two women to clash over stud George Nader.

Hedy Lamarr in *The Female Animal*

In *No Highway in the Sky,* screen actress Monica Teasdale's love of children and droll self-mockery (she calls her films "a few cans of celluloid on the junk heap someday") bring to mind the world-weary international star who portrayed her—Marlene Dietrich.

Marlene Dietrich in *No Highway in the Sky*

A. H. Trimble, "the man who looks like Will Rogers," famous for his impersonations of the late humorist, appears in the "Oh, Oh, Oklahoma" dance sequences of Universal's *You're a Sweetheart.*

FROM HERE TO ETERNITY

The names and faces that follow comprise a heavenly pantheon of cinema elite. They are the hallowed "late greats," screen stars gone to that big sound stage in the sky, martyrs who gave their all for show biz. Each was waylaid by his own notoriety, a sudden rise to the top, an on-again-off-again love affair with the public, too much of everything too soon. Flamboyant in death as well as in life the circumstances of their last hours on earth remain unclear, clouded with mystery and rumor of foul play. Many were involved with drugs and alcohol, although this appears to have been symptom rather than source of their cosmic blues, a way of filtering the binding glare of their goldfish-bowl existences. Each alternately courted and damned the public, protesting that they owed their fans nothing one minute and tearfully apologizing for an indiscretion the next. Many spent their last few years trying to die in order to escape the inevitable—character parts, sitcoms, and exile from Beverly Hills.

A few members of this select fraternity actually met their fate on backlot battlefields. Tyrone Power's career was on the wane when he died of a heart attack at forty-five after filming a strenuous dueling scene with George Sanders for *Solomon and Sheba,* but director King Vidor feels positive that the film could have effected a reversal in Power's plummeting popularity.

Mystery and legend surround the deaths of Jean Harlow, Marilyn Monroe, Lupe Velez, Bruce Lee, and George Reeves. The country was suspicious of the odd circumstances that led to Jean Harlow's death by uremic poisoning. According to the official studio explanation, Harlow's mother, a devout Christian Scientist, had refused medical treatment for her daughter until it was too late. The contradictions that had clouded the death of Harlow's second husband, Paul Bern, a few years earlier, made the account of her death just that much more difficult for a dubious public to swallow.

Like Marilyn Monroe, Bruce Lee is believed by thousands of fans to have been a victim of political assas-

sination. While Monroe was supposedly silenced by the CIA because she knew too much about the Kennedy assassination, international scuttlebutt has it that Bruce Lee was the target of the secret Kung Fu society of the Black Hand. Government officials in Hong Kong testified that Lee's death resulted from an allergic reaction to a painkiller, but friends back home in America believe that he suffered a brain hemorrhage from a blow inflicted while filming a screen fight.

Hollywood's Mexican spitfire, Lupe Velez, was a second-feature señorita when she decided to end her life, though her suicide note seems to indicate that she was more forlorn over a broken love affair and an ongoing pregnancy than her career. Rumors of a botched ritual suicide have outlived her films.

Preview audiences howled with laughter at the sight of television's "Superman," George Reeves, in his big scene in *From Here to Eternity,* causing the film's producers to cut most of the role Reeves had felt certain would reactivate his movie career and spring him once and for all from his cape and tights. When Reeves was found dead of gunshot wounds, the tabloids speculated that his tv success had never really compensated for his aborted film career, and that his death was a suicide brought on by his resulting despondency. However, his "Superman" costars have suggested that the real cause of Reeves's death was hushed up by authorities who feared that America's children would never be the same if they found out that Superman had been murdered.

Drugs and alcohol ended the misery of performers like Montgomery Clift, Marie McDonald, Nick Adams, Dorothy Dandridge, Gail Russell, and Bobby Driscoll when the public's affection turned to morbid curiosity about the seamy side of their personal lives and fading careers.

Gail Russell's continuous run-ins with the law for drunken driving made her mental disintegration all too public. The sensitive actress had been shuffled into films while still in her teens and had never really managed to catch up or cope with her instantaneous stardom. Her marriage to beefcake pinup Guy Madison (tv's "Wild Bill Hickok") was eventually destroyed by alcohol. When she spoke of her weakness for drink, she said it seemed to help since "everything had happened so fast" in her life and career. She died at thirty-six of natural causes, surrounded by empty bottles.

Rudolph Valentino died of peritonitis at the age of thirty-one, and yet there is still the lingering feeling that his death was an intentional act on his part. Film historian David Thompson said of Valentino, "Death rescued him from sordid scandal, thrust him instead into mythology, and, incidentally, saved him from the exposure that sound would have threatened."

It would seem that it was age that threatened Elvis Presley, who, like Valentino, was a simple, uneducated country boy when first catapulted into the public eye. His distress at being grotesquely overweight during the last years of his life wasn't the only reason for his debilitating pill habit, according to those close to him. It had begun when Elvis had first gotten hot during his early years in Hollywood. In *Elvis, What Happened?*, his bodyguard Red West told Steve Dunleavy several months before his death, "He takes pills to go to sleep. He takes pills to get up. There have been times when he was so hyper on the uppers that he has had trouble breathing, and on one occasion he thought he was going to die. His system doesn't work anymore like a normal human being's." His family continues to deny rumors of his drugtaking, but they refused to allow the findings of the Memphis coroner's report to be made public.

A sad end for what was becoming an increasingly sad existence awaited the fading sex symbol, Jayne Mansfield, on a Louisiana highway on a warm summer night in 1967. Besieged by law suits and personal problems, her last few films had been embarrassments, even for her. For some time, she'd sought escape from her troubles with pills and liquor. On this night she was headed to New Orleans for a nightclub engagement with three of her children and her boyfriend manager Sam Brody.

Laird Cregar was so distraught over being typecast as a hulking ghoul that he inadvertently stopped his heart while trying to diet himself into a svelte leading man. He was twenty-nine. Mario Lanza had eaten himself out of romantic parts, but temperament proved to be more damaging to his career than obesity, drugs, or alcohol. Like Lanza, Maria Montez had a reputation for being impossible to handle. After a number of years in Hajji-Baba type adventures, she was dropped by Universal and forced to seek work in European cheapies. While in Europe, she attempted to counter her advanced state of *avoirdupois* with hot saline baths. She died in one of a heart attack at the age of thirty-one.

We all know what happens to child stars, don't we? But we didn't know while we watched Judy Garland grow up on screen. "The experience of stardom when one is not old enough to deal with it," says John Kindon, professor of clinical psychiatry at UCLA, "causes a severe distortion not just of reality but of inner reality. For a child performer, there is almost a crippling of the normal developmental processes. They say things like, 'I only come alive when I work.' " For Judy, life was stardom; anything less spelled failure—and death. We were horrified as she succumbed to the very same stimulants and depressants that had allowed her to log more man-hours in her brief childhood than most people do in a lifetime.

Although John Garfield was never directly accused of anything other than sympathizing with left-wing causes, he was blacklisted for refusing to reveal the names of other Hollywood sympathizers. A friend remembers that, "When he wasn't able to work, he ran around in a violent, stupid kind of way. In the end he died of a heart attack. The blacklist killed him."

When Carole Landis's career failed to ignite with the public she told a reporter, "I know just how Lupe Velez felt. You fight just so long, then what have you got to face? You begin to worry about being washed up. You get bitter and disillusioned. You fear the future because there's only one way to go, and that's down." In addition to her lackluster career, there was her unhappy affair with British import Rex Harrison, who refused to leave his wife, actress Lilli Palmer. When it all became too much to handle, Landis swallowed a bottle of sleeping pills just before Harrison was to pick her up for a luncheon date. Harrison found her on the floor of her bathroom with a suicide note that made no mention of him. His fatal charm earned him the tag "Sexy Rexy" in the papers and sent him and Lilli back to England to wait out the furor.

Robert Walker never really seemed to recover from the loss of his beautiful and ambitious young wife, Jennifer Jones, to movie mogul David O. Selznick. He was dead at thirty-three, a tragic alcoholic whose sensitive face had hardened into that of a man twice his age.

James Dean became sullen and withdrawn after losing actress Pier Angeli to Vic Damone. Fond of quoting the John Derek character from *Knock on Any Door* who advised, "Live fast, die young, and have a good-looking corpse," he was dead within a month of predicting his own demise to a friend on the set of *Giant*. Pier Angeli also never really adjusted to Hollywood, to stardom, or to losing the young James Dean. Later she couldn't accept the decline in her fortunes. Just a year before she died, she told an interviewer, "I am still in love with Jimmy Dean." She blamed the specter of the dead teen idol for breaking up her marriages and keeping her from finding her own personal peace. She died of a barbiturate overdose at the age of thirty-nine.

The majority of these casualties suffered from a kind of universal Hollywood malaise, a premonition of impending obsolescence. They lived with the knowledge that for sex symbols and movie stars there is no such thing as a graceful decline. By dying at an untimely age, whether by their own hand or in some mysterious self-willed fashion, these special few have struck a bargain with time. Unlike other show-biz greats who have retired to their farms and tv residuals, missed but not mourned, they have invested themselves with an ironclad mythology, assuring perpetual adoration as long as there's a Late, Late Show.

CAROLE LOMBARD

How about Jeff Bridges in *The Wayne Morris Story*?

Rudolph Valentino

Jean Harlow

Lupe Velez

Laird Cregar

George Reeves

Dorothy Dandridge

Marie McDonald

Bobby Driscoll

Marilyn Monroe

Nick Adams

Tyrone Power

Jayne Mansfield

Pier Angeli

James Dean

Bruce Lee

Elvis Presley

Fantasy

Donald Duck cavorts with a bevy of Mexican beauties in *The Three Caballeros.*

AGE OF INNOCENCE

ho hasn't been disappointed when encountering the real-life model for a place or a thing first encountered in a vintage Hollywood movie? Don't bother to look for the Casablanca of Rick's Cafe Americain. It's not that it's no longer there. It never was.

Hollywood's technical perfection and attention to detail when rendering a New York street or a storm at sea were faithful enough to convince us that they were authentic even if we had seen the real thing. But if everything was beautiful at the movies and we weren't exactly sure why, it was because we'd forgotten that Hollywood's sensibilities had intruded on nature. We'd become so used to the artifice of Hollywood's backlot convention that we no longer recognized the deception involved. Life's truths paled by comparison.

On top of the synthesized reality that masqueraded as the real world, Hollywood often added a veneer of the fantastic or the supernatural without bothering to warn us in advance or explain why afterwards. Not only did ordinary people tend to burst into song in public places, for example, but elves, genies, ghosts, and devils inhabited the world of adults. Special effects and newfangled opticals allowed men to fly, animals to talk, and presences heretofore only hinted at to take shape before our very eyes.

Contemporary filmmakers have recently attempted to revive such components of film fantasy genres as musical numbers, fairytale creatures, and lavish special effects which became unstylish during the late fifties and sixties. However, these forays into our cinematic past rarely satisfy hard-core devotees of Hollywood's good old days, since the motifs and pacing of the newer efforts have been revamped to thrill a sophisticated, jaded, urban sensibility. *The Towering Inferno* and *Close Encounters of the Third Kind* were tremendous hits, but they look more like

tomorrow's front-page stories than yesterday's old-fashioned Hollywood make-believe. And *Star Wars*, the biggest grossing film in Hollywood's history, may dazzle the eye with the ultimate in special effects, but it makes no attempt to hide the fact that it's basically an overblown Saturday morning kid's show (with a touch of "Star Trek" thrown in); all that's missing are the cereal ads.

Even *New York, New York,* Martin Scorsese's *hommage* to the Hollywood musical, felt obliged to provide a context for musical numbers that old Hollywood would have offered up without reason or rhyme. Though it incorporated actual sets from the forties' films whose spirit it sought to evoke, it did so in a self-conscious manner that whispered we-know-that-you-know that things aren't really the same. De Laurentis's *King Kong* made a sincere attempt to update and repackage a venerable Hollywood fairy tale for adults (by adding hip talk, in-jokes, and liberal dashes of sex), but to a less spectacular reaction from the public than expected.

As far as film fantasy is concerned, aside from a few happily-ever-afters, it looks like the good old days are going to have to remain just that. The movie-going generation of the cynical seventies isn't likely to accept the presence of fanciful creatures in adult entertainment, nor is it capable of the kind of naiveté required to believe that a Berkeley musical extravaganza, too big from the looks of it to be contained in an airplane hangar, is actually taking place on a Broadway stage. This kind of conceit seems to have vanished along with free dishes on Wednesday. Apparently Little Miss Shopgirl of yesteryear was slightly easier to con than today's bionic children.

So, for the children of the sixties and seventies who never knew Hollywood fantasy, as well as for those who simply don't want to forget, we herewith present a few of the most delightful relics of an age when everyone believed in magic.

WILLIAM POWELL

Sets

Grace Moore and Emery D'Arcy in *When You're in Love*

Fred Astaire in *Royal Wedding*

Stand Up and Cheer

Nelson Eddy and Rise Stevens in *The Chocolate Soldier*

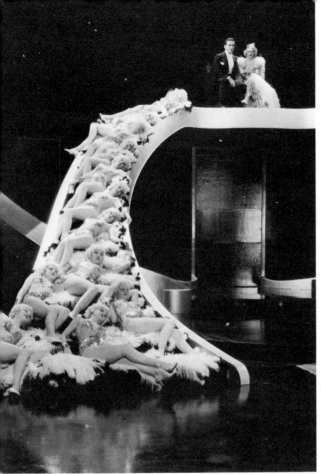

Art Jarrett, Ginger Rogers, and Berkeley Girls in *42nd Street*

Jeanette MacDonald in *The Merry Widow*

Born to Dance

College Holiday

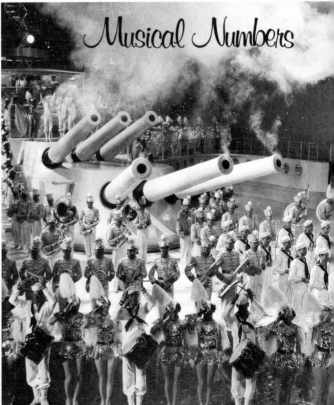

Scale

King of Jazz

Russ Tamblyn in *tom thumb*

156   Stan Laurel and Oliver Hardy in *Brats*

Grant Williams in *The Incredible Shrinking Man*

Janice Logan, Victor Kilian, Charles Halton, Frank
Yaconelli, and Thomas Coley in *Dr. Cyclops*

Darby O'Gill and the Little People

Beasts

Stan Laurel and Oliver Hardy in *Babes in Toyland*

Ben Blue and "Esky" in *Artists and Models*

Margaret Hamilton in *The Wizard of Oz*

Donald O'Connor, Julia Adams, Mara Corday, Mamie Van Doren, and Jean Willes in *Francis Joins the Wacs*

Philippe de Lacy and Nana in *Peter Pan*

Don Knotts in *The Incredible Mr. Limpet*

Dick Van Dyke in *Mary Poppins*

Sonja Henie in *My Lucky Star*

Danny Kaye in *On the Riviera*

Bobby Driscoll and Luana Patten in *Song of the South*

Puppets

Ghosts

Joan Blondell and Roland Young in *Topper Returns*

Jeanette MacDonald and Nelson Eddy in *I Married an Angel*

Don Ameche, Robert Lowery, Eugenie Leontovich, Alan Curtis, and George Ernest in *Four Sons*

Reginald Owen and Leo G. Carroll in *A Christmas Carol*

Rex Ingram in *The Green Pastures*

Heaven

Hayley Mills in *The Parent Trap*

Robert Young and Eleanor Powell in *Honolulu*

Gene Kelly in *Cover Girl*

Elvis Presley in *Kissin' Cousins*

Ginger Rogers in *Kitty Foyle*

Louis Hayward in *The Man in the Iron Mask*

Bette Davis in *Dead Ringer*

The Greeks Had a Word for Them

In Hollywood, a sex change doesn't necessitate a trip to Sweden. It's as close as the nearest wardrobe department. Drag as cinema gimmickry is a prank shared between audience and player in which the ever-present threat of disclosure creates a delicious sexual tension. The moment of truth, the final unveiling, usually occurs because a sexual encounter is imminent. The episodes are always fraught with a giddy suspense as to when and how the other characters will discover our secret. (Don't look for subtlety here, folks. This is the bureau of cheap laughs, no artistic pretensions allowed.)

A number of films have been built around drag: *Some Like It Hot*, *Sylvia Scarlett*, *Charley's Aunt*, and *Wings of the Morning*, for instance. But usually drag is encapsulated in a silly vignette like Bob Hope in *The Princess and the Pirate* or Danny Kaye in *On the Double*. We're talking pie-in-the-face school of comedy here, a carry-over from those bastions of corn, vaudeville and burlesque. And then there are the show-within-the-movie female impersonations by Ray Walston in *South Pacific* and Craig Russell in *Outrageous*.

You've probably noticed that a sex charade rates yocks only when the poseur is a man in chick's clothing. Female stars are very seldom allowed to be completely transformed; they hold onto their mascara and lip gloss. On the rare occasions when a real screen queen dons threads normally found on the opposite sex, the effect is a provocative twist of fashion. Dietrich will step into drag for a musical number with no explanations or apologies, just to add a little spice.

Women in men's clothing may be titillating, but you ain't never gonna catch John Wayne or Clint Eastwood in a dress (in a movie, anyway). With very few exceptions, female drag is the domain of the screen comic. Real he-men like Paul Newman and Charles Bronson have never been tempted to chance tarnishing their bankable macho mystiques.

But don't despair. Drag is one of the few examples of screen whimsy to survive the thirties and forties. Yes, drag is alive and well and living in Hollywood. Sexual UFO's like David Bowie and Mick Jagger are Dietrich's successors in the androgynous icon department. And it's reassuring to know that as long as there's a Mel Brooks, there will always be a man dressed in high heels and a tutu in the girls' dormitory.

Jack Oakie in *Let's Go Native*

Lou Costello in *Lost in a Harem*

Mike Kellin, **Jerry Lewis** in *At War With the Army*

Eddie Cantor in *Ali Baba Goes to Town*

Cary Grant, Ann Sheridan, and unidentified player in *I Was a Male War Bride*

Charles Chaplin in *A Woman*

Joe E. Brown and Victor Jory in *Shut My Big Mouth*

Charles Ruggles in *Charley's Aunt*

Jack Benny in *Charley's Aunt*

Ray Bolger in *Where's Charlie?*

Billy De Wolfe in *Isn't It Romantic?*

William Powell in *Love Crazy*

Lionel Barrymore in *The Devil Doll*

Melvyn Douglas in *The Amazing Mr. Williams*

Tony Curtis and **Jack Lemmon** in *Some Like It Hot*

James Coco in *The Wild Party*

Alec Guinness in *Kind Hearts and Coronets*   **Lee J. Cobb** in *In Like Flint*   **George Sanders** in *The Kremlin Letter*

Bob Hope in
The Princess and the Pirate

Stan Laurel, Oliver Hardy, and Vivian Blaine in *Jitterbugs*

Dudley Moore in *Bedazzled*

Alistair Sim and George Cole
in *Blue Murder at St. Trinian's*

Preston Foster and unidentified player in *Up the River*

Oscar Levant and **David Wayne**
in *The I Don't Care Girl*

Helmut Berger in *The Damned*

Irving Bacon and **Arthur Treacher** in *Up the River*

Tim Curry in *The Rocky Horror Picture Show*

Raquel Welch in *Myra Breckenridge*

Marlene Dietrich and Oscar Homolka in *Seven Sinners*

Annabella and Henry Fonda in *Wings of the Morning*

Miriam Hopkins and Lynne Overman in *She Loves Me*

Katharine Hepburn and Cary Grant in *Sylvia Scarlett*

Charlton Heston in *The Ten Commandments*

Joel McCrea in *Buffalo Bill*

Greer Garson in *Sunrise at Campobello*

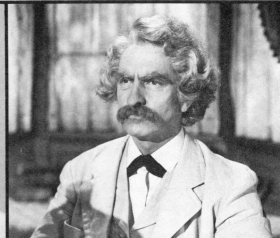

Fredric March in *The Adventures of Mark Twain*

Bette Davis in *The Private Lives of
Elizabeth and Essex*

Paul Muni in *A Song to Remember*

Irene Dunne in *The Mudlark*

Clark Gable and **Norma Shearer** in
Strange Interlude

Tyrone Power and **Maureen O'Hara** in
The Long Gray Line

Madeleine Carroll and **George Sanders** in
The Fan

Middle:
Dorothy Lamour in
Road to Utopia

Albert Finney in *Scrooge*

Bob Hope in
Road to Utopia

Agnes Moorehead on the set of *The Lost Moment*

Jennifer Jones in *Good Morning, Miss Dove*

Jean Arthur in *The Most Precious Thing in Life*

Ben Carter, **Virginia Weidler,** and Henry O'Neill in *Born to Sing*

Betty Grable and **June Haver** in *The Dolly Sisters*

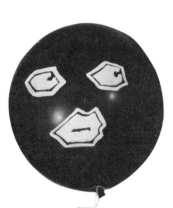

Ad shots to promote Moran and Mack in *Anybody's War*

Myrna Loy in
Ham and Eggs at the Front

Mantan Mooreland and **Frankie Darro** in *Up in the Air*

Gene Wilder and Richard Pryor in *Silver Streak*

Buster Keaton in *College*

Marion Davies in *Going Hollywood*   **Fred Astaire** in *Swing Time*   **Dan Dailey** in *You're My Everything*

Joan Crawford in *Torch Song*

June Haver in *Irish Eyes Are Smiling*

Marjorie Reynolds and **Bing Crosby** in *Dixie*

Moran and Mack in *Anybody's War*

Godfrey Cambridge in *Watermelon Man*

Yowsah!

177

Edgar Bergen and Charlie McCarthy in *Here We Go Again*

LET'S GO NATIVE

veryone knows that Hollywood took a few liberties with reality every now and then. It was kosher, for example, for industry tastemakers to tidy up America's history for the screen, to give the national character a facelift, or to contemporize historical periods in order to make them a little more palatable for the average moviegoer. And, of course, there was Hollywood's tendency to Americanize the rest of the planet by stocking it with actors and actresses of prominent and obvious Western origins. If you bought the gospel according to Hollywood, you were sure that those faraway places with strange sounding names were populated with English speaking natives who looked a lot like the folks up the block and sounded like them too. Even African headhunters spoke English. It would be easy to read more sinister motives into the film industry's exploitation of America's naiveté in this respect, but we choose to believe that the stereotypes, historical rewrites, and happily-ever-afters that have been dished up by Hollywood since *Birth of a Nation* have usually had less to do with proselytizing and politics than with a desire to show the suckers a good time.

When it came to the casting of exotic roles, there was a fine line between the imaginative and the absurd. We give you Helen Hayes as the little lotus blossom of *The Son-Daughter*, the inscrutable Lewis Stone (Judge Hardy) as her father, and Ramon Novarro as her ardent pigtailed suitor. A foreign accent, any foreign accent, could be adapted to any locale. Hedy Lamarr's Teutonic intonation qualified her to play a North African temptress, a Mexican peasant, and a Russian streetcar conductor. Any accent except the correct accent, that is. Chinese actor Keye Luke was fired from *Dragon Seed* because he made Katharine Hepburn look too artificial in her Peck and Peck pyjamas, Lilly Daché coolie hat, and oriental makeup.

It was in the interest of the studio bosses to keep high-priced contract players working, even if it meant plopping them into roles ridiculously ill-suited to their talents. Some actors rebelled against the rotten scripts and miscastings foisted upon them. Yet many felt that it was to their advantage to step out of type on occasion. When an actress like Luise Rainer took on the role of Chinese peasant in *The Good Earth*, it was to showcase her "versatility," the idea being that talent over matter would prevail. The trappings that accompanied this kind of tour de force—wigs, greasepaint, elaborate costumes—smacked of ornate stage productions. And that spelled class both to Hollywood actors and their keepers.

If this kind of thespian conceit leaves you feeling befuddled, allow us to offer a few rules of thumb that will enable you to cross-index actor to role. They'll make the going a little less treacherous, should you ever encounter one of these ethnic medleys on "Dialing for Dollars." If the actor is British, it usually means he's playing nobility of any descent, an American blueblood, or, last but not least, a British person. Enterprising Americans are usually Irish. Jewish actors will metamorphize into first-generation Italians or American Indians. (You don't have to be Jewish to play an Indian, but it helps.) Immigrant American farmers are Swedish; prewar Russians are German; prewar Chinese are everything but Chinese. Wartime Japanese are Chinese, Filipino, or Caucasian. Women of the South Sea Islands are from Mexico or Louisiana. Nazis are either German or British. Any intermingling of the races will produce a beautiful white girl (who's fated to die). Crooks and dopes are from Brooklyn. There are no Jewish people. The entire world, with the exception of the Belgian Congo, is white. God is a Catholic (and sounds like John Huston).

Theatrical artifice, when magnified on the screen, has become a humorous distraction for modern audiences. With the exception of the films of Marlon Brando, who loves to play dress-up, theatrical pretense and ethnic impersonation seem to have been deposed by fifties realism. Either the American public has had enough of exotic locales on the six o'clock news or we're all just a little too self-conscious to allow ourselves to swallow the old Hollywood nonsense. These days we see ten films a year in multiple theatre complexes with bomb shelter motifs and expresso bars. We've surrendered make-believe, along with The Roxy, to the wrecking bars of progress.

Charlton Heston in *The Savage*

Victor Mature in *Chief Crazy Horse*

Audrey Hepburn in *The Unforgiven*

Loretta Young and **Don Ameche** in *Ramona*

Boris Karloff in *Tap Roots*

Paul Newman in *Hombre*

Robert Taylor in *Devil's Doorway*

Linda Darnell in *Buffalo Bill*

Debra Paget in *Broken Arrow*

Burt Lancaster in *Apache*

Katharine Hepburn and **Turhan Bey** in *Dragon Seed*

Jennifer Jones in *Love Is a Many Splendored Thing*

Helen Hayes and **Ramon Novarro** in *The Son-Daughter*

Mickey Rooney in *Breakfast at Tiffany's*

Marlon Brando in *The Teahouse of the August Moon*

Alec Guinness in *A Majority of One*

Luise Rainer and **Paul Muni** in *The Good Earth*

Robert Donat in *The Inn of the Sixth Happiness*

George Raft in *Limehouse Blues*

John Wayne and Susan Hayward in *The Conqueror*

Dolores Del Rio in *Bird of Paradise*

Brian Aherne and **John Garfield** in *Juarez*

Marlon Brando in *Candy*

Hedy Lamarr in *White Cargo*

Natalie Wood in *West Side Story*

Sabu and **Jean Simmons** in *Black Narcissus*

Debra Paget in *Bird of Paradise*

Jeanne Crain in *Pinky*

The Spirit is Willing

Hollywood's zeal in transporting us to alien locales is matched only by its fondness for time-tripping through eras of yore. Unfortunately, very few actors look convincing in brocades and breastplates.

Frank Sinatra and **Kathryn Grayson** in *The Kissing Bandit*

Marlon Brando in *Desirée*

Rock Hudson in *The Desert Hawk*

Alan Ladd in *The Black Knight*

Clark Gable in *The White Sister*

Jeffrey Hunter and **Debra Paget** in *Princess of the Nile*

Hugh O'Brien and **Victor Jory** in *Son of Ali Baba*

Cornel Wilde in *A Song to Remember*

Janet Leigh and **Robert Wagner** in *Prince Valiant*

Ava Gardner in *The Bible*

Gene Tierney in *The Egyptian*

John Derek in *The Adventures of Hajji Baba*

Paulette Goddard, John Lund, and **MacDonald Carey** in *Bride of Vengeance*

Piper Laurie and **Tony Curtis** in *The Prince Who Was a Thief*

Howard Hughes Presents *The French Line*

DRESSED TO THRILL

I was presented with a great problem when my husband's sister from Russia came here with her family to make their home. The language, customs, and American clothes were all so strange to them. At first, I was horrified. Having a family of "greenhorns" saddened me. But through the medium of the movies, I found a wonderful way of quickly Americanizing them. My Russian in-laws are now on the road to becoming real Americans thanks to the movies—a magic world, embodying an all-round education.

Sincerely,
Mrs. Dora Pologiev
Brooklyn, N.Y.

—Photoplay
December 1932

Aren't you just the slightest bit curious as to whom the "greenhorns" from Russia chose to emulate in that wonderful year, 1932? Perhaps it was Jean Harlow in *Red Headed Woman*. Now there's an all-American girl for you. Or maybe it was Joan Crawford in *Letty Lynton*, the movie that asks the question, "Can a wealthy young socialite poison her lover, find love and forgiveness with another, and execute twenty-six costume changes in eighty-four minutes?"

For several decades, America and the movies grew up together, their destinies intertwined, each impersonating the other until fantasy and reality merged. The audience for Hollywood's Depression fantasies were working class heroes, salt-of-the-earth types who were anxious to embrace the good life in America, the America they saw in the movies.

So how you gonna keep 'em down on the farm, after they've seen Joan Crawford? The fact that Joan was pieced together with the precision of a Gaudi mosaic didn't occur to the hordes of greenhorns who rushed out to purchase 10,000 copies of the dress with the Ricky Ricardo sleeves worn by Crawford in *Letty Lynton*. While an economically depressed America treaded water, Hollywood's ravishing mannequins awakened the clotheshorse in every red-blooded woman, and provided the inspiration for Seventh Avenue's mass-produced cheap chic.

From the early twenties until the demise of the studio system in the fifties, Hollywood's formidable costume design braintrust would be the only enclave of haute couture in America. Just as the studios courted the great writers and stage actors of the day, they waged a thorough campaign to lure the major designing talents of the Broadway stage and fashion world to Hollywood. Of course, wealthy Easterners turned up their *nouveau riche* noses at the fairy-tale flash of Hollywood design. They were dressed in conservative elegance by Parisian couturiers. (Society columnists snickered in print at Miriam Hopkins's "vulgar" Hollywood wardrobe when she returned to New York after her screen debut.) A few stars patronized the French designers, especially those who, like Constance Bennett, had landed a title by marriage. And certainly the studio designers were not entirely immune to Paris's influence. But in the main, screen fashion was its own invention.

The designer's ultimate task was to create costuming that would be a credible ingredient of a coordinated whole as envisioned by the producer and the director. But his first consideration was to make the star look good. Monroe's belly, Grayson's oversized bust, Loy's thick legs, Garland's thick middle, and Davis's low-slung bosom had to be minimized; Ball's height, Grable's legs, Hayworth's bosom, and the faces of Leigh, Fontaine, and De Havilland had to be emphasized. The skills of the designers were so crucial to screen images that a star whose popularity depended on dazzle rather than talent might turn down even the juiciest part if denied the services of her fashion mentor.

In the tradition of the great design houses of Paris, a fashion master plan was developed for each star. A single costume or gown required sketches, fittings, screen tests, and endless conferences between designer, star, and director, and could end up costing as much as $10,000 to produce. Enormous amounts of money were expended on rare fabrics from Europe and the Orient. Meticulous beading and hand embroidery were exactingly applied to superbly cut and constructed costumes, creations of impeccable craftsmanship fashioned for the unblinking eye of the camera.

Costume sketch by Travis Banton for Marlene Dietrich in *The Devil Is a Woman.*

Joan Crawford with designer Jean Louis selecting jewels for *Queen Bee.*

Orry-Kelly fits Ava Gardner for *One Touch of Venus.*

Milo Anderson shows Joan Leslie his original prints from which he will create her gowns for *Rhapsody in Blue.*

Travis Banton confers with Marlene Dietrich.

Marlene Dietrich in *The Devil Is a Woman*

Walter Plunkett and Gene Tierney browse through sketches for *Plymouth Adventure.*

Edith Head and Gail Patrick

Joan Crawford in *Letty Lynton*. Costume by Adrian.

A national craze was often the lucky by-product of a designer's attempts to camouflage the figure flaws of a star. Adrian engulfed Joan Crawford's already broad shoulders with giant puffs of tulle to pull the eye up from her large hips and short legs. When the *Letty Lynton* dress became a national sensation, he launched the oversize shoulder by adding artificial fullness to blouses, coats, and even lingerie. There are those who say that Schiaparelli introduced the padded shoulder several seasons before Adrian, but, even so, it took Crawford's charisma to make it a classic.

Crawford was a contemporary of Clara Bow's, yet she outlasted the It Girl by some thirty years. Her talent easily eclipsed Bow's, but the endless fascination that Crawford held for movie audiences had more to do with her chameleonlike appearance and personality than her acting abilities. When flappers were the rage, she was the original hotcha kid; her rags-to-riches sagas made her the essence of Depression spunk a decade later; she was ready with shoulder pads, pin stripes, and gutsy determination during the war years; and she'd become a veritable screen institution by the fifties in her petticoats and Dior skirts. She was the apotheosis of talent and glamour—the movie star as fashion model.

Adrian with Joan Crawford in costume for *No More Ladies*

Adrian said of Crawford, "Joan is a very definite and bold person. That's why she is copied. There is not a negative thing about her. So thousands of women are impelled to copy her, not only because they think they can look like her, but because they hope they can achieve the positive quality that is her great attraction."

New directions in fashion sometimes evolved as a designer attempted to grapple with the technical problems encountered in filmmaking. For instance, when films were miked for sound, the popular fabrics of the twenties and early thirties, tulles and tissue taffetas, had to be sacrificed because their rustle was drowning out the dialogue. Voila! Bias cut velvets, satins, and crepes which molded the body provocatively and fudged censorship restrictions.

Carole Lombard in an early fashion shot

Extravagance paid off when a fashion tie-in like the *Sabrina* dress or Deanna Durbin's teenage duds could be used to boost a film's word-of-mouth advertising. It didn't take long for the studios to develop a modus operandi for selling movies with promotional fashion displays in department stores and fashion photography in fan magazines. As early as 1932, *Photoplay* offered its own shopping guide, "Hollywood Fashions," which directed its readership to the "hundreds of shops and department stores that carry faithful copies of fashions worn in Hollywood movies. . . . Now you too may wear the brown suede oxfords, brown alligator bag, brown jersey hat and brown gauntlet gloves worn by Miss Katharine Hepburn in *Morning Glory*."

Four Views of Womanhood

Anne Baxter in *The Ten Commandments.*
Costume by Edith Head.

Fifties glitz meets the Bible: Anne Baxter in Egyptian drag as Queen Nefritiri in *The Ten Commandments.* Producers were always worried when dealing with a costume picture that the styles of another era would be distractingly strange to modern audiences. So clothes, makeup, and hairstyles were adapted to suit the period in which the movies were made. The amalgams of style that resulted were often even more distractingly strange than the authentic would have been.

Ginger Rogers in *Kitty Foyle.*
Costume by Renie.

The typical American working girl, Ginger Rogers as *Kitty Foyle,* designed by Renie. Renie collaborated with Ginger to tone down her brassy image with a more conservative screen wardrobe, as well as a change of hair color. It got Ginger the Oscar.

Loretta Young in *The Accused.*
Costume by Edith Head.

Loretta Young as the repressed spinster of *The Accused,* designed by Edith Head. The designer's job was to flatter the star—even if a role called for deglamorization.

Joan Crawford in *The Women.*
Costume by Adrian.

In *The Women,* Joan Crawford played a shopgirl who'd hooked herself a wealthy husband. Her clothes for the film were deliberately vulgar, a lowbred working girl's idea of class.

Ginger Rogers in *Shall We Dance*

CHEAPER BY THE DOZEN

ong, long ago when movie stars roamed the earth, there existed within the Hollywood caste system the genuine article and the also-ran. The genuine article was the class act, the magic name that insured millions at the box office. The also-ran was the pretender to the throne, hapless victim of a star system that forced him into masquerading as a replica of the original.

This practice of cloning valuable stars and populating the studio roster with look-alikes, "threats," and "answers-to" seems silly by today's artistic standards, when an actor's value is measured not by the way his own personality overtakes a role but by his ability to literally metamorphose into the character he's playing. But for several decades the cult of the personality reigned supreme in Hollywood's dream factories, and the biggest stars were usually just playing themselves. More often than not, scripts were commissioned expressly to suit the talents or shortcomings of the big money-earners. This assembly-line mentality created a flourishing substratum market for a kind of poor man's version of the original—a unique Hollywood twist on the venerable American credo that you can't have too much of a good thing.

And so, when Garbo and Dietrich took Hollywood by storm, they started a run on sultry Slavs. Each studio had its own. There were Goldwyn's Anna Sten and Sigrid Gurie, Paramount's Isa Miranda and Sari Maritza, Warners' Lil Dagover, Universal's Tala Birell, RKO's Gwili Andre, and Fox's Lilian Harvey. Tyrone Power was Fox's "answer" to MGM's Robert Taylor, while Taylor had been groomed by Metro as a "threat" to their unpredictable roué Robert Montgomery. Rock Hudson would become the "new" Robert Taylor when the old model began to show his age.

Challengers were not only groomed to look like the prototype, but were cast in similar screen vehicles. In trying to take on an established star's screen persona, newcomers often fell into the trap of becoming typecast in the kind of roles the star himself would play. For instance, Dane Clark got stuck in John Garfield's shoes as a streetwise boxer, soldier, ex-con, etc., in supporting roles and second features.

Today the film industry can barely afford to pay the astronomical fees of its few reigning draws, let alone spawn a population of celluloid forgeries. Winning the game often has more to do with directors or expensive special effects than stars. And yet, even in this age of stripped-down backlots and professed nonconformity, Hollywood still manages to come up with multiple versions of the same stars.

But there is a difference. Since movie stars are models for ongoing cultural values, naturally types are going to overlap. If De Niro and Pacino seem interchangeable, it's because they share a certain style and certain qualities we admire. Their success may inspire self-styled imitators by the hundreds, whom Hollywood will rush to exploit when it can. (We give you the "prequel" to *Butch Cassidy and the Sundance Kid* starring William Katt, the latest of a batch of Redford look-alikes.) But these days the film industry can only react to the prevailing people style of the moment by searching out a particular type. The downfall of the star factories brought an end to the era of the mass-produced star.

GARY
COOPER

Whatever happened to Sonny Tufts?

Clark Gable

Sincerely,
John Carroll

John Carroll was hired in 1939 by Louis B. Mayer, who considered him the most likely rival to Clark Gable in Hollywood. But what good is a poor man's Clark Gable if the real thing is always around to grab all the juicy parts? The studio never bothered to package Carroll's unique screen personality properly. About the closest he ever came to playing a part fit for a King was Gable's old role in *Congo Maisie,* the remake of *Red Dust.*

John Carroll

Marlene Dietrich

Marlene Dietrich

Isa Miranda

Marlene Dietrich

Anna Sten

Sari Maritza

203

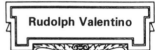

Rudolph Valentino

Ricardo Cortez

Ricardo Cortez (the former Jake Krantz) was developed by Paramount as their resident Valentino during the twenties. But, although he made the girls sigh, he could never seem to catch up to Rudy. As fate would have it, the rage for hot-blooded Latin lovers faded with Valentino, whose career was on the skids at the time of his death. But even if he hadn't been on the decline, his kind of screen posturing clearly would never have worked with sound. Cortez, on the other hand, was a survivor who maintained a solid career over the years in supporting roles and tv and movie direction.

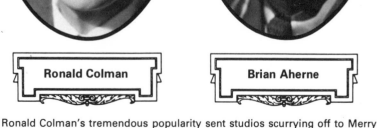

Ronald Colman

Brian Aherne

Errol Flynn

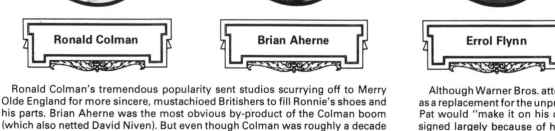

Patric Knowles

Ronald Colman's tremendous popularity sent studios scurrying off to Merry Olde England for more sincere, mustachioed Britishers to fill Ronnie's shoes and his parts. Brian Aherne was the most obvious by-product of the Colman boom (which also netted David Niven). But even though Colman was roughly a decade older than the newer models, producers usually sought him for a meaty role before his competitors. In his autobiography, Aherne tells of being awarded the starring role in *A Tale of Two Cities,* only to have it yanked away when Colman decided he'd like to have it after all.

Although Warner Bros. attempted to downplay Patric Knowles's function as a replacement for the unpredictable Errol Flynn, by assuring the fans that Pat would "make it on his own," it was widely known that he had been signed largely because of his resemblance to their popular swordsman. However, neither Knowles's life-style nor his screen presence were capable of titillating the public like Flynn's. He was wasted in second-lead parts with strong leading ladies.

Ginger Rogers

Jean Phillips

Jean Phillips was a dead ringer for Ginger Rogers, down to Ginger's chorus-girl sassiness. However, aside from the fact that she bore a striking resemblance to an established star, she aroused little comment. Paramount sang *I'll Be Seeing You* to Jean after only a couple of movies.

Paulette Goddard

Lynn Bari

Ingrid Bergman

Viveca Lindfors

Lynn Bari was a dimestore version of the brassy Paulette Goddard. Not genteel enough to be a leading lady, she drifted into bitchy, other-woman roles.

The healthy Nordic personality of Ingrid Bergman encouraged Warner Bros. to import a second large-boned Swede to these shores. Bergman herself had been compared to another Swede early in her career; she was nicknamed "The Palmolive Garbo."

Dane Clark has complained bitterly about being cast in a John ("Sure, sure; give everybody a break but me") Garfield mold by Hollywood's image makers since he was usually only offered roles that Garfield himself had turned down. Although not implicated in the Red Scare that ultimately KO'd Garfield's career, Dane's fortunes declined along with those of his competitor during the fifties.

John Garfield

Dane Clark

Cary Grant didn't patent male grace and worldliness—it just seems that way. Gig Young and James Garner (via television) attempted to follow his lead. And though it may have taken Cary a few years to polish his act, it took Young and Garner infinitely longer to achieve stardom. But when slick sophisticates became an endangered species on screen, they disappeared from the ranks of big movie names fast. Garner eventually returned to television and Young slid into several brilliant supporting roles (*They Shoot Horses, Don't They?* and *Lovers and Other Strangers*).

Cary Grant

Gig Young

John Gavin was a chip off the old Rock. Both heartthrobs were promoted by Universal at opposite ends of the fifties.

Rock Hudson

John Gavin

Mary Beth Hughes was a contemporary of Lana Turner's, but unlike Lana, whose star rose almost immediately, Mary Beth never really graduated from the B's at Fox. During the thirties and forties, she was usually cast as a tart or a tramp; in the fifties she became a Gladys George-type moll or madam. Talent notwithstanding, Mary Beth just didn't have a hot personal life to perk up the public's interest, like MGM's Sweater Girl.

Lana Turner

Mary Beth Hughes

The only explanation for Columbia's interest in Mary Castle was her uncanny resemblance to Rita Hayworth. When Rita was disobedient, she was threatened with replacement by her pallid look-alike.

Rita Hayworth

Mary Castle

After stunning appearances in *To Have and Have Not* and *The Big Sleep,* sultry Lauren Bacall's career rapidly lost steam after Warners, which had bought her contract from Howard Hawks, cast her in several lackluster films. Encouraged to be selective by her new husband Humphrey Bogart, she went on suspension six times in as many years to avoid mediocre scripts. In the meantime, husky-voiced Lizabeth Scott was groomed by Hal Wallis as his "answer" to Bacall. Scott, who made her debut just a year after her predecessor, churned out twenty-two films between 1945 and 1953, but few are particularly memorable.

Lauren Bacall

Lizabeth Scott

Maria Montez

Yvonne De Carlo

Both Yvonne De Carlo and Maria Montez could usually be found in lavish escapist entertainment of the harem pants variety during the forties. De Carlo had originally been invented by Paramount as a rival for tropical Dorothy Lamour, but she wound up at Universal where she would do for the yashmak what Dot had done for the sarong. Mexican born Montez started out in the mysterious East by traveling on the *Bombay Clipper* to *Sudan* and on to *Tangier*. De Carlo's itinerary eventually crisscrossed Montez's, starting in 1942 with *Road to Morocco* and on to the *Casbah, Hotel Sahara,* and *Timbuktu*. Unencumbered by temperament or accent, Yvonne ultimately inherited Maria's throne at Universal though Montez might have become the poor man's Yvonne De Carlo, had she lived long enough to ride out her filmography's descent.

Deanna Durbin and Gloria Jean were prim little screen songbirds who were forever warbling grand opera, even in the most unlikely surroundings. Both girls were under contract to Universal, and both were nurtured by producer Joseph Pasternak who used them in an attempt to bridge the gap between opera, which was considered to be an uppercrust diversion, and popular screen entertainment. Unfortunately for Gloria Jean, however, the big budgets and Cinderella roles went to Deanna. Although the plots of their films were virtually interchangeable, Deanna's screen persona was that of a sparkling debutante type, while Gloria Jean usually came across as the talented, but boring, girl-next-door.

Deanna Durbin

Gloria Jean

Hope and Crosby

Morgan and Carson

Warner Brothers exploited the phenomenally successful "Road" pictures by producing the "Two Guys" series starring Dennis Morgan and Jack Carson. Paramount held on to the crooner-and-stooge formula with Martin and Lewis.

208

Robert Redford

Julie Christie

Nick Nolte

Suzy Kendall

John Beck

Judy Geeson

Robert Redford may have cultivated his shaggy haircut and mustache around the same time as the average accountant, but one isn't so sure about the Butch Cassidy do's of Nick Nolte and John Beck.

Does anyone remember Suzy Kendall and Judy Geeson, two British birds of the Julie Christie feather?

Clark Gable as *Tarzan*.

PICK A STAR

obert Blake would've given his right bicep to have played Lenny Bruce on the screen. But did he have a shot at the role? "No chance, man," Blake complained. "The way things work here in Hollywood, I'm surprised they didn't give it to Mark Spitz."

When you think about some of Hollywood's near misses, it might not have been all that extraordinary if they had. Consider the fact that, if left to their own tastes, the men at Hollywood's helm would have given us Paul Muni

as *Dracula*, Clark Gable as *Tarzan*, and Greta Garbo as *Dory-Ann Gray*. The fact is that hundreds of cinematic coups which carry the mark of inspired casting were actually a producer's second or third preference.

That's just the beginning of a seemingly endless list of Hollywood success stories that came breathlessly close to having completely different casts. Would it have been all wrong, or a thousand times better, if these pics had been made starring Hollywood's original choice?

Hurd Hatfield and George Sanders in *The Picture of Dorian Gray.*

Erich von Stroheim and Gloria Swanson in *Sunset Boulevard*

During the thirties and forties, the big-name stars couldn't begin to do all the scripts that had been written with them in mind. The careers of a gaggle of actors were kept afloat by the overflow. Paramount and Goldwyn boarded a whole stable of studs—Cary Grant, Joel McCrea, Randolph Scott, Fred MacMurray, Ray Milland, and Robert Preston—just to fill Gary Cooper's pumps when there wasn't enough of Coop to go around. Over at Warner's, Bette Davis got first crack at the coveted scripts, but if HRH Bette was in a snit, Jack Warner might award one of her roles to Ida Lupino. Ann Sheridan was next in line if Ida demurred, and Alexis Smith achieved a kind of peripheral stardom by accepting whatever was left.

Eleven actors rejected the role of the down-in-the-mouth detective of *Double Indemnity*, giving Fred Mac-Murray the chance to make it one of his most memorable. Rosalind Russell won the role of Hildy Johnson opposite Cary Grant in *His Girl Friday* only after director Howard Hawks was rebuffed by Carole Lombard, Ginger Rogers, Jean Arthur, Claudette Colbert, and Janet Gaynor. Mae West was Billy Wilder's first choice for the fading silent star, Norma Desmond, of *Sunset Boulevard*, and Robert Montgomery, Fredric March, Constance Bennett, Myrna Loy, Carole Lombard, and Miriam Hopkins all turned up their noses at *It Happened One Night* before Gable and Colbert were nudged into their Academy Award-winning roles.

Stars usually come equipped with radar for spotting roles suited to their particular talents, but there are always hapless souls like Miriam Hopkins, who dismissed *Twentieth Century*, a film which proved to be the turning point of Carole Lombard's career, as "just another silly little comedy." Doris Day might have rejuvenated her waning career had she accepted the part of Mrs. Robinson in *The Graduate*, but playing a sexual predator was simply out of the question for the image-conscious Dodo. And would Marlon Brando really have looked any sillier as *The Egyptian* than he did as Napoleon in *Desirée*? Or as the Sundance Kid than as Lee Clayton, the hired gun of *The Missouri Breaks*?

Becoming a star in Hollywood has sometimes meant making sure the other guy didn't. Katharine Hepburn has confessed that when she first came to RKO she deliberately accepted roles just so Ann Harding wouldn't get them. And Joan Crawford climbed to the position of Queen of the MGM lot on a stack of Norma Shearer's hand-me-down scripts.

The role that was to become the chance of a lifetime for someone was often tossed from star to star on a turbulent sea of temperament and studio politics before coming to rest with its rightful interpreter. Lana Turner reneged on her commitment to do *Anatomy of a Murder* when Otto Preminger wouldn't let her dress her character, a low-rent army wife, in gowns by Jean Louis. The part went to Lee Remick. Dean Martin walked out on *Something's Got to Give* when Monroe was fired, and Bette Davis vetoed the idea of doing Scarlett if Errol Flynn was hired. The

216

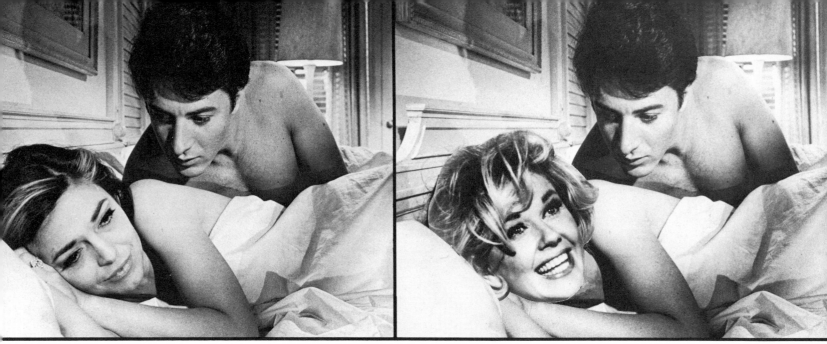

Anne Bancroft and Dustin Hoffman in *The Graduate*

forgettable Edmund Purdom was engaged to lip sync the Mario Lanza soundtrack of *The Student Prince* when Mario grew too fat to button his uniform. And it would have been Georgie Jessel, not Al Jolson, threatening that "You ain't heard nothin' yet!" in the very first talkie if he hadn't haggled with Jack Warner over bread. And if Jessel had gotten the part of *The Jazz Singer*, then maybe Danny Thomas could've starred in *his* life story. As it was, Danny missed out on *The Jolson Story* because he refused to have his nose shortened for the role.

As you can see, more often than not it was fate, not a producer, that matched an actor to the role he'd been "born to play." During the fifties, the young Paul Newman was a self-styled Brando type who always seemed to lose out to James Dean when vying for angry-young-man parts. He lost the coveted role of Cal in *East of Eden* to Dean (the film had originally been planned for Brando and Clift). But when Jimmy cracked up in his Porsche, Newman inherited *Somebody Up There Likes Me* and the mantle of Boy-Most-Likely for millions of female fans.

To this day, Claudette Colbert maintains that Bette Davis is the only star who didn't get where she is via the proverbial casting couch. Claudette may or may not be overstating the case, but there's no doubt that Hollywood's romantic intrigues have had as much to do as talent with determining who got the juiciest roles. Evelyn Keyes says that His Crudeness, Columbia boss Harry Cohn, used to handicap the distaff front-runners for a starring role according to who was the easiest lay. But

score one for the girls, courtesy of Veronica Lake, who's supposed to have blackmailed producer Arthur Hornblow (the ex-Mr. Myrna Loy) into giving her her first starring role in *I Wanted Wings* in return for keeping the lid on their affair. Only the fittest survived Hollywood's intricate sexual intrigues. Vera Zorina's film career was catapulted into oblivion when David O. Selznick pulled strings to have her replaced in *For Whom the Bell Tolls* by his special "protégée" Ingrid Bergman. Paramount claimed that it didn't approve of the way Vera looked in the rushes with her newly shorn freedom-fighter crewcut, but Vera knew better. And then there was Glenn Ford, who subscribed to Charles Bronson's sentiments that "kissing someone you don't love in front of the camera can be hell." Glenn decided that if the part of Queenie Martin in *Pocketful of Miracles* didn't go to his current girlfriend, Hope Lange, he'd back out of his commitment to director Frank Capra to star in the film. It made no difference to him that he'd already agreed to star opposite Shirley Jones and that Capra was going to have to pay Shirley seventy-five thousand clams whether she played the role or not. When Capra was given Glenn's ultimatum, he exploded, "Fuck Glenn Ford. We'll replace *him*!" But a tangled financial setup prevented Capra from standing by his convictions. "What choice could I make? Principle or money? I was sixty-four years old and it was a young man's game. I opted for the money."

Jon Voight and Dustin Hoffman in *Midnight Cowboy*

Like most Hollywood producers, David O. Selznick was known to cast feminine roles with his glands on occasion, but he, more than anyone else, deserves the credit for making casting an art. As an independent producer obliged to cast film projects from his competitors' stables, he canvassed both stars and unknowns with a painstaking plodding that drove his underlings mad. When he staged his fabled search for Scarlett, he cunningly exploited his perfectionist's image with carefully timed progress reports, photographs of the front-runners in costume for their screen tests, and write-in polls whereby the fans could cast their vote for the stars they thought should be cast in the leads.

Selznick couldn't get Goldwyn to loan him his first choice for Rhett, Gary Cooper, but he was able to get Clark Gable because Gable needed the bread for his impending divorce from Ria Langham (leaving him free to marry Carole Lombard).

The story that Selznick discovered Vivien Leigh only days before his deadline remained, until his death, the best kept publicity secret of his career. Correspondence discovered among his personal effects has revealed that he made overtures to Leigh about playing the part many months before their actual meeting. There had been problems to iron out, of course, but from the first minute he'd seen her in *A Yank at Oxford*, the die was cast. Yet, to this day, the legend of Selznick's last-minute discovery of Scarlett lives on.

Stars have been born overnight thanks to roles that

Marlon Brando and Karl Malden in *On the Waterfront*

Joan Crawford and Zachary Scott in *Mildred Pierce*

were intended for another, totally different actor. Until *Coming Home*, Jon Voight's reputation rested almost exclusively on his stunning performance in *Midnight Cowboy*, a role originally intended for Michael Sarrazin. Faye Dunaway became one of the few women to capture screen stardom during the sixties by filling in for Tuesday Weld in *Bonnie and Clyde*. And Jack Nicholson's career was rescued from motorcycle movies and cheapo horror flicks by Rip Torn's last minute decision to bow out of *Easy Rider*.

A startling number of Academy Award-winning performances came about as the result of a producer or director making do with a smallfry when the big fish couldn't be hooked. Montgomery Clift couldn't relate to the role of the dull-witted ex-prizefighter of *On the Water-*

front which then brought Marlon Brando an Oscar. Olivia De Havilland and Loretta Young won Academy Awards for *To Each His Own* and *The Farmer's Daughter*, respectively, in roles that Ingrid Bergman had declined. Ingrid walked away with two Oscars in secondhand parts herself, for *Gaslight*, which had been originally intended for Hedy Lamarr, and *Anastasia*, which was to have gone to Jennifer Jones. Katharine Hepburn, not Ginger Rogers, had been the first choice for *Kitty Foyle*. Joan Crawford made her comeback in *Mildred Pierce* by grabbing it when Bette Davis turned it down and fighting to keep it from going to Barbara Stanwyck as planned. And Elia Kazan was forced to use Vivien Leigh as his Blanche du Bois in *A Streetcar Named Desire* when Olivia De Havilland informed him that a lady just didn't say and do those things on screen.

Joseph Cotten and Loretta Young in *The Farmer's Daughter*

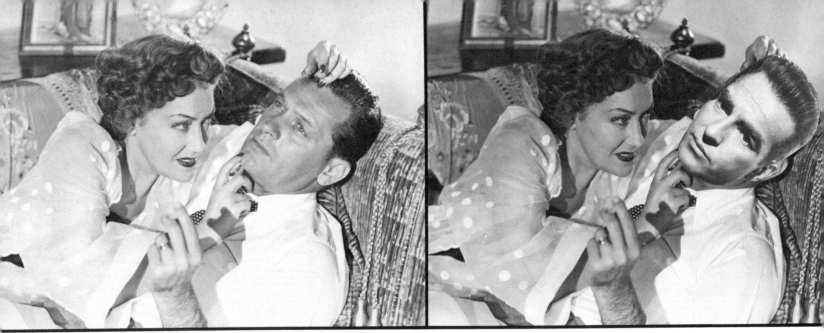

Gloria Swanson and William Holden in *Sunset Boulevard*

Hollywood almost succeeded in luring Audrey Hepburn back from her Swiss retreat for *Forty Carats*, but she backed out at the last minute. The trades reported that Hepburn would sign only if the film's producers secured the services of her favorite director, William Wyler, but columnist Leonard Lyons suggested that the tale of a middle-aged divorcée's affair with a much younger man hit too close to home for Audrey, who is married to a man several years her junior. Years before, Montgomery Clift had shied away from doing *Sunset Boulevard* for similar reasons. The part was a chance in a lifetime, but Clift found distasteful parallels between his real-life friendship with the notorious Libby Holman and the script's central relationship between a young opportunist and an aging star.

Producer Robert Evans had optioned *The Great Gatsby* for his wife, Ali MacGraw, as a follow-up to their immensely successful collaboration on *Love Story*. He wanted either Jack Nicholson or Warren Beatty for the part of Gatsby, but there was just one catch—neither Jack nor Warren was interested in the role as long as Mrs. Evans was to play the lead. Nothing personal; they just didn't think she could act. The business was settled when Ali decided to ditch Bob for her co-star in *The Getaway*, Steve McQueen. Evans then attempted a Selznick-style

Mia Farrow and Robert Redford in *The Great Gatsby*

Judy Holliday and William Holden in *Born Yesterday*

search for a new star; the role eventually went to Mia Farrow, who cabled Evans from London to ask, "Can I be your Daisy?"

Harry Cohn paid a record sum for the movie rights to *Born Yesterday* as a vehicle for Columbia's greatest asset, Rita Hayworth. But a lovestruck Rita passed up the chance to demonstrate her flair for comedy when Prince Aly Khan crooked his royal finger in her direction. The part went instead to Judy Holliday (whom Cohn referred to as "that fat Jewish broad"). Another example of a fairy-tale marriage getting in Hollywood's way occurred when Grace Kelly hotfooted it to Monaco, leaving *Cat on a Hot Tin Roof* and *Designing Woman* to Elizabeth Taylor and Lauren Bacall, respectively.

Frank Sinatra abandoned *Carousel* after only three days' work. According to insiders, Old Blue Eyes' voice and ring-a-ding-ding style just weren't up to the demands of the semi-operatic Rogers and Hammerstein score. Frankie, however, maintains that the walkout had nothing to do with his pipes. He resented the fact that Fox planned to shoot two versions of the film simultaneously, in Cinemascope and in Todd-AO, and he was being paid for only one. The more malleable Gordon MacRae replaced him.

Gordon MacRae and Shirley Jones in *Carousel*

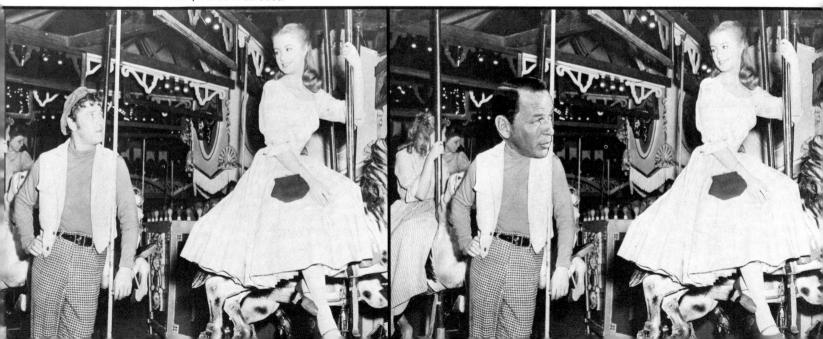

Burt Lancaster and Deborah Kerr
in *From Here to Eternity*

Ida Lupino and Humphrey Bogart in *High Sierra*

Joan Crawford's official reason for withdrawing from the role of Karen Holmes in *From Here to Eternity* was her supposed lack of enthusiasm for her costumes. Probably more to the point was the fact that Crawford was used to essaying title roles such as *Letty Lynton*, *Sadie McKee*, *Mildred Pierce*, et al., and *Eternity* was an ensemble movie containing several equally important starring roles. Perhaps if the movie had been retitled *From Karen Holmes to Eternity*, it would've been Joan, instead of Deborah Kerr, on the beach with Burt.

George Raft KO'd his own career by allowing his superstitions and insecurities to dictate his script selections, while Bogart thrived on playing his rejects. Raft refused to play the gangster in *Dead End* because the character's code of ethics conflicted with his own; he didn't feel confident enough in *The Maltese Falcon*'s young director, John Huston, to take a chance on the part of Sam Spade, or in the script of *Casablanca* to accept the role of Rick; and his notion that it was bad luck to die on the screen kept him from doing *High Sierra*. He opted instead for *Spawn of the North*, *The Lady's from Kentucky*, and the like.

Mary Astor, Humphrey Bogart, and Peter Lorre in *The Maltese Falcon*

James Mason and Judy Garland in *A Star Is Born*

Born starring Judy Garland was offered to a number of big names before producer Sid Luft finally settled for the reliable James Mason. The story is that Marlon Brando, Cary Grant, and Henry Fonda, among others, couldn't face competing with Garland's tantrums or her scene-stealing tactics, no matter how strong the script. It was the same kind of apprehension that kept Elvis Presley from accepting the corresponding role in Barbra Streisand's remake of the remake of *Star*. Presley, surrounded by his usual retinue of bodyguards and hangers-on, listened politely as Barbra outlined her ideas for the film in his Caesar's Palace dressing room during a between-show break. His friends bubbled over with enthusiasm for the project after Streisand had gone, but Elvis had already decided that the deal wasn't as good as it sounded. First off, he wasn't thrilled about playing a rock star on the skids. But the bottom line was that no matter what Barbra promised, he knew that there was room for only one star in a Barbra Streisand movie. And besides, he wasn't about to let a woman like that think she could boss him around.

Shortly before his death from a heart attack and several long-standing illnesses, malaria, hepatitis, gonorrhea, and tuberculosis among them, Errol Flynn had made tentative plans to star in the film version of *Lolita*. Aside from the obvious drollery in casting Flynn, with his well-known predilection for virgin flesh, in the role of a like-minded professor, there was the added irony of Flynn's recent announcement of his plans to marry his own Lolita—seventeen-year-old Beverly Aadland. Some say he ended up turning down the part when his future fiancée was denied the starring role opposite him.

Sue Lyon, James Mason, and Shelley Winters in *Lolita*

Joanne Woodward and Richard Beymer in *The Stripper*

Just before Marilyn Monroe's death from a drug overdose, a number of Hollywood columnists had written that her suspension from Fox meant that her career was washed up for good. But, quite the contrary, her death robbed a stack of scripts from their intended star. One, *Goodbye Charlie*, was a rather flimsy comedy which eventually starred Debbie Reynolds, and probably would've remained so, even with Monroe. *The Stripper*, however, might have been a turning point for Monroe, since it would've been the first film to show her as a sexpot slightly past her prime. But life and Hollywood go on, and Joanne Woodward, the Duchess of Downbeat, took over the role and converted an essentially endearing figure into a depressing loner.

Cary Grant laughed when Jack Warner offered him the role of Henry Higgins in *My Fair Lady*, reminding him that a Cockney was hardly the person to teach elocution to Eliza Dolittle. Cary added that, not only would he not play the role, but he wouldn't even buy a ticket unless his friend Rex Harrison was allowed to recreate his Broadway success in the film. Warner also tried to interest James Cagney in the part of Eliza's father, but Cagney opted to hang out with the chickens back on his farm.

When Darryl Zanuck refused to loan out Number One Box Office Star Shirley Temple for the role of Dorothy in *The Wizard of Oz*, Judy Garland was chosen to take her place. (As fate would have it, *Oz*'s success caused Zanuck

Rex Harrison, Audrey Hepburn, and Wilfrid Hyde White in *My Fair Lady*

nt to do Air Force *in a submarine.*

—Bryan Foy
Production Head, Fox B-Unit

Xanadu's massive doors from *Gunga Din*, as well as a few bats from *Son of Kong*? No matter. We accepted the fact that these bits and pieces of studio reality were intended to survive from one movie to the next.

Part of the reason for the sense of continuity that can be felt from one Hollywood film to another was the particular style established by each studio's creative and technical people. Composers, art directors, set and costume designers had extraordinarily long careers as compared with those of, say, actors or screenwriters, on whom the Hollywood power game usually took a devastatingly swift toll. Their special genius is easily recognizable even in their earliest work.

If you didn't spot a Warners' production by the presence of supporting players like Alan Hale or Frank McHugh, you couldn't fail to recognize the distinctive musical scoring of the master composer and arranger Max Steiner, whose churning orchestrations and tinkling bell chimes trademarked the Warner's product for over thirty years. Steiner was the first to create the musical scoring of films by developing and intercutting individual themes for each of a film's major characters as well as its crucial plot sequences. When one of these character themes was especially well suited to a particular star, it was carried over into his following pictures. For instance, the rakish tune that accompanied Errol Flynn throughout *The Private Lives of Elizabeth and Essex* was used for Flynn again in *The Loves of Don Juan*. And then there were Steiner's familiar stock musical touches, like the swell of the heavenly chorus to announce the coming of death. (Remember Bette Davis's dying scene in *Dark Victory*?) In addition to these familiar elements, Steiner often resurrected melody lines both from his own past work and from outside sources. For example, Melanie's theme from *Gone With the Wind* was "borrowed" by Steiner from the 1934 Ann Harding melodrama, *The Fountain*, while the surging la-

ment of *Flamingo Road* was, in fact, his own composition of eleven years earlier for *Crime School*.

The practice of reviving tunes from past pix was customary at every studio because it minimized the expense of commissioning new ones and served to subtly reinforce the memory of a studio's former hits in the minds of the audience. MGM, for instance, had a special fondness for "Easy to Love" which had been written for *Born to Dance*; whenever there was a nightclub scene in an MGM movie, the club's orchestra was sure to strike up a few bars. Sometimes film characters might share a joke with their audiences by way of a musical allusion, as in MGM's *The Philadelphia Story* where a slightly inebriated Katharine Hepburn warbles "Over the Rainbow" while her sister sings a chorus of "Lydia the Tatooed Lady," both classics from past MGM films. Today, what with rights and royalties, we can probably assume that it was dollar considerations, not subtlety, that motivated Paramount to revive "Football Hero," the lively anthem of *Million Dollar Legs*, for their 1975 Burt Reynolds comedy, *The Longest Yard*.

Just as a set decorator could go into the prop department and pull out a particular style of lampshade, a casting director could thumb through his directory to shop for a certain character type from the many actors under contract. Studio policy underlined the importance of displaying as many contract players as possible, and scripts were chosen accordingly. This constant piecing together of well-known supporting players with props and effects from past productions was responsible for giving each major studio's product a familiar stock company feel.

The world of the Hollywood movie clearly had a moral and physical terrain all its own. It was a well-ordered environment inhabited by lots of old friends. "Haven't we met somewhere before?" Cary Grant asks Ralph Bellamy in *His Girl Friday*. They have . . . three years earlier in similar roles in *The Awful Truth*. These kind of allusions work because they focus on what we all know: the movies are a world unto themselves, a mythology composed of a limited number of best loved tales, a country of familiar faces.

And if the faces themselves changed over the years, the roles didn't. Hadn't we met *The Pleasure Seekers* (1964), Ann-Margret, Pamela Tiffin, and Carol Lynley, somewhere before? Most definitely we had. They're the same three gold diggers who've been panning for rich husbands on the screen for the last forty years. We first saw them in 1932 in *The Greeks Had a Word for Them*, followed by *Ladies in Love* ('36), *Three Blind Mice* ('38), *Moon Over Miami* ('41), *Three Little Girls in Blue* ('46), *How to Marry a Millionaire* ('53), *Three Coins in the Fountain* ('54), and *The Best of Everything* ('59). We knew just what to expect from these films. They served up the same old corny platitudes and implausible endings in film after film, and

that's exactly what kept us coming back for more.

We can usually count on a respectable waiting period between an original screen hit and its official reprise, but during that interval the very same formula might be reworked unofficially four or five times. In *Don't Say Yes Until I Finish Talking*, Mel Gussow recounts the method by which one studio boss, Fox's Darryl F. Zanuck, squeezed one film after another from a handful of favorite formulas:

The theory was that there were only a limited number of plots in the first place. *Love Is News*, which Zanuck made with Tyrone Power and Loretta Young in 1937, was about an heiress who falls in love with a reporter who has been criticizing her. Zanuck remade it as a musical, *Sweet Rosie O'Grady*, in 1943, with Robert Young and Betty Grable, and again in 1949, as a straight comedy again starring Tyrone. He briefly considered naming it *Love Is Still News*, but changed his mind and called it *That Wonderful Urge*. Gene Tierney played the girl. Actually the relationship is at least as old as *It Happened One Night*, which wasn't Zanuck's, and was made in 1934. A typical variation was in the musical *On the Avenue*, in which Dick Powell played a singer-playwright who satirized an heiress (Madeleine Carroll) in his latest play. Another favorite Zanuck theme was the hick who shows up the city yokels (as in his *Telephone Girl* episode, Sherlock's Home). He used it in *Thanks for Everything* (Jack Haley in 1938) and in *The Magnificent Dope* (Henry Fonda in 1942), although it had already been done, by Columbia in *Mr. Deeds Goes to Town* (Gary Cooper in 1936). *The Bowery* in 1933 moved across the river in 1943 to become *Coney Island*, and both were really *What Price Glory* in civilian dress. Zanuck's *Kentucky* of 1938 moved all the way to Rio de Janeiro in *Down Argentine Way* in 1940, taking its horse farm with it, although leaving Walter Brennan behind. Probably the most durable Zanuck Remake began in 1935 with a movie called *Folies Bergere*, in which a *Folies-Bergère* star (Maurice Chevalier) is mistaken for a Parisian financier (Maurice Chevalier). The movie co-starred Merle Oberon as the financier's wife and Ann Sothern as the star's girl friend. In 1942 Zanuck moved *Follies* to Rio de Janeiro and made *That Night in Rio*. Don Ameche played a Brazilian financier and an American vaudevillian, with Alice Faye and Carmen Miranda as the wife and the girl friend. In 1951, Zanuck dug up the property again and set it *On the Riviera*. Danny Kaye played a French flying ace and an American entertainer and Gene Tierney and Corinne Calvet were the wife and the girl friend.

Once Zanuck hit on a successful gimmick, he twisted it, disguised it, and turned it inside out until he'd exhausted every possible angle. Fledgling screenwriters Phoebe and Henry Ephron were told shortly after their arrival at Fox by the head of the B-movie unit that the only cocksure method of getting a script into production was to milk one of the boss's pet plot devices. Their first B-assignment, consequently, was to rework Zanuck's beloved country-boy-outfoxes-the-city-slickers bit, which had just been done for the umpteenth time with John Payne in *To the Shores of Tripoli*, into *Rip Goes to War*, with an Airedale in the John Payne part.

Hollywood had no shame when it came to disguising hits of the not-so-distant past and pronouncing them the latest, the greatest, the newest, and the best. This policy of remaking the same pictures over and over wasn't limited to any one studio; they all practiced it to a degree. Ring Lardner Jr. told Kenneth Geist in an interview in *Film Comment* that the system of Bryan Foy, the then head of the B-unit at Warners, which cranked out thirty films a year, was to "rotate a huge pile of scripts stacked alongside his desk. When a picture was completed, its script would return to the bottom of the pile, and when a writer came into Foy's office to be assigned a project, he was simply handed the script at the top of the pile, and asked to switch the background."

Current fads, fancies, and fashions are always a good excuse for a blast from Hollywood's past. An ongoing infatuation with the style of an earlier era, for instance, can act as the catalyst for a whole spate of trendy re-do's, as the present-day nostalgia for forties fashion and Bogart-style movie shamuses has done for the revivals of *Farewell, My Lovely* and *The Big Sleep*. During the fifties, the country's love affair with television was inadvertently responsible for the overhauling of vintage hits by the droves. It seemed that the only way for Hollywood to compete with the small screen was to mount *big* pictures—musicals, swashbucklers, etc. MGM started the ball rolling in '51 and '52 by scoring resounding hits with old favorites like *Ivanhoe*, *Showboat*, *Scaramouche*, and *The Prisoner of Zenda*.(This, the second remake of *Zenda*, didn't take any chances. It reproduced the popular '37 version almost frame-for-frame. Its fidelity was achieved courtesy the '37 *Zenda*, which was shown to the cast and crew on a movieola kept handy on the set.)

And who says a sequel's never equal? Certainly not the folks out there in Hardy Family America who, like today's sitcom and soap fans, enjoyed staying current with such series favorites as Maisie, Blondie, Charlie, Torchy, and, last but not least, Lassie. Providing a sequel for a hit movie wasn't always that simple, however, especially if you'd killed off a popular character in the original. But no matter, you could always bring him back under another name or as a bittersweet memory via a film flashback, as Warners did with John Garfield in the Lane Sisters flicks.

Dress it up. Dress it down. Keep a straight face and pray that the critics will look the other way. You shouldn't have any problems with the Fourth Estate so long as you appeal to their theatrical snobbism by excavating a stagy "classic" like *Dr. Jekyll and Mr. Hyde* or *The Hunchback of Notre Dame*. The critics tend to sanction the refurbishing

of this kind of thing time after time. But a word to the wise: when attempting to revive an old nag, you'll have much better luck if you don't attempt to exploit its bloodline. The critics always seem to favor the original fossil, no matter how ambitious the next try. *Force of Arms*, a loose reworking of Paramount's *A Farewell to Arms*, which made no formal reference to its source of inspiration, was shrugged off by reviewers as a passable war film, whereas the much ballyhooed Selznick remake of the popular original, with the original title and pedigree intact, was a financial and critical fiasco. This isn't to suggest that it wasn't a clunker, but had it not invited comparison between itself and its classy antecedents, it might not have landed with such a loud thud.

Think that just because the days of the bigtime studios are over you won't be seeing remakes and sequels and other soft core cinematic rip-offs? Don't bet on it. This year alone we're going to see the rebirth of such favorites as *Here Comes Mister Jordan* (*Heaven Can Wait* with Warren Beatty), *The Champ* with Jon Voight in the Wallace Beery role, and *The Wiz*, a remake of *The Wizard of Oz* with Diana Ross as Dorothy. Lassie will be back in *The Magic of Lassie* and Benji may run for president. As for sequels, they've never been healthier. Damien, the bad seed of *The Omen*, is already back for a return performance, with two more visits planned. There'll be *More American Graffiti* and a new *Invasion of the Body Snatchers*, a continuation of *Love Story* (blecch), and of *National Velvet*. We'll find out whether Scarlett and Rhett got back together in *Tara: The Continuation of Gone With the Wind*. Those cute kids from *Goodbye Girl* will go to Hollywood for *Goodbye Girl 2*. *Star Wars* will be back; production on the sequel began after just a few weeks of the first's astounding box office business. And we'll probably be seeing more of Peter Sellers as Inspector Clouseau long before we're ready. And get this. There's even a "prequel" to *Butch Cassidy and the Sundance Kid* entitled *Butch and Sundance: The Early Days* starring Redford-clone William Katt.

So if it looks familiar, it probably is. Yes, even today the unwitting movie-goer can come down with a case of Hollywood remakitis. But there's one saving grace—the cure is simple and quick: just drink lots of liquids and stay away from the Late Show. You'll feel better in the morning.

What you will be seeing on the following pages is a pictorial record of a number of Hollywood's most popular variations on a theme. We should caution you, however, that, much as we'd like to, we can't begin to follow up all the detours that a popular plot device or other basic film component might take from one incarnation to the next. Here then is an abbreviated survey of the interchangeable plots, stars, sets, and costumes with which Hollywood recycled Hollywood.

A. Gloria Swanson and Lionel Barrymore in *Sadie Thompson* (1928)

B. Joan Crawford and Walter Huston in *Rain* (1932)

C. Rita Hayworth and Jose Ferrer in *Miss Sadie Thompson* (1954)

D. Adolphe Menjou, Pat O'Brien, and Maurice Black in *The Front Page* (1931)

E. Cary Grant, Rosalind Russell, and Ralph Bellamy in *His Girl Friday* (1940)

F. Douglas Fairbanks, Jr., Cary Grant, Joan Fontaine, Victor McLaglen in *Gunga Din* (1939)

G. Dean Martin, Frank Sinatra, Peter Lawford, and Ruta Lee in *Sergeants Three* (1962)

H. Walter Matthau and Jack Lemmon in *The Front Page* (1974)

I. Shirley Temple, Warren Hymer, and Adolphe Menjou in *Little Miss Marker* (1934)

J. Mary Jane Saunders and Bob Hope in *Sorrowful Jones* (1948)

K. Claire Wilcox and Tony Curtis in *Forty Pounds of Trouble* (1962)

A. Bette Davis and Leslie Howard in *Of Human Bondage* (1934)

B. Eleanor Parker and Paul Henreid in *Of Human Bondage* (1946)

C. Kim Novak and Laurence Harvey in *Of Human Bondage* (1964)

D. Margot Grahame and Walter Abel in *The Three Musketeers* (1935)

E. Pauline Moore and Don Ameche in *The Three Musketeers* (1939)

F. Gig Young, Van Heflin, Robert Coote, and Gene Kelly in *The Three Musketeers* (1948)

G. Richard Chamberlain, Frank Finlay, and Oliver Reed in *The Three Musketeers* (1973)

H. Ian Wolfe, Charles Laughton, and Clark Gable in *Mutiny on the Bounty* (1935)

I. John Wayne, Montgomery Clift, and Walter Brennan in *Red River* (1948)

J. Marlon Brando, Richard Haydn, and Trevor Howard in *Mutiny on the Bounty* (1962)

A. Theda Bara in *Cleopatra* (1917)

B. Claudette Colbert in *Cleopatra* (1934)

C. Elizabeth Taylor in *Cleopatra* (1963)

D. Lowell Sherman, Neil Hamilton, and Constance Bennett in *What Price Hollywood* (1932)

E. Janet Gaynor and Fredric March in *A Star Is Born* (1937)

F. James Mason and Judy Garland in *A Star Is Born* (1954)

G. Kris Kristofferson and Barbra Streisand in *A Star is Born* (1977)

H. *State Fair* (1933)

I. Donald Meek (center) in *State Fair* (1945)

J. Pamela Tiffin, Alice Faye, Bobby Darin, and unidentified player in *State Fair* (1962)

A. Warren William and Marie Wilson in *Satan Met a Lady* (1936)

B. Humphrey Bogart and Lee Patrick in *The Maltese Falcon* (1941)

C. George Segal and Lee Patrick in *The Black Bird* (1976)

D. Vera-Ellen, Vivian Blaine, and June Haver in *Three Little Girls in Blue* (1946)

E. Dorothy McGuire, Maggie McNamara, Louis Jourdan, and Jean Peters in *Three Coins in the Fountain* (1954)

F. Hope Lange, Suzy Parker, and Diane Baker in *The Best of Everything* (1959)

G. Pamela Tiffin, Ann-Margret, and Carol Lynley in *The Pleasure Seekers* (1965)

H. Jean Harlow and Clark Gable in *Red Dust* (1932)

I. Ann Sothern and John Carroll in *Congo Maisie* (1940)

J. Ava Gardner and Clark Gable in *Mogambo* (1953)

A. Irene Dunne and Cary Grant in *My Favorite Wife* (1940)

B. Doris Day and James Garner in *Move Over Darling* (1963)

★

A. Frances Dee, Jean Parker, Katharine Hepburn, and Joan Bennett in *Little Women* (1933)

B. Margaret O'Brien, Elizabeth Taylor, June Allyson, and Janet Leigh, in *Little Women* (1949)

A. Cary Grant and Katharine Hepburn in *Bringing Up Baby* (1938)

B. Ryan O'Neal and Barbra Streisand in *What's Up Doc?* (1972)

★

A. Greta Garbo and John Barrymore in *Grand Hotel* (1932)

B. Walter Pidgeon and Ginger Rogers in *Week-End at the Waldorf* (1945)

A. Irene Dunne and Cora Sue Collins in *Magnificent Obsession* (1935)

B. Jane Wyman and Judy Nugent in *Magnificent Obsession* (1954)

★

A. Ronald Colman in *Lost Horizon* (1937)

B. Peter Finch and Michael York in *Lost Horizon* (1973)

A. Ramon Novarro in *Ben Hur* (1925)

B. Charlton Heston in *Ben Hur* (1959)

★

A. Betty Field, Alan Ladd, and Barry Sullivan in *The Great Gatsby* (1949)

B. Bruce Dern, Mia Farrow, and Robert Redford in *The Great Gatsby* (1974)

A. Fredric March and Norma Shearer in *The Barretts of Wimpole Street* (1934)

B. Bill Travers and Jennifer Jones in *The Barretts of Wimpole Street* (1957)

★

A. Claudette Colbert and Clark Gable in *It Happened One Night* (1934)

B. June Allyson and Jack Lemmon in *You Can't Run Away From It* (1956)

A. Ronald Colman, Mary Astor, and Douglas Fairbanks, Jr., in *The Prisoner of Zenda* (1937)

B. Stewart Granger, James Mason, and Jane Greer in *The Prisoner of Zenda* (1952)

★

A. Joel McCrea and Dolores Del Rio in *Bird of Paradise* (1932)

B. Louis Jourdan and Debra Paget in *Bird of Paradise* (1951)

Cary Grant and Lew Ayres in *Holiday*

Cornel Wilde and Ginger Rogers in *It Had to Be You*

Sets are constructed so that all of their different elements are detachable. Walls, bookshelves, staircases, etc., can be stored for future use. Elaborate sets, especially exteriors, are often kept standing. Here, the medieval Paris streets used in 1939's *The Hunchback of Notre Dame* are put into service for *The Master Race* (1944). Adjustments have been made by the set dressers to meet the requirements of the picture. At budget conscious RKO, the spacious mansion built for Orson Welles's *The Magnificent Ambersons* became a New York apartment house for *Cat People*. The Ambersons' house, like the *Meet Me in St. Louis* house, was used again and again. Among the productions that moved in were *Experiment Perilous* and *The Spiral Staircase*.

Agnes Moorehead and Tim Holt in
The Magnificent Ambersons

Jane Randolph, Tom Conway,
and Kent Smith in *Cat People*

Sir Cedric Hardwicke and
Charles Laughton in *The Hunchback of Notre Dame*

The Master Race

Claire Trevor in *Murder My Sweet* (1944)

Jean-Pierre Aumont, Ginger Rogers, Mona Maris, and Adolphe Menjou in *Heartbeat* (1946)

A costume for a star often has a busy future after its screen debut. It may find itself on the back of another star, a supporting player, or an extra. The vampish gown designed by Edward Stevenson for Claire Trevor in *Murder My Sweet* showed up a few years later on Mona Maris in *Heartbeat*. Marilyn Monroe's scanty outfit designed by William Travilla for *Bus Stop* didn't have quite the same witchcraft on skinny Leslie Caron in *The Man Who Understood Women*. Another Monroe castoff, Orry-Kelly's beaded soufflé from *Some Like It Hot*, was bounced around by Barbara Nichols in *The George Raft Story*.

Don Murray and Marilyn Monroe in *Bus Stop* (1956)

Leslie Caron in *The Man Who Understood Women* (1959)

Marilyn Monroe in *Some Like It Hot* (1959)

Barbara Nichols in *The George Raft Story* (1961)

PURELY COINCIDENTAL

The foolish story [of Where Love Has Gone*] seems to have been suggested by the abrupt demise of Johnny Stompanato. The gang at Embassy and Paramount, therefore, are probably congratulating themselves on their monumental restraint and good taste—simply because they didn't try to cast Lana Turner in the role.*
—Newsweek

an cannot live by Walter Cronkite alone; he must have Rona Barrett. White House transcripts, bedroom tapes, and supermarket journalism can barely keep pace with the public's appetite for the latest intimate revelations about the rich, the famous, and the powerful. Yet even the *National Enquirer* and other like-minded gazettes are unable to give us the real lowdown on the stars, pols, and powerbrokers until death or public scandal intervenes to alleviate the threat of legal retaliation. But leave it to Hollywood to find a way to package this morning's front page story with all the lurid details intact—or better yet, improved upon. By changing the names "to protect the innocent," Hollywood claims dramatic license to invent cogent details that are missing from the headlines, or to alter and embellish the known facts in the interests of a more entertaining product.

Imagine how thrilled audiences must have been to get what appeared to be keyhole views of some of the world's most celebrated marriages. *The Barefoot Contessa*, for instance, allowed us to slip unnoticed into the boudoir of that famous royal couple, Rita Hayworth and Prince Aly Khan. Like the real-life Rita, Maria Vargas was a Cinderella who had risen from humble origins to stardom, but her story ends bleakly with an impotent Prince Charming and death. We get a similarly intimate and unflattering insight into the marriage of Marilyn Monroe and baseball star Joe DiMaggio, courtesy *The Goddess*, in which Kim Stanley portrayed a sex symbol incapable of giving or receiving love. Although Marilyn's baseball player was transformed into a rather thickheaded prizefighter, and many denials were issued to the contrary, it was difficult for audiences to miss the connection. Both these movies served the important purpose of telling people what they wanted to hear: the rich weren't really happy at all; they were grasping, greedy, and loveless. Hollywood was expert at rearranging reality to suit the public taste. This didn't always mean demythicization; sometimes a dash of romance or heroism could make the truth a little easier to

swallow. In the 1943 film *Flight for Freedom*, Hollywood confided that aviatrix Amelia Earhart (Tonie Carter) had not been lost at sea at all, but had purposely crashed her plane, knowing that the subsequent search for her remains would lead to the discovery of enemy Jap installations in the South Pacific. Or, as Bosley Crowther put it in *The New York Times*, "the film loudly asserts that our present naval actions in the Pacific have been made possible because of 'one pretty girl.'" RKO denied the connection between Tonie and Amelia, but it paid Earhart's husband $7,500 for his permission to do the film nonetheless.

Such denials were a necessary, and tantalizing, part of the game. Twentieth Century-Fox insisted that it had had no intention of inviting comparison between Fanny Brice and the torch singer with a weakness for underworld types (played by Alice Faye) in *Rose of Washington Square*. But if this was so, then what was Alice doing moaning "My Man" (Fanny's signature song) to her gangster boyfriend Tyrone Power? It didn't take much persuasion on the part of Fanny's lawyers to convince Fox's Darryl Zanuck that such a coincidence called for a sizable out-of-court settlement.

Screenwriter-director Joseph Mankiewicz still shrugs off the numerous similarities between his *Barefoot Contessa* and Rita Hayworth, for obvious reasons. He's been a bit more helpful on the subject of his inspiration for Margo Channing, the bombastic Broadway star of *All About Eve*, whom he claims to have based on stage and screen actress Elisabeth Bergner. But in 1950, as far as audiences were concerned, everything about Bette Davis's Margo, from her temperament to baritone voice, was Tallulah Bankhead to the core. Even Tallulah herself couldn't help noticing the resemblance; her mock indignation over the matter got her more attention than she'd had in years. She told her radio listeners on "The Big Show," "Don't think I don't know who's been spreading gossip about me and my temperament out there in Hollywood, where they made that film, 'All About Me.' And after all the nice things I've said about that hag [Bette Davis].

When I get hold of her, I'll tear every hair out of her mustache." As for Bette, she still insists that even if her voice did happen to boom like a foghorn throughout all of *Eve*, it didn't necessarily mean she was doing a Tallulah impression. It's just that she'd been a trifle hoarse during the filming, owing to the shouting matches she'd been having with her then husband, William Grant Sherry.

All About Eve couldn't possibly exploit Tallulah; she'd been doing that herself for years. But many showbiz personalities have been profoundly displeased to find themselves the "thinly disguised" subject of a biographical Hollywood treatment. No strangers to exploitation themselves, both Harry Cohn and L. B. Mayer were enraged by the portrait of the odious movie producer carved by Rod Steiger in *The Big Knife*. It wouldn't have been quite so humiliating if Rod hadn't gone around telling anyone who'd listen that he'd used them as models.

Judy Garland was terribly hurt by the obvious similarities between herself and the pill-popping Neely O'Hara in Jacqueline Susann's *Valley of the Dolls*; but that didn't stop her from agreeing to play a role in the film. (Ironically, her amphetamine addiction did.) And you probably shouldn't bring up the subject of *The Godfather* the next time you're making the scene with Sinatra. Ol' Blue Eyes gets so worked up on the subject that just the sight of *Godfather* author Mario Puzo at a stylish Hollywood watering hole not long ago sent him into paroxysms of rage. But who could blame him. Puzo and co-screenwriter Francis Ford Coppola practically had their Mafia-protégé singer, Johnny Fontaine, humming rooby-dooby-do.

Al Jolson was so furious with the references to his courtship of showgirl Ruby Keeler while she was the mistress of Forty-Second Street gangster Johnny Irish Costello, in Walter Winchell's story for *Broadway Thru a Keyhole*, that he ended up attacking the columnist in front of a crowd of—appropriately enough—prizefight fans. Winchell, however, was shielded by his wife June, who wielded her high-heeled shoe with such conviction that Joly ended up with a permanently crooked pinkie.

Bing Crosby turned to his lawyers for protection when Hollywood aimed its camera sights at his turbulent marriage to singer Dixie Lee. But his attempt to protect his family's privacy with threats of legal action was ignored by the higher-ups at Universal. They took the gamble that Bing would back down, since he'd have a tough time proving his case without exposing his private life to an even greater degree. And that's essentially just what happened. Crosby did, however, attempt to thwart the production of *Smash-Up: The Story of a Woman* by putting the word out in Hollywood that anyone participating on the film would be doing great harm to him and his family. This was probably the most effective approach he could have taken, since he was particularly well liked in the film community. Several influential actresses did turn down *Smash-Up*'s pivotal role of the alcoholic wife of a successful songwriter who is destroyed by her husband's career, before it was accepted by Susan Hayward. (By the way, one of *Smash-Up*'s screenwriters is said to have written a great deal of her own alcoholic unhappiness into its script—humorist Dorothy Parker.)

The Reynolds tobacco family also tried everything within its awesome power, including litigation, to prevent Universal's screen adaptation of the sensational novel *Written on the Wind*. Robert Wilder's bestselling book dealt unofficially with the mysterious circumstances surrounding the death by gunshot of Zachary Smith Reynolds, heir to the family fortunes. Little is known of Reynolds himself other than the fact that he appears to have been a high-strung emotional young man of ambivalent sexuality who married young torch singer Libby Holman in 1931. A year later he was dead. His wife, who was carrying their first child at the time of the shooting, was indicted with first degree murder. Although the charge was later dropped entirely, it was too late to stop the landslide of scurrilous coverage that had begun in the tabloids. Shortly thereafter, the film *Reckless* created a stir by casting Jean Harlow as a Libby Holman–type entertainer whose life is thrown into turmoil by the suicide of her husband. When *Written on the Wind* threatened to revive the story once again several years later, the Reynolds understandably tried to kill it, but with scant success. As for Holman, she was eventually forced into retirement by the scandal. For years thereafter her sole connection with show business was her enigmatic friendship with actor Montgomery Clift.

Sometimes the pointed distortions with which Hollywood tried to evade charges of libel could backfire, doing the subject of a fictionalized cinematic portrait a far greater disservice than the truth. Years after filming *Citizen Kane*, probably the most famous movie *à clef* ever made, Orson Welles swore in a court affidavit that neither he nor veteran screenwriter Herman Mankiewicz had had any intention of using the lives of publisher William Randolph Hearst and his mistress Marion Davies as models. But as far back as when Mankiewicz was first hammering out ideas for the script, he'd confided to friends that he was, in fact, doing just that. He confidently discounted any fuss over the matter, since he'd disguised the publisher's mistress as an untalented opera singer with the personality of a simpering twit, when everyone knew that the real Davies was a gifted comedienne and one of the best-liked figures in the film colony. But *Kane* contained so many chunks of information about Hearst and Davies which movie audiences knew to be accurate, that the distortions, too, eventually came to be accepted as truth. This was particularly so for Davies, since audiences which have viewed *Kane* over the years remain largely unfamiliar with her screen work. Until *New Yorker* film critic Pauline Kael undertook to restore Davies' reputation in the late sixties, the image of her which had remained with the public was that of Kane's mistress, the whining and opportunistic Susan Alexander.

Not every movie *à clef* relies on audience recognition of the real-life counterparts of its protagonists. It wouldn't have meant much to audiences in 1964, for instance, to have known that Stanley Kubrick had made a special trip to Harvard to meet Dr. Henry Kissinger while researching the title role for his screen adaptation of *Dr. Strangelove*. Kissinger was still several years away from Nixon and his shuttle diplomacy. Even when a film does draw much of its material from the life of a well-known celebrity, the public is sometimes thrown off the track by other associations. Most moviegoers thought that director Martin Scorsese was exploiting the Judy Garland mystique by casting her daughter Liza Minnelli as the hard luck singer who becomes a star in *New York, New York*, but what they were really seeing was Liza Minnelli in *The Doris Day Story*. The traumatic events in the life of the band singer married to a high-strung musician were easily recognizable to anyone who'd read Doris's recent autobiography. For instance, the scene in which the pregnant singer is beaten by her enraged husband as he simultaneously attempts to keep his auto under control is almost identical to an episode in Doris's story. And, like Doris, Liza works her way up from one-night stands to glorious movie musical stardom. Here the similarity ends, however, as *New York*'s screenwriters chose to delete the suicide of Doris's real-life husband, choosing instead to let both Liza and Robert De Niro walk, more or less, into the sunset, though not together.

The kind of treatment a celebrity gets on film is a matter of personal prejudice and artistic interpretation on the part of the filmmaker. Aimee Semple McPherson was depicted as everything from martyr to calculating charlatan. She was portrayed by Jean Simmons as a ruthlessly intelligent businesswoman in *Elmer Gantry*, but in *Miracle Woman* she's made out to be the unwitting victim of a scheming business manager. *Miracle Woman*'s original script had taken a tough, uncompromising look at the evangelist's life and career, but then director Frank Capra got squeamish. "The thought of a wicked evangelist deliberately milking poor, adoring suckers for money in the name of Christ was just too much for my orthodox stomach. I weaseled. I insisted on a 'heavy' to take the heat off the evangelist."

Another subject of multiple screen interpretations, Walter Winchell, had been delighted to find himself the inspi-
ration for the high-powered columnists of *Blessed Event* and *Okay America*, both released in 1932. However, he maintained a conspicuous silence on the subject of the comparisons drawn between his career and that of the viperish Broadway columnist of *Sweet Smell of Success*. In the tough Clifford Odets–Ernest Lehman script, the Winchellesque character played by Burt Lancaster is a sadistic, power-mad show-business scribe who thrives on vicious exposés. His only weakness is the lovely and sensitive sister whom he has attempted to protect from the big, cruel world, just as Winchell had unsuccessfully attempted to keep his trouble-prone daughter Walda out of the public eye.

Howard Hughes accepted cinematic invasions of privacy as part of the game. In fact, he even gave his blessings to Robert Ryan when he asked for permission to play the cold-blooded Hughes-like tycoon in *Caught*. With one stipulation—that Ryan promise not to wear tennis shoes.

Warner Bros.'s affectionate spoof of Charles Lindbergh's meteoric rise to fame was guilty more of bad timing than of bad taste. The film, complete with an unfortunate title—*It's Tough to Be Famous*—was released just a few weeks before the Lindbergh baby kidnapping. It was withdrawn within days of the tragedy and permanently shelved. The public was in no mood for satire.

The movie *à clef* is one of the few cinematic conventions to have survived the endless shifts in moviemaking technique as well as the meanderings of the public taste. It is, of course, the public's insatiable curiosity about the rich and famous that keeps this particular brand of film fantasy alive. Movies like *The Greek Tycoon* and *Rose* continue to offer up gossip and innuendo in the guise of intimate revelation, and true or untrue, they continue to shape our perception of reality.

You probably had no trouble identifying the widow of the slain politician who marries a ruthless Greek shipping magnate in *The Greek Tycoon*, nor the hard-living, hard-drinking rock star of *Rose*, since the celebrities on which they were modeled are still newsworthy today. But you may have seen many of the films we've mentioned without making the connection between the protagonists and their real-life counterparts. Because celebrity, no matter how sensational, has a way of fading with the passage of time, we've assembled a pictorial index of who's really who in the movie *à clef*. As far as we can tell, the first movie of this kind was made in 1917 by Raoul Walsh as *The Woman and the Law*, the thinly disguised story of Blanch De Saulles, a young South American woman who shot her husband, millionaire playboy Jack De Saulles, in an argument over the custody of their child. We think you're going to be surprised at how many films have incorporated touches of the Bad and the Beautiful into their scenarios since then.

Broderick Crawford in *All the King's Men*

Huey Long

Douglas Fairbanks, Jr., in *It's Tough to Be Famous*

Charles Lindbergh

Peter Sellers in *Dr. Strangelove*

Henry Kissinger

Lew Ayres in *Okay America*

Walter Winchell

Liza Minnelli in *New York, New York*

Doris Day

Best wishes Doris Day

Kirk Douglas and Lana Turner
in *The Bad and the Beautiful*
(**David Selznick** and **Diana Barrymore**)

Shari Robinson in *You're My Everything* (**Shirley Temple**)

Nanette Fabray and Oscar Levant
in *The Band Wagon*
(**Betty Comden and Adolph Green**)

Rip Torn in *Payday* (**Hank Williams**)

Ronee Blakley and Henry Gibson in *Nashville* (**Loretta Lynn and Red Foley**)

Jacqueline Bisset in *Day for Night* (**Julie Christie**)

Robert Montgomery in *The Saxon Charm*
(Jed Harris)

John Barrymore in *Twentieth Century*
(Jed Harris)

Lucille Ball and Bob Hope in *Critic's Choice*
(Jean and **Walter Kerr)**

Barbara Stanwyck in *Miracle Woman*
(Aimee Semple McPherson)

Agnes Moorehead in *What's the Matter With Helen*
(Aimee Semple McPherson)

Geraldine Page in *The Day of the Locust*
(Aimee Semple McPherson)

Lauren Bacall in *Written on the Wind*
(Libby Holman)

Joey Heatherton and Susan Hayward in *Where Love Has Gone* **(Cheryl Crane** and **Lana Turner)**

Carroll Baker and George Peppard in
The Carpetbaggers
(Jean Harlow and **Howard Hughes)**

Doris Day and David Niven in *Please Don't Eat the Daisies* (**Jean** and **Walter Kerr**)

George Sanders in *All About Eve* (**George Jean Nathan**)

Burt Lancaster in *Sweet Smell of Success* (**Walter Winchell**)

Faye Dunaway in *Network* (**Lin Bolen**)

Dyan Cannon in *The Last of Sheila* (**Sue Mengers**)

Warren Beatty in *Shampoo* (**Jay Sebring and/or Jon Peters**)

Martin Sheen in *Badlands* (**Charles Starkweather**)

Sylvester Stallone in *Rocky* (**Chuck Wepner**)

The Harder They Fall (**Primo Carnera**)

Leo G. Carroll and Mara Corday in *Tarantula*.

ONE STAR THEATER

(A long shot of a revolving globe. Over this shot is superimposed newsreel footage of World War II combat—bomb blasts and artillery attacks. During this shot the voice of the narrator is heard.)

NARRATOR: The American nuclear attack left millions homeless.

(CUT TO: Newsreel footage of fleeing refugees and South American earthquake victims.)

But it had at last brought an end to the devastation wrought by the giant crab monsters!

(CUT TO: newsreel footage of war-torn European cities.)

But what about their eggs? The clever aliens had hidden their offspring in a godforsaken hell high in the treacherous Himalayan Mountains where no man had ever gone before.

(CUT TO: aerial shot of a snow-capped mountain range.)

Once again, the job of wiping out the invaders fell to America's military titans. . . .

(CUT TO: exterior shot of the Pentagon and then to interior shot of five-star GENERAL HORACE WHITEHEAD's office. The general's office includes a large desk and several folding chairs. The general stands in front of a map of the world, pointer in hand, and is about to address a gathering of the joint chiefs of staff.)

WHITEHEAD: *(ominously)* Gentlemen, we've managed to blast these creatures back to the alien planet from which they came, but the only way to wipe out the threat of a new generation of crab people is to mobilize a search and destroy mission immediately. *(Looks around the room)* Are we in agreement?

(The various commanders pause to reflect for a moment and then nod their agreement.)

WHITEHEAD: *(to his attaché)* Get me the President!

(The scene changes to the laboratory of the world-famous scientist, DR. FRANZ O'HOOLIHAN. The doctor, along with his colleague, DR. STEVE KIRK, and his daughter HELGA, a respected scientist in her own right and a former Miss World, is peering into a microscope on an otherwise uncluttered table. Behind the doctor is a world map very much like the one in General Whitehead's office.)

DR. O'HOOLIHAN: *(animatedly)* If I could only find the answer! Ach! To be so close and yet so far!

HELGA: *(reassuringly)* Now, father . . . you've never failed before, have you? Has he, Steve?

(DR. KIRK shakes his head.)

Maybe if you got some rest. You can't go on this way. You're exhausted. Isn't he, Steve?

(DR. KIRK nods.)

DR. O'HOOLIHAN: *(more animatedly)* No! No! I will not rest until I have conquered this . . . this . . . thing! Don't you see . . . it was I who first made contact with the aliens. It is I who is responsible for the destruction they have wrought. It is I who must go to their spawning grounds and destroy them before it is too late!

HELGA: *(determined)* Well, if you go, then I'm going too.

DR. O'HOOLIHAN: *(frantically)* No! No! It will be no place for a woman. You, Helga, you must stay here and continue the work I've begun.

HELGA: *(more determinedly)* I'm going with you and I don't want to hear another word about it. Subject closed. Now I'll just go and pack our things. You see, a woman *can* make herself useful if she wants to.

Sound familiar? Of course it does. It's the kind of thing that you're used to hearing through a speaker perched on the window of the family station wagon or seeing on television at three a.m. when you can't sleep. Unless it's a *Beach Party* romp or an Italian muscle flick, it's usually in glorious black and white with one or more of the following features: exotic locales courtesy rear screen projection, papier mache monsters, harem girls, cheap special effects, a film clip of two magnified lizards fighting on a fake set, the same musical score as "Sky King," post dubbing, women behind bars, harsh lighting, cramped sets, lowbrow comedy, murder, mayhem, and Mamie Van Doren.

This then is a One Star Theater presentation. A uniquely American cinematic tradition, conceived in mediocrity, produced in haste, and devoid of any artistic pretension, its single *raison d'être* is to turn a quick buck. It's the first cousin of the B-movie and the great-uncle of the porno film. Its creators had every intention of making a bad movie. They've gone to inordinate lengths to make sure that its budget and production values are low enough so as not to intimidate a drive-in audience, but not so vile that the average Joe couldn't take the missus along.

These films—*High School Confidential*, *Johnny Stool Pigeon*, *Beach Blanket Bingo*, etc.—were the logical progression of the Hollywood B-movie production system for which quantity, not quality, was the byword. But unlike the B-movies of the forties, which were studio-made copies of hit formulas cranked out by the thousands, the One Star movie got its foothold in the fifties, around the time that labor unions and inflation were putting a crimp in the studio's bankrolls and television was putting a crimp in the nation's brain. Their uniqueness stemmed from the fact that they were usually independent productions. The founding fathers of the movement, Hugo Haas, Albert Zugsmith, and William Castle, might have been beholden to the majors for distribution, but it was they, and they alone, who were responsible for maintaining the unremittingly high standards of tastelessness that would mark the genre.

And what about the stars of these productions? They certainly weren't in it for the money. Their salaries were and are so low as to be almost nonexistent. More often than not, the pay isn't much more than three squares a day or a trip to Hong Kong. But still, it's the movies . . . well, sort of. And for most of the names and faces that you associate with this genre—Beverly Michaels, Keith Andes, etc.—it was the next best thing to genuine stardom. They'd come to Hollywood to make it big, but either they didn't click or they'd arrived just in time to see what was left of the movie industry lumbering to a standstill. A part in a grade-Z cheapie was their only hope. There was always the possibility of getting a break and being discovered in one of the things. It's doubtful that Gloria Talbott and Frank Lovejoy intended to make a career out of things like *The Wasp Woman* and *Shack out on 101*. But very few graduated to the big time. Anne Bancroft managed to extricate herself from *Gorilla At Large* and *The Girl in Black Stockings* to become *The Miracle Worker* via her stage success with that role. And Jack Nicholson moved on from Roger Corman's company and films like *The Little Shop of Horrors* and *Hells Angels on Wheels* to win an Academy Award. But these two were exceptions.

It should be noted that there are stars like George Hamilton and Joey Heatherton who can convert even a big budget extravaganza into a One Star debacle. Jayne Mansfield, for instance, was the very embodiment of the One Star school. She managed to wreak havoc on several otherwise first-rate productions before producers realized where she really belonged.

Yes, while the more respectable Hollywood institutions — the studios, the star system, musicals, costume pictures—have faded away into a beautiful memory, it's the One Star tradition, the last and least venerated, that survives. It has its own stars, its own *auteurs*, and its own classics, like *Night of the Living Dead*, the *Citizen Kane* of the movement. Its influence can be observed all over the world, most especially in Japan with its atomic monster creations and in England with its Hammer Films. Some of the most memorable One Star productions have, in fact, come about as the result of an independent American company joining forces with similar groups in Italy, Japan or Spain. These collaborations have given us such stunning exercises as *The Frozen Dead*, starring Dana Andrews and a post-dubbed Italian cast, and the Japanese monster flick *Godzilla*, starring Raymond Burr. *Tentacles*, one of 1977's biggest One Star hits, was a product of footage featuring two newcomers to the One Star company, John Huston and Shelley Winters, shot in what appears to be San Diego, and then intercut with footage shot in Italy with a completely different supporting cast. Another recent hit, *It's Alive!*, was a low-budget thriller deemed so awful when first completed back in 1971 that it was peremptorily shelved. It was discovered six years later by a Hollywood promotion genius who repackaged it with a new title and a clever ad campaign; a few months later, it was breaking attendance records at drive-ins all over the country. Yes, whether home grown (*The Texas Chain Saw Murders*, *Truck Stop Women*) or foreign born (*Kung Fu Stallion*), the hits just keep coming. The One Star musical, which started with Gloria DeHaven movies, followed by the fifties rock-and-roll flicks like *Rock Around the Clock* and *Because They're Young*, is flourishing again today with films like *Carwash*, *Thank God It's Friday*, and *FM*. And contrary to the predictions of industry soothsayers, the growth of the porno market hasn't affected business in the slightest. Of course, the One Star production has itself grown a bit more provocative since its beginnings but, for the most part, it continues to lean toward repressed sexuality and fetishism with heavy doses of blood and guts rather than hard-core thrills.

A One Star movie has its own special kind of élan. It may be awful, but at least it's honest. And wouldn't you really rather see *Bikini Beach Girls Meet the Monster* than *Airport* any day? Of course, there are those who still laugh at the efforts of directors like Roger Corman and George Romero, but not for long. Film students all over the world are beginning to study and write about the work of these and other great One Star innovators.

What follows here, however, is the first time ever salute to the stars of the One Star Rep Company, those unique talents who've labored for years in things like *I Suck Your Blood* and *Kiss, Kiss, Kill, Kill* without so much as a nod from the elitist film critics' community. They've given us some of the funniest, scariest, and worst moments in the history of the movies, and now it's time to show our gratitude. We love you Hugh Beaumont, Arthur Franz, and all the rest. This may be the first tribute to you, but it certainly won't be the last.

Fay Spain

Rondo Hatton

Steve Reeves

Cleo Moore

Beverly Garland

Richard Denning

Hugh Beaumont

Joey Heatherton

257

Annette Funicello and Frankie Avalon

Clint Walker

Keefe Brasselle

Diana Dors

Dorothy Provine

Turhan Bey

Frank Lovejoy

Marie Windsor

Keith Andes

Beverly Michaels

Hillary Brooke

David Brian

Jon Hall

Barbara Steele

Deborah Walley

Raymond Burr

Whit Bissell

Eva Bartok

Richard Carlson

John Agar

Kerwin Mathews

Vera Hruba Ralston

Arthur Franz

Arthur Lake

A doll-like **Myrna Loy** leaves her trailer to resume work on *So Goes My Love*.

STUDIO TOUR

Good afternoon, ladies and gentlemen, and welcome to the Amalgamania Studio Tour. We ask that you heed all signs and refrain from wandering away from the group. Don't be alarmed if your wristwatches stop as the gates close behind us, for movies are timeless and so is our studio.

Our tour will allow you to observe the stars up close— in front of the cameras, on the sidelines of their newest movie, or in their dressing rooms taking a break between scenes. You'll see them being made up, snacking, sketching, signing autographs, greeting visitors, reading, playing games, posing for publicity photos, or just waiting.

The information provided by your tour guide at each stop comes directly from official publicity material issued by the studio.

So now, if there are no further questions, our studio tour will commence. . . .

Norma Shearer's portable dressing room is the envy of the lot.

That's **Ruth Hussey** poised in the doorway of her dressing room, pausing to smile for our studio tour. She's taking a break from *Our Wife.*

Break time for the leading lady of *Vice Squad,* **Kay Francis.**

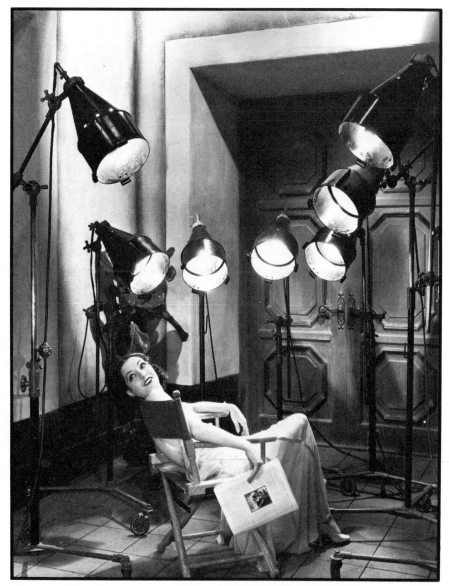

Lupe Velez lounges during a hard day's work on *The Broken Wing.*

Crooner and businessman **Bing Crosby** is checking *Variety's* Top 50 Grossers during a break in the filming of *Here Is My Heart.*

Bette Davis is probably shopping for future movie material as she reads on the set of *The Little Foxes.*

Alice Faye in costume for *Poor Little Rich Girl*

You're right, it's beautiful **Constance Bennett** awaiting her next scene in *The Affairs of Cellini.*

Elizabeth Taylor during a lull in the production of *Elephant Walk*

Oops . . . we seem to have wandered into **Humphrey Bogart**'s dressing room. Sorry, Bogie.

Magnificent Obsession's star, **Irene Dunne**, checks her makeup.

Joan Crawford has received birthday gifts from her fans all over the world. She's taking a break from filming *Queen Bee*.

Glamorous **Marlene Dietrich** and her bicycle are a familiar sight on the backlot. She's working on *The Flame of New Orleans*.

Dick Powell as Lysander in *A Midsummer Night's Dream* is enjoying some ice cream with some of his pickaninny retainers.

Looks like **Buster Keaton** has lost the toss to **Jimmy Durante** and has to pay the check. The two comedians are lunching on the porch of the studio commissary.

Gary Cooper cruises around the [Amalgamania] lot.

John Wayne and **Jean Arthur** find time to eat during the making of *The Lady Takes a Chance*.

Cary Grant and stand-in on the set of *The Awful Truth*

Cary Grant and stand-in (seven years later) on the set of *None but the Lonely Heart*

Cary Grant and **June Duprez** socialize while their stand-ins pose for a lighting setup during the filming of *None but the Lonely Heart.*

Deanna Durbin confers with *Can't Help Singing* director William Seiter, while her stand-in takes her place under the hot studio lights.

Humphrey Bogart says "hello" to stand-in Mike Morelli's little daughter on the set of *Dead Reckoning.*

Joseph Cotten and stand-in at work on *I'll Be Seeing You*

Ella Raines and stand-in celebrate El▮

Carmen Miranda and stand-in

Carmen Miranda takes it easy while her stand-in takes her place for a lighting check on the set of *Something for the Boys*.

Rosalind Russell entertains her stand-in during a break from filming *Roughly Speaking*.

Ralph Bellamy and stand-in on the set of *The Awful Truth*

Alan Ladd and stand-in on the set of *Two Years Before the Mast*

Joan Crawford and stand-in

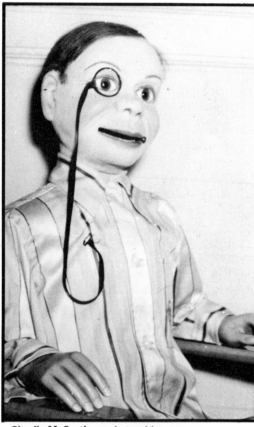

Charlie McCarthy and stand-in

Dorothy Lamour and stand-in go over the script for *Swing High, Swing Low.*

The ever-gracious **Claudette Colbert** presents her stand-in, Pluma Noisom, with a prize bull terrier pup in appreciation for her work on *She Married Her Boss.*